HOLY WAR

A Brady James Novel

William J. Millman

SB

Sunset Beach Press

SB

Sunset Beach Press

Copyright © 2013 by William J. Millman

Manufactured in the United States of America

Cover photo: Colourbox

Library of Congress Control Number: 2013949233

ISBN: 978-0-9857918-2-7

To my Mom and Dad,
Who always believed

PROLOGUE

The room was darkened, with shadows from the dozens of flickering candles painting ever-changing images on the walls and ceilings.

"As-Salāmu `Alaykum."

"Wa `alaykumu s-salām."

"Are you ready? Have you given yourself to Allah and to the army of martyrs who have died for Islam?" a soft but powerful voiced asked, as it had many times before in the previous weeks.

"I have."

The youthful reply was tense but confident.

"You know what you must do."

"I do."

A thin bearded man in long, flowing black robes handed a backpack to the young man standing before him.

"Then take this, and wait for our call."

"I will, in Allah's name."

"Ma'a salama."

The young man hefted the backpack over his shoulder and with a subtle bow, turned and left the room. The bearded man watched him leave without expression. But the moment the door closed, he smiled.

CHAPTER 1

The smell of curry permeated the tiny Adams Morgan restaurant.

Brady James and his girlfriend, Anne, sat at a two-person table near the very back of the crowded room. With crossed bronze swords mounted on the wall just over their heads, heavy purple draperies blocking out most of the exterior light, and high-pitched musical wails erupting from the sound system, there was little doubt that this was an authentic Middle Eastern restaurant, not a sterile re-creation like so many of the fast food wanna-be's that had sprung up all around DC in recent years. That was one reason why it had become one of their favorite places, why they'd been coming there the first Tuesday of every month for over a year now.

"I really do love this place," Brady said as he glanced around the room. "No tourists, good prices, and the food's so spicy it burns you twice – once going in, and then..."

"I think that's more than we need to know," Anne interrupted with a tolerant smile. "Or at least more than *I* need to know."

"Such a delicate flower. How'd you ever wind up with a slob like me?"

"Just lucky, I guess."

Brady knew that it was he who had been the lucky one. In the 18 months since Anne had first appeared at his door to describe what she believed to be the murder of her Senator boss, Brady's life had taken a real turn for the better. Not only had the Hoch story vaulted him back into the front pages of the Washington Post, and through syndication to papers and Internet sites all over the world, but his personal life had gone from zero to 60 mph in a matter of weeks. As he looked over at Anne he marveled how such an attractive, intelligent, cultured woman could choose him over the thousands of younger, trimmer, more couth alternatives that slithered through the corridors and alleyways of DC. He was a lucky SOB, that was for sure.

"Margie was telling us about the new Woody Allen film that just came out," she was saying when Brady's attention returned to the present. "Same basic story: funny geek meets beautiful girl and charms her with his erudite psychoses. But this time she says it's actually pretty funny. What do you think? Want to give it a try?"

"You think it's theater-worthy?" (He knew Anne would understand his shorthand. He questioned whether it was worth all the hassle of dressing up, driving, parking, and then shelling out 12 bucks or more, as opposed to Netflick-only, which was the designation of any flick that cost more than $10 and didn't push the needle past 65 on Rotten Tomatoes.)

"Sure, let's go wild!" she said with a broad grin. "You only live once, right?"

"Okay. When do you want…?"

He was interrupted in the middle of the sentence by a waitress bringing their meal. Brady stopped, not because anything he was saying was so important or secretive, but because he thought the woman might explain a bit about the dishes she was bringing. That's what they usually did. It was one of the things he really liked about this place. He liked to hear about food. About anything, really. Details were what made life interesting. Otherwise, it was all Wonder Bread and Fox News. Bland nothings creatively packaged.

"The Harira and Lahm Lhalou?" she asked in heavily accented English. Brady glanced up to see a woman wearing the trademark server's costume: a loose-fitting deep blue dress topped by a matching Niqab, leaving only a narrow slit through which he could see intense dark brown eyes. He knew that the native costume was one of the restaurant's big drawing cards, but it still took him aback every time he came into close contact with one of their female employees.

"That…that's got to be her," he said, indicating Anne with a bob of his chin. "I had the…"

But before he could finish, the woman leaned down close to his face and whispered: "Help me. Please!"

The pain in her eyes made more of an impression than her words. She dropped a piece of crumpled white paper in Brady's lap and before he could say a word disappeared straight out a back doorway.

"What the hell was that?" he asked as he turned to watch the flowing blue robes disappear behind him.

"I don't know. But I can tell you I didn't order Lahm Lhalou," Anne said with a frown. "You probably frightened her."

"Somehow I don't think that's it," Brady mumbled, staring out the window in thought. He was about to continue along the same lines, when out of the corner of his eye he saw the crumpled piece of paper the woman had dropped, a brilliant white blotch on the red cloth napkin in his lap. He picked the paper up and began to unfold it.

"Now what?" he griped. He hated to be interrupted at the dinner table. His temper didn't improve as he read:

'My son is in trouble, bad trouble. Maybe al-Qaeda. Please, PLEASE help us!' And a phone number.

"Fan mail?" Anne asked, watching him closely.

"Another nutcase," he said with a heavy sigh. But Anne noticed that he didn't re-crumple the note and toss it on the table, but instead folded it carefully and tucked it in his breast pocket.

"What kind of nutcase?"

Brady shrugged. "Claims her son is somehow in trouble with al-Qaeda – maybe. Probably just got bullied by a Middle Easterner at school."

Anne's eyes narrowed and Brady knew she was about to make a point he hadn't considered. "How did she know you'd be here?"

Now it was Brady's turn to squint. "Good question. I mean, we do come here every month…"

"Do you really think the average waitress knows you were a big-shot reporter?"

He hated when she came to obvious conclusions before he did.

"How do I know?" he answered, sounding defensive even to himself. "Maybe Fareed mentioned it to his staff." Fareed Hassan was the owner of the Golden Crescent, and someone Brady had known for nearly 20 years. He'd interviewed the Algerian immigrant way back then for a feature on gangs that had been shaking down shop owners in Adams Morgan for protection money. They weren't exactly best buddies, but when Fareed opened this new place, Brady had received an invitation for a private first meal with just a handful of other friends, family and associates. He probably thought Brady might talk to some of his Washington Post friends and get the restaurant a mention. Whatever the reason, Fareed was the only person in the place James knew well enough to mention his good ol' days at the Post.

"Could be," Anne said, but her tone suggested she wasn't convinced.

"I don't know any other way..." Brady began, but just then a young waiter appeared from nowhere to stand less than a foot from the plump ex-reporter, waiting for him to finish his sentence while inspecting the food still sitting untouched on their table.

"So *there* it is," he muttered to himself.

James looked up at the waiter. "Excuse me?"

"Please forgive us," the waiter apologized with a slight bow of his head as he indicated the Harira and Lahm Lhalou. "This food goes to another table. Your food comes in just a minute." Before either Brady or Anne could say a word, he scooped up the two dishes and scurried off to a table across the narrow room.

"What was that?" Anne asked, perplexed.

"This gets curiouser and curiouser," James said, more to himself than Anne. He glanced around the room and then back to his girlfriend. She watched him closely, waiting for an explanation. "Did you notice anything unusual about our server – I mean, the first one?" he finally asked.

"Aside from the fact that she brought the wrong food, left you a note and disappeared out the back door? Nope, pretty much our standard fare."

"Yeh, all that too. But I meant how she was dressed. Notice anything…different?"

Anne thought back to the young woman. She hadn't really paid all that much attention to her. "No, I don't think so. Why?"

"Her headdress – it was blue. Matched her dress, which was very dark blue as well."

"And?"

"Look around. Both the other waitresses are wearing black hoodies. And their dresses are a lighter blue, I think."

Anne looked more closely at the women as they served and took orders. "You're right!" she said. "At least about the head covering. I really don't remember if the dress was that blue or not."

Just then the male server reappeared carrying a large tray with both their orders.

"Excuse me," Brady asked as the young man began to take covers off each dish, "but how many waitresses do you have working tonight?"

The waiter looked at him inquisitively. He glanced over his shoulder to be sure it wasn't a trick question. "Just those two," he said with a nod in their direction. "Why? We are very sorry about the mix-up with the orders…"

"No, no, it's not that," Brady said. "When did they start their shifts?"

"Their 'shifts'?" the waiter asked, his accented English suggesting he wasn't familiar with the term.

"When did they start working tonight?"

He shrugged. "I don't know. Around 5:30, I think. I can check with them, if you like."

"No, that's okay," Brady said easily. "Just wondering."

The waiter's left eyebrow shot up involuntarily. He explained the contents of each dish and then stepped away with one last glance back at the two strange regulars.

"She wasn't a waitress," Anne said as soon as the server was out of earshot.

"Doesn't seem like it. She probably just grabbed those two dishes when no one in the kitchen was looking and brought them over here."

"Pretty elaborate plot just to give you a note – costume, planning…"

"Yeh, A lot of work for a nutcase." He tapped his breast pocket absently.

Anne knew then that they hadn't heard the last from the woman.

CHAPTER 2

Derek chugged a Budweiser while he read the crumpled note. The bottle looked unnaturally large in the little man's hand, but the contents disappeared all too quickly.

"So, are you gonna call this mystery woman?"

Brady took a deep breath. "Yeh, I guess I am. Against my better judgment."

"Just can't resist the lure of a big story, can you?" the diminutive private investigator jabbed. "A sucker for a pretty byline."

"Be nice to have something attractive around here," James muttered. He'd called his old friend as soon as he and Anne had gotten home the night before to let him know about the strange goings-on at the restaurant. They'd decided to meet for brunch at the PI's apartment. Brady would have suggested breakfast, but he knew Derek only ate breakfast when he was still awake from the night before. Otherwise, brunch was the earliest meal on the agenda, at least when he wasn't working a case. And at the moment, he wasn't.

Brady grabbed the note from his friend and studied it, again.

"What are you doing, looking for secret codes?" the PI prodded. "Come on, call the broad already. If – or more likely when – she turns out to be the typical cuckoo clock, maybe we can catch the Nationals at Cincinnati this afternoon. Strasburg is on the mound."

Brady had to admit the possibility of seeing the Nationals' prize jewel go up against the Reds was appealing.

"All right, pass me the phone."

"What do I look like, the butler here?"

Brady sighed heavily and walked over to the where the phone was parked – on a side table just three feet from where Derek was sipping the last dregs of his first beer of the morning.

He dialed and steeled himself for the disappointment he was almost sure he'd feel when the woman told him the whole story. The phone rang six times, twice more than he usually allowed. He was just about to hang up when a woman's voice answered in a whisper:

"Hello?"

"Uh, yeh, good morning," he began. "My name is Brady James, and I was given a piece of paper with this phone number on it…"

The woman interrupted him. Her quiet voice was energized, anxious.

"Subhan' Allah," the woman said with obvious relief. "I thank you so much for your call. It is my son – he is in trouble. Very bad."

"Yes, I got that from your message. You know, ma'am, if he's really in a bad spot, I would suggest you call the local police. I'm just an old retired reporter…"

"You stopped that rich man, that Mr. Hoch. If you can stop him, perhaps you can stop these devils."

Hoch again. Ever since he had helped break up the oil billionaire's plot to steal the Presidential election and install his own man in the White House, he'd been getting these kinds of cold calls. Everything from lost kids to whack-job plots by aliens to take over the universe. Up til now, not one of them had panned out to be anything worth giving up his comfy seat in front of the big screen TV to watch any of DC's pathetic sports teams struggle to eke out a victory.

"Look, lady, I'm sure your troubles are bad. I wish I could help you, really. But that's what the cops are for. That's their job."

"No police!" Her voice turned icy. He could feel her fear right through the receiver. "They kill him if they find out police are involved."

"Who? Who will kill him?"

"I don't know, maybe al-Qaeda, maybe other group. But they are bad, very, very bad." At this, her voice dropped to a bare gasp. "They want him to blow himself up."

Brady felt the hairs stand up on the back of his neck.

"How? When?" He couldn't help himself. Even though it was a one in a million longshot, the possibility of a terror attack in the District was too big a story to give up without a question or two. There was a pause, during which he heard the sound of a door shutting and a male voice calling out in the background.

"I cannot talk more," the woman said. "Meet me at the Lafayette Square, tomorrow at 3 in afternoon."

Brady was about to object, to insist that she tell him all about it on the phone, when the call disconnected. He was tempted to call right back but hesitated, considering the possibility that the woman had hung up because someone had come into the room and she couldn't chance being overheard talking to him.

"So?" Derek asked as Brady slowly put the phone back in its cradle.

"How'd you like to go for a walk in the park tomorrow afternoon?" Brady asked.

Derek rolled his eyes.

*****

It was a hot, hazy, take-two-steps-and-your-clothes-are-drenched August day in DC. Brady had been in a lot of hot places during his 62 years, but only in DC could the air get so thick, grey and ugly that you could barely see the Washington Monument from the Capitol Building. A deep breath sandpapered your lungs. He wouldn't have been all that surprised to see a Tyrannosaurus Rex emerge from the noxious leaden haze. Or at least one of the dinosaurs that occupied the big domed building on the Hill. In his opinion, the 100 Senators and 435 Representatives had become little more than dandified raptors, and politics a destructive bloodsport. But that didn't mean he wanted to see all politicos dead. Maybe just neutered...

"A cold one would taste pretty damn tasty right about now," Derek said as he and Brady sat on a bench near the corner of H and Madison streets. Looking past the grand bronze statue of the venerable Revolutionary War-era French general astride his rearing warhorse, the White House was clearly visible in the distance. Brady wondered if the woman hadn't chosen this park for its symbolic value.

"She's possibly Muslim and it's three in the afternoon. Might be better to hold off until after this little get-together," Brady responded to his friend's lament with all the sarcasm he was so richly known for.

The tiny PI grumbled but said no more. James ignored him and scanned the park for the woman. He caught himself looking for someone wearing a traditional Middle Eastern costume, complete with some sort of concealing headgear. *'Probably the last thing she'd wear here,'* he thought, and readjusted his expectations. But truth was, he really had no idea what she looked like. Just a general idea of her height and a very specific remembrance of intense brown eyes. Hard to make out from a distance.

"How long are we gonna wait for her?" Derek asked after several minutes of idle watching.

Brady glanced down at his watch. He realized that wearing a watch was an anachronism in this age of cellphone time keeping, but he didn't care. Perhaps as a holdover from his journalist days, he hated those little electronic leashes and tried to use his as little as possible. Besides, when did a cellphone ever stand on its own as a work of sculpture, like the Breitling he now saw indicated 3:07 with appropriately archaic pointing hands.

"She's only seven minutes late. Give her a break," he said.

No sooner had he said the words, than a small, thin, olive-skinned woman wearing a long dark grey skirt, black blouse and purplish headscarf walked into view, looking cautious at best, frightened at worst.

"Possible at ten o'clock," Derek sang out before he could open his mouth. That was one thing Brady really admired about his little friend: nothing got past him. N-o-t-h-i-n-g.

"All right. I'm off," James said. Following their pre-arranged plan, he left the PI sitting on the bench while he headed off on an intercept course. From what he could tell, the woman hadn't identified him yet. *'Might be near-sighted,'* he deduced, but it might also be true she simply hadn't gotten around to him yet. There were probably two dozen other people either sitting, strolling, or snapping pictures in the park. The woman was busy trying to eye each of them without calling attention to herself.

As he approached to within thirty feet or so, he saw the woman's eyes meet his. "Contact," he whispered into a small lapel mike hidden beneath his collar. He knew without looking behind him that Derek would be holding his hand to his ear to screen out wind noise from any further communications.

Feigning a tourist's interest in the towering statue, Brady shaded his eyes and stared up at General Lafayette even as he continued walking. He kept track of the woman's trajectory with an occasional glance out of the corner of his eyes; her look of confused hesitation grew as he seemingly ignored her. But just as they were about to pass on the dusty dirt pathway, Brady leaned in just enough to bump her shoulder hard, eliciting a sharp cry of dismay from the surprised woman.

"I'm so sorry! I guess I wasn't looking where I was going," Brady apologized, even as he bent down to pick up imaginary belongings the woman had supposedly dropped. As he stood, he handed her a crumpled piece of paper not unlike the one she had passed to him at the restaurant.

"Are you okay?" he asked solicitously.

"I...I am fine," the woman stammered, glancing down at the piece of paper that had been thrust into her hand. Brady touched her arm and looked into her eyes to draw them up from her hands.

"Well, again, I'm so sorry," he said a little too loudly as he smiled and nodded. "Don't read it here," he whispered through clenched teeth. "Go to a bathroom."

With that he continued on his way, staring once again at the statue.

The woman hesitated just a second, before stuffing her hand into a pocket and scurrying across the park past where Derek was still sitting.

"So far, so good," he whispered into his clip-on mike.

Brady pretended to read the plaque on the base of the statue as he watched the woman depart toward H Street. "I'm getting a hankering for a nice strong cup of coffee," Brady muttered into his mike.

"Make mine a Slurpee," the PI said as he wiped beads of sweat from his forehead. "I'm cooking over here."

With that he stood and followed their 'contact' across H.

*****

Brady got to Koala Coffee on 17th Street before the woman. They'd chosen the small local coffee house because it was easily found, usually uncrowded, and the coffee was cheap. Not all that good, but cheap. Most importantly, the shop played Australian pop music constantly, so eavesdropping was virtually impossible.

He found a small, rickety table toward the back of the joint and sat down to await the woman, and Derek – who'd been following her at a safe distance to make sure she hadn't been tailed. The note they'd given her told her to go up 16th to I, turn left, then left again at 18th, and left once again on Pennsylvania to the coffee shop. The odds of anyone accidentally taking that circuitous route were just about zero.

Brady had nearly finished his first, and probably only cup of coffee when the door opened and the woman from the park finally entered looking hot and nervous. He waved, and as soon as her eyes adjusted to the darkened room she exhaled visibly and made her way to his table.

"Alma, how are you!?" Brady said loud enough so that anyone in the shop would think they were old buddies.

The woman's face showed confusion, but she took the chair Brady offered her and sat.

"Mr. James, I cannot thank you enough…" she began, until Brady cut her off with a wave of his hand.

"What would you like to drink?" he asked with a welcoming smile. "I can't really recommend the coffee, but the water might be okay."

"I…do they have juice?"

"I think they might." He lowered his voice so that it couldn't be heard more than two feet away over the Men at Work song blaring through tinny speakers. "An associate of mine will be joining us momentarily… Hey, could we get a juice over here!" he called out loudly to the bleached blond 20-something stationed behind the coffee bar. "Anything in particular?" he asked the woman.

"Orange?"

"Make that orange juice, please. In fact, make it two."

"Make it three," a familiar voice called out from just inside the door, "and lots of ice."

Derek, red-faced and sweating profusely, waddled over to the table and sat down next to the woman, much to her obvious consternation.

"Hey, how ya doing?" he said reaching out his hand.

The woman looked at him as if he'd just descended from an alien spaceship.

"My 'associate'," Brady said, glaring at the extended hand until the PI shrugged and withdrew it. "Derek DiLaurain, this is…" He looked at the woman for some assistance.

"Nyla. Nyla Jacobson," she said softly. "My pleasure to meet you." She glanced repeatedly at Derek, who smiled demonically at her discomfort.

"Jacobson? Not very…Middle Eastern," Brady said to break the awkward silence.

"My husband was Jacobson, Allāh yarHamu. He died five year ago. Heart."

"I'm sorry," Brady said. "So you've been raising your son by yourself?"

At the mention of her son, Nyla looked as if she would cry. "He is a good boy. But he is young. They take advantage of him."

"I'm sure he is, Mrs. Jacobson," James tried to calm her. "Now why don't you tell us all about this…problem your son has."

She took a deep breath and was just about to launch into her explanation, when the blonde barista appeared with three oj's. Nyla looked down at her hands and remained completely silent as the young woman delivered their drinks.

"Can I get you anything else?" the blond asked with the spunky insincerity common to all such servers.

"What'd you have in mind?" the PI leered.

Brady kicked his friend under the table, hard.

"Hey!" Derek fumed. "I was just…" Brady's glare cut him off in mid-sentence. "…just kidding around. I think that'll do for now, thanks."

As the blond made her way back to the coffee bar, Derek pouted. Brady ignored him.

"You were about to tell us about your son?" he gently prodded Nyla.

The woman nodded thoughtfully. "It all began four, maybe five month ago. Marid, that is our son's name, although everyone call him Chip. Like 'chip off old block', you know? He look just like Andy, my dead husband. Maybe skin is darker…"

"How old is 'Chip'?" Brady interrupted, desperate to keep her on point.

"He is 22. Graduate from college last May. American University. Good school."

"Yes, it is. So how did he meet these people who are deceiving him?"

"I do not know. All I know is that four or five month ago he start going to local mosque, not just once a week, but many time. Too many time."

"Was he always religious?" Derek asked. Nyla started as though she had forgotten he was there.

"Marid? No, not really. I mean, we go to mosque for Ramadan and Eid, but, no, not like the last few month. Something change…"

"Why do you think he's in trouble?" Brady pressed. Attending services regularly was a problem that a lot of parents he knew wished they had.

"First, he grows beard. Then he say that I must wear hijab. Then, he insist I do not drive. Me! I taught *him* how to drive! He tell me that my non-Muslim friends are non-

believers and I should not see them!" Her indignation came
through clearly. But then, she lowered her voice and
glanced around warily. "I found this in his bedroom," she
said softly, and reaching into the deep pockets of her dress
pulled out a small sheath of papers. "I made copies." She
handed them to Brady. One look told him why she was so
upset. Although most of the documents were in Arabic, the
few in English were recipes for explosives and diagrams for
bomb-making. And a tourist map of the District, including
the Capitol, the Smithsonian Museums, and the White
House.

He whistled out loud in spite of himself.

"What?" Derek asked. Brady handed the papers to
him.

"Did you tell him you found this stuff?" he asked her.

She nodded. "I did. He was very, very angry. He said
things I never hear him say before. Bad things."

"Did he explain why he was looking at these kinds of
sites?"

"Not then. But later, two weeks ago, I hear him say
on telephone that they will 'slay the Great Satan.' All
Muslims know Great Satan."

Derek raised an eyebrow. "So that's it? Do you have
anything else? Anything that would suggest that he's actually
involved in some kind of plot or plan? I mean, lots of kids
threaten to do bad things."

"He doesn't see his old friends. He spends all free
time with people he met at mosque. He doesn't even watch
basketball games on TV. I know my son. Something is very
wrong, and I am afraid."

Nyla clasped her hands before her on the table top. Brady glanced over at Derek before turning back to face her.

"Can we meet the boy?" he asked.

Derek's eyes widened in ill-concealed surprise.

The woman made a questioning face. "I will try to make him meet with you," she said quietly, "but I am not sure he will. He is...so different."

Brady nodded understandingly. "It's important, for us to judge just how bad this all is. Perhaps it's just a passing interest."

"Maybe he just wants to show off to his new friends," Derek offered.

Nyla stared at her hands. "I will try. But what should I tell him?"

Derek and Brady exchanged another look. Derek shrugged.

"How about telling him that a journalist from the Post got into contact with you through local Muslim organizations," James suggested. "Tell him I'm doing a story on young Muslim men in DC – how the wars in Iraq and Afghanistan, the Egyptian Spring, the terrorism concerns all impact them, and I'd like to interview him. How about that?"

"You should be a reporter," Derek said with a teasing grin.

"Perhaps. Perhaps he will talk to you. He very much has opinions," she said shaking her head.

"Good. Use that. Tell him that if he really wants people to know about Islam and about Muslims in America, he should talk to me."

"I will. I will talk to him. And you will help him, yes?"

Brady swallowed visibly. "We will…do our best to see first of all what this is all about…"

"If anything," Derek added.

"…and if it is something serious, we'll try to help. Yes. Definitely."

For the first time since she'd arrived, a smile appeared on Nyla's face. "I knew you are good man. I knew it." She took his hand in hers. "Thank you. Shokran."

"Your son doesn't know how lucky he is to have a mother like you," James said, patting her hand. "Now, can you give us a little more background info so that we can better understand where this whole thing is coming from?"

"What kind of 'info'?"

It turned out that Nyla had met Andrew Jacobson, an American petroleum engineer, in the UAE back in 1988. He was there looking for oil, she was a secretary in the company's Abu Dhabi headquarters. He spoke little Arabic, her English wasn't too good, but the attraction was mutual and just over a year later they were married. In 1990 they moved back to the U.S., and 14 months later their son Marid was born.

"Do you have a photo of him, by any chance?" Brady asked.

Her face lit up. "Of course! He was such a beautiful child." She dug into a pocket and produced a black leather wallet. She flipped through several sheets of vinyl wallet protectors until she found one she liked. "This at age 6," she said, handing it to Brady. James took one look at the blue-eyed, sandy-haired boy and knew at once why a terrorist organization would try to recruit him.

"Do you have anything a bit more recent?" he asked, showing it briefly to Derek before handing it back to her.

"This one is his graduation picture – just last year."

Brady could still see the same little boy in this latest photo, but the warm smile and welcoming gaze were gone. The young man that stared back at him looked solemn at best, dangerous at worst. Derek's eyes widened when he saw the picture.

"He seems to have become a bit more…serious," he commented, glancing up at Nyla as he handed it back to her.

Her smile faded as she stared at the photo. "I don't know what happens to him. My poor son, my poor Marid."

"That sweet little boy is still in there somewhere," Brady reassured. "We just have to find him. Now go home, and persuade him to see us."

"I will. I will do that," she said. She took two large gulps of orange juice, shoved the papers she'd produced back into a hidden pocket in her skirt, and pushed away from the table.

"Oh, one other thing," Brady said. "Why the waitress get-up in the restaurant? Why didn't you just call me?"

Nyla smiled sheepishly. "Our community is very small here in Washington," she said. "There are many from Middle East, but it is small all the same. That is how I knew that you and your woman ate at Fareed's restaurant. I could not risk that someone could see me talk to you. So, I wear the outfit like servers. And you are not so easy to call on the telephone. They tell me you are 'unlisted.'"

'For just this sort of situation,' Brady thought. "Sorry about that," he said.

"Speaking of phones, can you get access to your son's cellphone?" Derek interjected out of the blue.

She shrugged. "I might. Why?"

"How familiar are you with computers?"

"I have laptop."

"Excellent. Do you think you can follow these instructions?" He handed her a small slip of paper. "It will allow us to identify the people your son is talking to."

"I think so," she said when she'd glanced at them. "How long will this take?"

"Two minutes. Once you download the file and open it, you're done."

"And he will not know? He would be *very* angry."

"Not unless he monitors his programs a lot more carefully than most people."

She looked doubtful, but finally made up her mind. "I will try."

"Good. Let us know how you make out."

"I will. Ma'a as-salaama." She nodded briefly to the two men and then turned and left the coffee shop without even a glance back at them.

"Sweet little boy? That kid has bin-Laden eyes," Derek said doubtfully as soon as the door closed behind Nyla. "And how do you know she's not just another over-the-top paranoid control freak?"

"I don't. But those papers she showed us weren't Spiderman cartoons. They looked to me like the real thing." At that he reached under his right thigh and pulled out a familiar looking piece of paper. "But just to be sure, let's get this over to that explosives guru of yours, what's his name again?"

"Graves. Eddie Graves. Yeh, ok. I'll see if I can get to him this afternoon. And you?"

"I think I'll do a bit of background research on Islam in DC. If we get to talk to the kid I want to have all my ducks in a row."

"Shouldn't we contact the Feds? Secret Service, FBI?"

"Too early. If it turns out the kid's just pissed off at the world and is play-acting the role of bigshot terrorist, I don't want to stir up a bees' nest of trouble for him. Or his Mom."

"How about Chez?" The DC cop was a good friend and their main contact in the police world.

"Maybe. Let's talk to a few people, and then the kid. We'll decide from there."

"As long as we don't wait too long."

Brady sighed.

CHAPTER 3

Eddie Graves lived in a moderately fashionable area of northern Virginia, in the Starbucks-ridden no-man's land between the yuppie neighborhoods of northwestern Arlington and spooky Langley. A large number of Beltway Bandits lived in the area, most of whom looked to the east and the District for their bread and butter, though more than a few looked west to the George H.W. Bush Intelligence Center. Graves had once called Langley home, but for twelve years had been out on his own, billing ungodly hours to everyone from foreign governments to Congressional committees for sharing his expertise on explosives. Derek had met him through mutual friends.

Graves had been stationed in Iraq and Afghanistan before the average schmo in the U.S. even knew where the two countries were located. He was a 'security consultant' in each country, placed there by the Agency to make sure that Saddam and the Taliban never got too comfortable and always had something to concentrate on beyond oppressing their own people. He'd enjoyed his time in the desert. But one day, after the third time a sniper put a bullet too close for comfort – this time through his backpack less than a foot from his head, he realized that he could make more money with a lot less effort, and minimal personal security worries, by starting his own firm back in the DC area.

Derek's big old Cadillac rumbled to a stop in front of the two-story brick and siding home just after 1 pm. He hopped down off the riser he used to see above the steering wheel and slid down to the pavement. He was in a good mood. He only half-believed that this Arabic kid was really into anything seriously dangerous, and in any case, Graves usually had the best selection of beer of any of his friends.

He was whistling as he reached up to press the doorbell.

"Well, well, well, if it isn't the Munchkin Sam Spade," Graves said jovially as he threw open the door. At six-foot four, 220, with scarce an ounce of fat on him, Eddie would make even a normal-sized guy feel a bit under-sized. Luckily, Derek *never* felt small.

"Hey Eddie, blow anything up yet today?" he said, reaching out his hand to shake Eddie's even as he proceeded to march past him into the living room.

"Was saving that for your arrival," Graves said as he shut the door. "I thought that piece of crap out there in front of the house would be a good place to start."

"Hey, be my guest – it's insured," the PI said as he hopped up onto the surprisingly fashionable sofa.

"Wouldn't waste the explosives. Want anything to drink?"

"Does a pig fly?"

"He will before you pay for a beer," Graves muttered as he went into the kitchen. "Pretzels too?" he yelled back.

"Sure, why not."

Moments later Eddie came back into the living room carrying three different beers in one hand, and a green porcelain bowl filled with pretzels in the other.

"Take your pick," he said, dropping the three beers onto the coffee table in front of Derek.

"You mean, which one first, right?"

Eddie shook his head with a smile. "Do I look as stingy as a certain little PI I know?"

"You're a prince among men," the PI responded as he inspected the bottles and made his selection. He popped a top and took a deep gulp.

"So, other than to hit me up for beers that cost more than you're willing to pay, what brings you out of the District? You said something about an Arab kid and a bomb?"

Derek quickly outlined the situation. Graves listened carefully, asking for clarification when necessary.

"You've got the paper that James lifted?" Eddie asked when he'd finished.

"Right here." He pulled the paper out of his inside jacket pocket and handed it over.

Graves slipped on a pair of reading glasses and inspected the single piece of paper closely. With his carefully groomed greying hair and beige button-down shirt, he looked more like a college professor than an explosives expert. Derek saw his eyes narrow and his lips purse unconsciously, and knew right then that this story wasn't going to disappear as quickly as he'd hoped.

"What? Bad news?"

"Not good. As you may or may not know, the majority of al-Qaeda and copycat 'terrorist' sites are just junk, eye candy meant to recruit loser assholes into thinking that they're religious superheroes who are going to save the world for Allah, or whatever. More than a few of the sites are hosted by the FBI and some lesser-known agencies that are trolling for domestic goofballs with a predilection for that kind of nonsense. The schematics for explosive devices on those sites are either complete junk, or they're impossible for the average John Q. Rughead to assemble."

"And this one?"

"This one looks like the real thing – both the site and the instructions. I'm pretty sure I've seen the site before – I'll have to check a database to be sure. And the explosive vest seems to be classic suicide bomber stuff dating all the way back to pre-Iraq days. Basic, not very sophisticated, but effective. The blast will kill or maim anyone in the immediate vicinity, but the ball bearings and nails will cause significant casualties within a fifty foot radius, and will continue to draw blood out to four or five times that distance.

"If your kid is hanging out with folks who know how to access this shit, he's in deep – whether he knows it or not."

Derek sighed. Just his luck.

"If need be, could you hook us into some of the guys who are tracking this stuff? Someone we can bounce ideas off of and who can let us know if we're letting our imaginations get the best of us?"

Eddie didn't hesitate. "Absolutely. At the very least I can serve as a go-between, taking requests from you and Brady and bringing back the feedback. A lot of these guys are a little...media shy," he explained with a smile.

"Can't understand why," the PI said with wide-eyed innocence.

"Here, have another one of these," Graves said, passing him an unopened beer. "Maybe this will help you see the light."

Derek accepted the bottle and immediately spun the top off between his thumb and index finger, sending the cap sailing across the room.

"You've been practicing," Eddie said with real admiration.

"It's all in the wrist."

*****

Brady didn't have a lot of contacts in the DC Muslim world. Not that he had anything against them. It was just that he never seemed to run into them in either his work or social circles. That's why when he wanted a quick rundown on what was what and who was who in Islamic DC, the only person he could really go to was Professor Shaid Mansoor.

Mansoor was an Associate Professor of Middle Eastern studies at George Washington University. James had met him while working on a story about modern day middle-class slave labor in greater DC nearly ten years earlier. Maids kept locked in garages. Factory workers whose passports were taken away when they set foot in this country, and weren't returned until they'd paid off huge sums supposedly fronted to them for food, housing and medical care. Sex slavery. Real ugly stuff. Middle Easterners were found on both sides of the equation: both as victimizers and victimized. Mansoor seemed to know them all, or at least knew how to get to them all.

His knowledge about that community wasn't all that surprising, since George Washington was one of the biggest schools in DC and had longtime roots in the Middle East. An expensive, top-50 private university located in downtown DC just a stone's throw from the Department of State, GWU uses its proximity to tap big-time former government officials for lectures and visiting professorships and has a poli-sci department that regularly ranks among the nation's best. Mansoor was their Middle Eastern guy, with a sub-specialty (largely unspoken) of terrorism.

Brady drove around the campus for fifteen minutes looking for a parking space, until he finally found one on 22nd street with enough shade from an old elm to keep the worst of the sweltering sun off his roof. He walked the long block to the grey four-story building that housed the Political Science Department, sweating every step of the way. He breathed a loud and heartfelt sigh of relief when he stepped into the soothing coolness of Monroe Hall.

Mansoor's office was on the top floor. Brady wondered if the location of the office indicated the stature of the professor. Knowing the petty politics of university life, he wouldn't be surprised. What did surprise him, however, was the utter lack of visible security in the Hall. He found it ironic that Mansoor would specialize in terrorism and yet have his offices in a building that any two-bit malcontent could terrorize pretty much at will. 'Freedom of movement,' he was sure the university administrators would claim, until that Virginia Tech day when all the touchy-feely idealism would explode in a hail of bullets and bombs. Brady hoped it wouldn't be today.

He waited impatiently for an elevator, looking around as he did at small groups of students coming and going, the expensive artwork, the city itself in full swing outside the large windows. He wondered how many of those kids, or their parents for that matter, ever thought about all the political, religious, or just plain insane crazies out there who would need just the slightest push to do them harm in the name of some unfathomable belief or impossible goal. It was a scary world, if you bothered to stop and think about it.

The ding of the elevator bell returned his focus to the task at hand. Two co-eds who shared his car tapped their cellphones as if possessed, with complete disregard for anyone or anything around them. He wondered if they were texting each other. Thankfully, he had the car all to himself by the time he got out on the fourth floor, turned right, and then left to a short hallway that could have easily been transported from a 1970's psychiatric hospital.

'Nice,' he thought as he scanned nameplates looking for his guy. He'd been down on the second floor last time they'd met. Maybe his story had helped Mansoor move up the professorial pecking order.

Finally he found the door and knocked. A familiar voice invited him to enter.

"Mr. James!" the professor said warmly, standing to kiss the nonplussed James on both cheeks. "It has been too long."

"Professor. It has indeed. Nice digs," he said, eying the large, tastefully furnished room with the requisite power desk and just enough eye-catching handicrafts from the region to season the piles of papers and books with the flavor of the Middle East. "Weren't you on the second floor, in a somewhat more…modest office last time we met?"

Mansoor smiled. "The world moves in strange and mysterious ways," he said. "Sit, sit. May I offer you a cup of tea?"

Brady still didn't understand the whole tea thing. Why would anyone drink a tannic, bitter-tasting concoction that did little more than make you want to pee, when they could have the buzz of a coffee or the soothing refreshment of a nice cold beer instead? He realized he'd have to wait a while for the latter, but chanced a call for the former.

"Sorry. I'm all out," the professor explained. "I don't drink the stuff myself, and so I rarely remember to buy more."

"How about water?"

"Ah, a healthy alternative. Am I not the only one whose circumstances have changed in the past few years, then?"

Brady shrugged. "Actually I've been trying to keep my girlish figure."

"Quite successfully, I see."

James sucked in his gut as Mansoor poured a glass of water.

"So what is this about a possible terror plot?" the professor asked as he handed the glass to Brady.

James reiterated the story about Nyla and her son. "I'm no expert on bombs and suicide vests," he said as he finished, "but the information her son had in his room looked like the real deal to me. His mother's scared, and I don't blame her."

"I understand. So what would you have me do?"

"First of all, give me a quick rundown of the situation here in the DC area vis a vis immigrants from the Middle East."

Mansoor shook his head and sighed. "You talk about the Middle East as if it were just one big country. There are immense social, cultural and religious differences between communities within most of those countries, let alone between those that are thousands of miles apart. For your purposes, Middle East really means 'Muslim', am I right?"

Brady started to object, but caught himself. "Radical Muslim," he corrected. "But yeh, I guess it does."

"Then we're talking about people from as far east as Senegal, as far west as Pakistan – if we ignore the Uyghers and Kazakhs of China, as far north as Kazakhstan, and as far south as Nigeria, Kenya and Tanzania. And that's not even including Indonesia, with the largest Muslim population in the world. Islam is just as diverse as Christianity, although we here in the States have come to identify the term mainly as Middle Eastern or South Asian."

Brady listened patiently. He was not quite the Islamic neophyte Mansoor seemed to think. He'd read his share of news articles and commentaries over the years, and had already Googled Islam for dozens of articles about the mainstream religion and the radical offshoots that now threatened jihad for offenses real and imagined. What he needed to know more about was the local scene. But he knew the professor well enough to know that he'd eventually get around to it, once he'd made his own points.

"And that doesn't even include the Sunni-Shia divide, or the Salafi-moderate gulf. I could talk about any one of those groups for hours." He looked at Brady and smiled. "But of course that's not why you're here. You want to know about our local Islamic scene, and who might be involved in some of the more radical aspects."

"As much as I'd love to hear all about the rest," he said with just the right mix of respect and sarcasm, "yes."

Mansoor leaned back in his chair and steepled his fingers. "You know, of course, that talk about jihad does not equate to terrorism. There are a lot of people in this country, and everywhere else, who have axes to grind but will never take up arms to make their point."

"You're preaching to the converted, Prof. Look, I'm not a cop, and I promise you that no names will appear in any story. I just need a starting place if I'm going to try to learn more about Marid's new friends."

The professor hesitated a second as if evaluating Brady's motives. "If I were looking for people who might not like the U.S. government, I'd try the Masjid Al-Taqwa mosque in Southeast," he finally said. "They have a reputation for aggressive 'outreach'."

"Anyone there in particular I should talk to?"

"I doubt he'll talk to you, but try Ali al-Tumani. He's made some public statements that suggest he's not America's best friend. And he loves the spotlight."

"Do you know anyone who knows him?" Brady pressed. He'd learned long ago that even a lukewarm introduction from a barely-known associate is usually better than a cold call.

"You don't make it easy, do you?"

"Sorry. I just don't have a lot of contacts in that particular mosque."

Mansoor chuckled. "I bet. Let me make a few calls. I might be able to at least get you in the door. After that, it'll be up to you."

"Can't ask for anything more than that."

"You can, and sooner or later you will," the professor contradicted. "But, what the heck, if we can help keep one kid from getting caught up in all their jihad mumbo-jumbo, it's worth it."

"Thanks, Prof."

"Don't mention it. And I mean that literally: don't mention our little talk to anyone. This is a small town and a small community."

"So I've heard."

"I'd appreciate it."

"You got it. And Prof, tell the man that I'm doing a story on young Muslims in DC. Ok? I don't want to stir up a lot of attention over what may still turn out to be a false alarm."

"I understand. I'll tell him."

*****

By the time Brady caught up with his PI friend it was after four in the afternoon. Derek was sprawled out on his sofa watching a 2007 Redskins game when James arrived.

"You think they're gonna win this time?" Brady teased.

"As much chance as any other game lately. How'd it go with the Prof?"

"Good. He gave me a couple of leads in the Muslim community. How about you?"

"Eddie vouched for your boy's schematics. They're the real thing. If he actually makes that vest it could work."

"Damn. I was still hoping that Nyla was overreacting. I guess we'd better talk to her Chip. And the local radicals."

"Grab yourself a beer," Derek said, waving toward the kitchen. "Get in the right frame of mind."

"Tempting, but I think I'll wait a bit. Might need a clear head if I need to convince old Chip that it would be in his best interest to talk to us."

"I always thought you lied better after a couple of cold ones."

"Might be true. But I think I still have enough game when sober to sway a 22 year old."

"Go for it."

Brady made himself a cup of coffee and settled down next to the telephone. He rehearsed his argument and dialed Nyla's number.

The phone rang six times and he was just about to hang up when she finally answered.

"Hello?"

"Nyla, it's me – Brady James. Did you talk to your son?"

Her voice dropped to a whisper. "I did. He's not convinced, but he said he'll talk to you."

"When?"

"I'll see if he'll talk now."

"Nyla – I think it'd be better if we talked in person."

There was a longish pause. "I don't know...maybe you can persuade him."

He heard her call for her son. He waited. He was beginning to think he'd been stood up when the telltale sound of a young male voice could be heard saying something away from the receiver in Arabic. Nyla answered in a tone that suggested she was still insisting that he talk to Brady. Then the rustling sound of the phone being passed.

"Mr. James?" the voice asked. "This is Marid al-Zabaar. My mother tells me you'd like to interview me for a story you're working on." The voice was cool, not openly hostile but definitely not warm and fuzzy.

"You're her son, Chip?" he asked, hoping to get a feel for where the kid was politically.

"I'm her son, Marid," he corrected.

"Right. Well thank you for agreeing to let me interview you," Brady began, but Marid cut him off before he could finish the sentence.

"Not yet, I haven't. I told my mother that I'd be willing to talk to you, not be interviewed. I'm not sure I want to appear in the press."

"Then we'll make it anonymous. It's your story that I want to tell, of what it's been like growing up Muslim in DC. We don't need to use your name."

"Somehow I don't think you really want to tell my story," Nyla's son said so matter-of-factly that Brady was afraid that he'd somehow divined the real reason behind the interview request. He was about to tap dance all around the truth when Marid bailed him out. "Like Jack Nicholson said in 'A Few Good Men', I don't think you can handle the truth. Or your readers."

"Why don't you let me decide that," Brady answered. "You might be surprised what I can handle, and what my readers find interesting."

He hoped the long pause was a good sign. It was. "Do I get to read the article before you print it?"

"You can read it, but I won't promise that I'll change anything, unless there are factual mistakes." He wanted the kid to know that he wasn't in charge.

Another pause. "Look," Brady continued, sensing that he had the kid on the ropes, "you can tell it like it is. You can let all the non-Muslims out there know just how they've treated you, and your friends. You can help them understand about Islam."

"They are infidels," Marid growled. "How can they understand?"

"They are people. It's up to you to *make* them understand."

Brady heard a snort of what he took for derision.

He decided to push the ego button. "What, you don't think you can do it?"

"Most of them will never understand, no matter who explains," Marid said with a hint of defensive irritation.

"Maybe so. But even if you only convince a handful, isn't that better than nothing?"

Another pause. "Yeh, maybe. All right. When do you want to do this thing?"

"You tell me."

Brady wanted to get together as soon as possible, before the kid could change his mind or one of his new friends could forbid him to do it. Marid couldn't make it the next day, but the day after was a possible. They agreed to meet at noon. Agreeing where wasn't so easy. "No place public," Marid insisted. Brady thought about Anne's apartment, or Derek's, but thought better of it. A mosque was out. Brady had an idea. A little odd, but the price would be right, if it were available, and it wouldn't draw any prying eyes.

"I have a doctor friend. How about if we meet at his office?"

Marid hesitated. "Yeh, okay, that works," he agreed after due consideration.

Brady gave him the specifics. "See you there."

"No cameras, and just you – no one else."

"You got it."

"Okay. See you then."

As Brady hung up he wondered if maybe Nyla had been a bit overanxious after all. Her son didn't sound much different than a dozen other young guys he'd interviewed. Of course, most of them were felons, and none of them were studying suicide vest construction. He pursed his lips and sighed.

*****

By the time he got home to Anne's apartment, Brady was hot, tired and bothered. He couldn't for the life of him figure out why this young, seemingly well-adjusted young guy would suddenly give up the good life of suburban DC and set out to bomb anyone – let alone the White House.

"Maybe it's something that happened in Afghanistan, or Pakistan, or Iraq, or Iran, or Syria," Anne said as she rubbed his shoulders. "There's so much going on over there, we might not even know about it."

He groaned and flinched a bit as she hit a particularly tender spot. "Maybe. But I've been watching everything online pretty closely, and I haven't seen anything in the last few months that would take a recent college grad with lots of friends and turn him into a suicide bomber. Of course, maybe some of their operatives got to him and fed him a line of bs that he believes so fervently that he's ready to die for it."

"Or maybe his mom thought he was a lot happier than he really was," Anne said softly. "Moms have been known to make that mistake."

"Occupational hazard." He threw up his hands. "Nothing we can do about it now," he added, grabbing her by the waist to pull her around to face him. "How about we reverse roles: I'll give you a rubdown."

She couldn't help but smile at his leering grin. "Why do I think it won't end there?"

"Don't know," he said with a straight face. He was just stretching upwards to kiss her when the phone rang.

"Don't answer it," he said quickly.

"What if it's something important?"

"They'll call back."

But Anne was already reaching for the receiver. *'Must be her secretarial training,'* he thought. She couldn't let a phone ring long enough for the voicemail to kick on.

"Shaid Mansoor?" she asked, covering the mouthpiece with her hand.

Brady nodded and took the phone.

"Prof, what's up?"

"I made those calls I promised you, and low and behold, Mr. al-Tumani will deign to speak with you."

"Great. You must have been very persuasive."

"Actually, I just told him who you were and that you were researching a story about young Muslims in DC, and he agreed right then and there. No argument, no lecture."

"Out of character?"

"Very. In fact, just about 180 degrees out."

"Any chance that he might be involved with whoever is playing the kid?"

"Hard to say. Definitely not impossible."

By the time Brady hung up he had the imam's phone number but was wondering just what he'd gotten himself involved in.

"Bad news?" Anne asked from the expression on his face.

"Don't know yet. Not good."

"Then you need something to get your mind off your work," she cooed, pulling his head in close between her breasts and massaging his temples.

For just an instant he was about to say he needed to make a call first. But for just an instant. He'd make the call tomorrow.

CHAPTER 4

Dr. Benjamin Weiss was not only Brady's urologist, but an old poker buddy and almost as crazy about the DC sports scene as his retired journalist friend. James called him at 8:30 sharp. He knew Ben always got into the office by that hour, to review patients' files and return calls before his first appointment at 9:00. The receptionist, his wife Rachel, passed him through after just a few words of friendly chit-chat.

"Mr. James, how the heck are you?" the familiar voice said. "Still having problems getting the old hose to drain?"

"Hose is just fine, thanks," Brady answered, cringing a bit. "How about you? Check out any good prostates lately?"

The doctor chuckled. "You squeeze one, you squeezed them all."

"That's not a pretty picture."

"In the eye of the beholder, I guess. So, if it's not about business, what's up? Don't tell me you've got tickets to the Nationals."

"A very rare commodity, but no, actually I'm calling for a favor."

"What can we do for you?"

Brady quickly explained that he was working on a story about young Islam males in DC and needed a 'neutral' spot to hold an interview.

"Here? Sure, I suppose that'd be fine. We can make one of our examination rooms available. But are you sure your guy won't feel that the offices of a Jewish urologist aren't exactly neutral?"

In truth, Brady hadn't even considered the possibility, but he didn't have another place in mind that would work as well, especially for free. "Well, I suppose the only way to know is to ask him. I'll let you know. Tomorrow at noon?"

"Fine. See you then."

Even as he was hanging up, Brady decided that he wouldn't bother to tell Marid about Ben's ancestry. Just the Arlington address. He'd deal with the rest then and there.

*****

No sooner did he hear the dial tone than Brady dialed al-Tumani.

"Salam Alaikum," a gruff voice on the other end of the line answered.

"May I speak with Mr. al-Tumani, please?"

There was a delay. "This is the reporter, isn't it?"

"It is. Is this Mr. al-Tumani?"

"Mullah al-Tumani. Yes."

"Mullah," the reporter quickly adjusted, "as you already know, my name is Brady James. I'm a journalist doing some research for an article about young Muslim men in the DC area."

"Yes, Professor Mansoor has told me. What is it I can do to help you with your story?"

"Well, you have something of a...reputation as an activist in the area..."

"You mean as a radical cleric, don't you?" he interrupted.

"Well, yes as a matter of fact. I was hoping you might talk to me about your work, and about the young men who follow your teachings."

"You understand that I cannot name names or talk about specific situations."

"I do. I'm looking for some context: how many young Muslim men attend your services, some demographics, why they attend your services and not others, what they're looking for, that kind of thing."

It didn't take long for him to make up his mind. "Fine. When shall we meet?"

"Well, are you available today?"

"How long will this take?"

"An hour, maybe less. Depends on you, actually."

"How about 5:30 – after Asr and before Maghrib."

"Afternoon and evening prayers?"

"I'm impressed," al-Tumani said with more than a hint of sarcasm. "Yes, between prayers. Can you come here to the mosque?"

"I can. Thank you."

The mullah gave him the address and they finalized the interview. Brady felt his heart pounding as he hung up.

*****

Brady had been tempted to ask Derek to ride along with him to the Mullah's place in Southeast, or at least shadow him in his own car, but upon further reflection he decided to go it alone. He didn't want to spook al-Tumani, at least not until he could learn more about the sub-culture that he – and perhaps Nyla's son – inhabited.

Southeast DC is not a pretty place. A lot of African-Americans shy away from the decrepit neighborhoods across the Anacostia River. Most white District dwellers have never even visited. Military installations dot the area, barbed-wire protecting our nation's soldiers from the poverty, drugs and despair that infect many of the surrounding streets. As James crossed the John Phillip Sousa Bridge on Pennsylvania Ave, he couldn't help but think that it was neighborhoods like Southeast that served as breeding grounds for so many of the violent anti-establishment groups that had sprung up in the U.S. and elsewhere. And if violence was the disease, then people like al-Tumani were the viruses that took simmering discontent and turned it into a religious experience.

Brady turned off of Pennsylvania onto Q St SE and into a parking spot in front of a rundown two-story brick building fronted by a hand-painted sign that read 'Southeast Mosque'. He locked the doors carefully and scanned the neighborhood. Not so bad. A little beat-up, everything in need of paint, but generally speaking the homes and other buildings weren't as dilapidated as some other areas of the city he'd seen. The lawns were mowed; not too many boarded windows.

The mosque, on the other hand, looked like an abandoned office building. The grass was overgrown, the few scraggly bushes hadn't been trimmed forever, and a window on the ground floor was cracked. Brady ignored the condition of the building and walked up to the entrance door. A well-worn pair of shoes and a pair of sandals sat on a rickety shelf just outside the door. They reminded Brady of the necessity of removing his own shoes before entering.

As soon as his shoes were shelved he knocked loudly. He waited patiently for a minute or two until at last the door swung open to reveal a young black man, no more than 22 or so, with a full beard, wearing a white, full-length galabiyya and matching turban.

"Yes?" he said with no more of a welcome than if Brady were selling life insurance door to door.

"Mullah al-Tumani?"

"Is he expecting you?" the young man asked with obvious incredulity. Brady got the distinct impression that not too many white beardless visitors made their way to the Mosque.

"He is. Would you tell him that Brady James is here?"

"Wait." The brusqueness was just this side of insulting.

It was nearly five minutes later, with sweat running down Brady's back and accumulating on his upper lip and forehead, that the young man reappeared.

"Come with me," he said, somehow making it sound like he was doing Brady a favor.

The inside of the building was a pleasant surprise. They entered directly into a large open room with a number of candles burning around the periphery. As opposed to the exterior of the building, this room, though far from luxurious, was clean, recently painted, with what appeared to be fairly new carpeting. Best of all, it was cool inside. They passed through the main room to the back of the building and a small office. Inside, sitting behind a large and surprisingly expensive looking desk, sat a small middle-aged Middle-Easterner whose black beard was streaked with grey.

He wore the same clothes as his assistant, though with considerably more embroidery on both the galabiyya and hat. He did not smile and did not stand as Brady was ushered into the room.

"Mr. James," he said with a curt nod.

"Mullah?" Brady asked, to be sure he was in fact speaking with al-Tumani.

"It is. Please, be seated."

He nodded to the sole chair sitting in front of the desk. Brady did as he was told, glancing around at the nearly bare walls as he did. The young aide disappeared silently back out through the door, which he shut behind him.

"So, you are writing a story about our Muslim youth, is that right?" al-Tumani asked, his black eyes locked on James'.

"That's right. Specifically about the trials and tribulations of young Muslim men living in DC."

"Why do you think there are tribulations?" the Mullah asked, his voice absolutely neutral, revealing nothing of his own feelings.

Brady had not expected any disagreement with his basic premise and was taken aback; he quickly regrouped. "What I've read, what I've heard, and what other young men I've interviewed have told me. Ever since 9/11 there have been... disagreements, some of which have come to blows."

"Most of which the Muslims in question had little to do with instigating," the mullah said in a tone that broached no argument. "May I ask where you've been interviewing? I haven't heard anything through our little grapevine about a famous journalist talking to young men in our community."

"Northern Virginia and southern Maryland," Brady said immediately, hoping the lack of hesitation and specificity would provide cover for his blatant lie. "But I've only spoken with three young men so far. I hope to meet more."

"And so you are here." The mullah certainly didn't beat around the bush or hide behind niceties.

"Well, yes. Mainly I'm here to get some context from someone who knows the community, but I'm also hopeful that you might be able to help me contact several young Muslim men – both those who've had problems, and those that haven't."

"In which group would you place your first three interviewees?"

Brady wasn't used to answering more questions than he asked, but he understood that the mullah was just feeling him out.

"A little of both," he said. No need to commit just yet.

Al-Tumani nodded thoughtfully. "I am not surprised. I should think that most non-white, non-Christian young men in this area, or anywhere in this country for that matter, would have some problems."

"And why do you think that is?"

"America is a hypocritical country. Most people claim to value individualism and freedom, but what they really value is their own beliefs. Anyone different than they are is dangerous. Anyone who is a Muslim is doubly dangerous because they might be a terrorist, and young Muslim men are even more dangerous than that."

"If you don't mind me being the devil's advocate, where isn't that the case? From what I understand, non-

Muslims in many Muslim countries are persecuted, denied basic rights, even killed. Surely things are much better for Muslim men here."

"The Koran says 'Let there be no compulsion in religion.'"

"I'm not talking about theology, but reality. Do you deny that non-Muslims are persecuted in many Muslim countries?"

"There are Muslims who do not follow the letter of the Koran."

"Aren't there governments in Muslim countries that do not follow the letter of the Koran?"

"Individuals. True believers follow the words of the Prophet, Allah bless him, and do not allow their personal biases to affect their actions."

"Like you?" Brady knew he was pushing the envelope, but he wanted to see the man's reaction. What greeted him was a cold stare.

"I was young, once. I made mistakes that young men make. I have grown wiser with the help of Allah the almighty."

"And now you counsel young men to follow the letter of the Koran?"

"It is the only way."

"Do they listen? I understand that some young Muslim men look upon the West in general, and the U.S. in particular, as an evil to be destroyed. Through jihad, if I'm not mistaken."

Al-Tumani waved his hand dismissively. "There are always hotheads. They are not in the majority and do not reflect the true face of Islam. Islam is a religion of peace."

"I read somewhere that words such as 'kill', 'fight' and 'murder' occur in the Koran over 35,000 times. It doesn't sound all that peaceful."

"How many times do such words occur in the Bible?"

"I have no idea. But I think anyone who's read the Bible would agree that there is a lot of violence in there. I never hear any Muslim admitting the same about the Koran."

"Because the main themes of the Koran are peace and understanding."

James wasn't getting anywhere. "Okay, let's leave the Koran for now. How about here in DC? How would you characterize the local Muslim community in general, and young Muslim men in particular?"

"How do you mean?" The mullah wasn't going to give up anything easily.

"Are they content? Do they feel welcomed, or at least accepted as full and equal members of the community? Do they think they are looked down upon, or discriminated against because of their religion?"

"Some yes, some no. Muslim is not a monolithic entity, any more than Christianity. But if you mean do young men seem to have a harder time of it here than their elders or women relatives, I'd say yes. For all its churches, America is not a holy place. Just take one look at all the drugs, the prostitution, the way women dress and display themselves in public places. How can our young men not be outraged?"

"You do know that most of the heroin in this country comes from Afghanistan, a Muslim country?" James countered. "And I'm pretty confident that prostitution is not unknown in Islamic countries."

The mullah's eyes narrowed. Brady could tell he wasn't used to anyone contradicting his words. "In Muslim countries, women are revered and protected. Here, they show themselves like whores, and so they are treated like whores."

Finally the gloves were coming off and his tone hardened. "So young men would be justified in their anger?"

"Absolutely."

"And what, exactly, should they do about it?"

Just as Brady prepared to be assaulted by an angry rant, the mullah took a deep breath and leaned back in his chair. He closed his eyes for a moment to collect himself.

"They should register to vote and elect leaders who reflect their ideals and beliefs," he said calmly, the red in his cheeks fading slowly. "They should protest. They should write in newspapers and blogs. They should change their world."

"Do you know any young men who are doing that? Changing their worlds?"

"I might. I take it you'd like to interview them?"

"I would."

"Why should they want to talk to you? What's the benefit for them?"

Brady had been prepared for the question. "Publicity. They can get their message out to the world, or at least our little corner of it. If they want to change things, they'll need other people to help them. If they're persuasive, my story might help them convince others."

"So your motivation is strictly altruistic?" The cynicism was not disguised.

"Of course not. I want to sell papers. But I also want people to understand their world. That's *my* job." Of course, his *real* job was to find leads to the shadowy world that Marid had apparently stumbled into, but he wasn't about to share that reality with al-Tumani.

The mullah stared for several seconds. "All right. I will see if some of our brothers will speak with you."

"Thanks. I appreciate it."

"Just be sure the article is fair and balanced. That is all I ask."

"I'll do my best."

The way the mullah cocked his head, Brady was fairly certain he wasn't entirely convinced. *'As long as he puts me in touch with some of his 'brothers'*, Brady thought.

CHAPTER 5

Dr. Weiss had scheduled his last morning appointment at 11:30, so that by the time Brady arrived a little before noon there was no one in the waiting room. Nyla had left him a voicemail that she had been able to install the tracking software on her son's phone, so Brady was confident that they could monitor the kid. But he wanted to meet him, talk face to face. That's how he'd always learned the most about the people he'd profiled, whether criminal or cop.

Just minutes before Marid was scheduled to arrive, Mrs. Weiss showed the last patient out the door and accompanied her husband to an early lunch. James was left alone in the office. On one hand, he thought it might be easier to get the kid to open up if no one else was there. On the other, if the kid really had gone over to the dark side, he wasn't sure he was thrilled to be there with no one within earshot. He'd soon know if he'd made the right decision.

He sat and flipped through a Time magazine as he waited, trying to give the impression – to himself as much as to Marid – that he was relaxed and in charge. Only problem was, he found himself flipping through page after page without remembering a word he'd read. Noon came and went. 12:10. Then 12:15. He was about to give up hope when the door finally opened and a familiar face, albeit partially covered by a curly blond beard, walked into the waiting room.

"Marid?" he asked, standing to greet the young man.

"Yes. You're Mr. James?" He seemed polite, calm, not at all the firebrand Brady had expected.

"That's me. Hey, thanks for meeting me like this. I appreciate the interview."

"It's for an article on young Muslim men in DC, right?" He wanted to be sure.

"It is. Trying to give a good, rounded picture of what it's like growing up Muslim during these difficult times."

"And how did you come to contact me?" the young man asked. Brady thought he recognized a hint of defensiveness.

"Just by asking around the neighborhood. Someone mentioned that your mother had married an American oil worker…"

"A 'real' American, is that what you mean?" The defensiveness was full-blown.

"An American born here. It made for an interesting difference between you and so many of the other young men who either were born in the Middle East or South Asia, or both their parents were born there. A different angle."

Marid digested the information and seemed to relax a bit.

"Okay, so what now?"

"Now we sit and talk a bit. Okay?"

"Yeh, sure."

"Let's go in back, though. It'll be a bit more private."

He led the way through a door next to the reception desk to the small office Ben had lent him. He pulled a big leather chair out from behind the desk and motioned for Marid to sit. Then he pulled a smaller chair over to face him.

"I really appreciate your coming today," Brady began. "It's important that people understand just what young Muslim men in the DC area are confronted by."

"No problem. I'd like people to see the way things really are as well."

The kid seemed a little tense, less defensive, but above all surprisingly controlled.

"Good. Then we're on the same side."

"I doubt that." Simple. Direct.

"We'll see. So, tell me a little about yourself – age, childhood, where you went to school, that sort of thing."

Marid seemed to relax a bit and leaned back in the chair. "Not much different than a lot of kids, I suppose, except that I was raised Muslim. As you already know, my Mom married my Dad overseas and then moved here – or to Texas, actually. Then I came along a little over a year later. We lived in Texas until I was 9, and then moved to this area."

"Did being Muslim cause any problems in your younger days?"

"Not really. I mean, I knew even then that we were different – my Mom and me, not my Dad who really didn't practice any religion – but I don't remember anyone bullying me or calling names or anything like that."

"So then you came to DC. What then?"

"Well, from the view of being Muslim, what happened then was 9/11. Suddenly we went from nobody really paying any attention to Muslims, to all of a sudden we were the bad guys. Terrorists. Trying to destroy the West."

"How did that impact you?"

Marid took a deep breath and stared off into space for a moment. "Actually, I kind of kept quiet about being Muslim. I mean, most of my friends were Christians, and we didn't really talk about religion all that much."

"And you have light hair and blue eyes."

Those eyes locked onto Brady's. "I didn't pretend to be a Christian. I just didn't bring it up in casual conversation. I really wasn't all that religious."

"Did your friends know you were Muslim?"

"Some."

"Did they say anything, do anything…?"

"Not to me directly, no. I guess they didn't see me as one of *them*, the terrorists. But yeh, I heard a lot about rugheads and nuking the Middle East, and all of that."

Brady could see the pain in the kid's eyes. "How did that make you feel?"

Marid looked up at Brady with a quizzical glance. "I thought this was an interview, not psychoanalysis."

"Readers want to know what you felt, not just the cold facts. The whole point of the story is to show the human side of Islam in DC. So?"

He shrugged. "So, I kind of felt like…well, kind of like a traitor to my Mom's heritage, you know? Sure, some crazy people using Islam as their excuse crashed those planes, and I couldn't understand how they could do such a thing. But there were millions of other Muslims out there who hadn't done a thing who were suffering for the actions of a dozen madmen. And, I didn't really do anything about it."

"One person can't always change the world."

"Change always begins with one person," the kid answered, and once again Brady caught a glimpse of the tough, determined young man behind the blue eyes.

"Okay. So you laid low for a while. What then?"

"Then, I went off to college, and for the first time met people like me – Muslim Americans. It was eye-opening."

"How do you mean?"

"Well, first of all, where we lived in DC I only knew a handful of Muslims, and I really didn't spend any time with them."

"But in college…"

"In college it was different. The kids that go to a specific school are all sort of similar to begin with, so I had a lot in common with most of the other Muslim kids beyond religion. Then the atmosphere of the school lent itself to philosophical and political discussions. We spent a lot of time staying up late, talking about al-Qaeda, bin Laden, the whole mess. For the first time in a long time, I didn't feel like being a Muslim was something to be ashamed of. As a matter of fact, I realized it was something I should be proud of." He sat up straighter in his chair and stared at Brady as if daring him to contradict him. "I suppose you could say I had an epiphany."

"How did the other students, the non-Muslims, react to this new you? Were they understanding, or confused, or what?"

"Most of my close friends were okay with it. I wasn't really into proselytizing or anything. I guess the main difference was that I attended mosque, prayed on a daily basis, and observed the holy days more strictly. To my friends it wasn't that big a change. No big deal."

"And to you?"

"Once you've seen the path, you must take it." His voice was so calm it was almost mechanical. It was like listening to a different kid. Brady tried to keep his expression unchanged.

"Do you mean something more than prayer and the like?"

"When you allow Allah into your heart, it changes you. You see things differently. You see the world differently."

"How do you mean? What kinds of things?"

"Just about everything. When you're raised here in the States, like I was, you're taught that freedom and democracy and wealth are the ultimate goals of life. They're not. Or they don't have to be. Faith, family and friends are the true goals of a Muslim's life. The western philosophies are all about the self. Islam is about the community, about our interconnections, about Allah and the life after this one."

"And how has this revelation played out in your life? Has it changed what you do, or how you do it, or has it just changed your point of view?"

Marid paused as if considering carefully his next words. "A man must ultimately be judged by his actions. It is easy to cry out against injustice, or crimes against humanity. It is something else to take action."

"Admirable. But what kinds of action? What can one person do?"

"I volunteer at the mosque twice a week. I read to little kids. Help them understand the big world out there."

"What do you read to them?

The young man looked at James out of the corner of his eye. His skepticism was ill-concealed.

"From the Koran. Other, similar books."

"Do you ever…take part in protests, anything like that?"

He scowled. "You've been talking to my mother, haven't you?"

"We talked briefly, yes, but she didn't mention anything in particular."

"That's a surprise. But, to answer your question, yes, I have participated in protests. We picketed the Pentagon after the shooting of those 16 innocents in Afghanistan, and the State Department, the White House, Congress…"

"You get around. Ever been arrested?"

"There is no shame in going to jail for a just cause," Marid said with more vehemence than Brady would have anticipated.

"I take it that means yes?"

"Yes. I was arrested twice, for trespassing and public disturbance."

"I bet your Mom was very upset."

"She worries too much."

"Isn't that what mothers do – worry?"

"I suppose."

"What are you doing these days?"

"How do you mean?" he asked, and Brady heard the defensiveness once more.

"Just what I asked. What are you doing these days? Do you have a job? Do you have a girlfriend? How is your life in general?"

"Not too bad. I lost my job at a consulting firm a little over a year ago. They downsized."

"Last in, first out?"

"Something like that." Brady heard anger and jotted a note to follow-up with Nyla. "I get some part-time work every now and then through some friends."

"Also Muslims?"

"Yeh. Muslims take care of their own."

"Girlfriend?"

"No," he answered, his voice softer. "It is not easy to find the right person to share your life."

"You can say that again." Brady glanced down at his notepad. "How about recent happenings in the region – the Egyptian Spring and all the changes it has brought, any impact on you or your friends?"

"Not so much. Maybe a little more pride, that Muslims are changing their lives without the west leading the way." Brady could see that pride in the boy's eyes.

"But no difference in the attitudes of the non-Muslims in your life?"

"No, not really. Their lives are very inward looking. They see what is happening throughout North Africa and the Middle-East, but it doesn't touch them."

Brady nodded. He'd asked most of the questions he'd wanted to touch upon. "Anything else you'd like to add? Any message for other Muslims, or non-Muslims for that matter, in DC?"

Marid thought for a moment. "Not really. Oh, maybe one thing. They shouldn't judge all Muslims by the actions of just a few, any more than they'd judge all Christians because of a handful of troubled souls. And even those few may have their reasons. They might not be obvious, but they might still be valid."

"Anyone in particular," James asked, "who might be misunderstood?" He stared at Marid, hoping to get a strong reaction. All he got was a shrug.

"Not really. We all have our reasons."

"Yes, I'm sure we do," Brady said, closing his notebook. "Well, that's about all I have. Thanks again for coming by. How can I get ahold of you if I need some clarification or additional info?"

"You can call my Mom. You obviously have her phone number."

"Nothing more direct?"

"I don't like cell phones."

Brady tried to hide the surprise from his face. "E-mail?"

He thought a moment. "Yeh, all right. You can reach me at ShahidM83@yahoo.com. But I don't check it very often."

"I'll keep that in mind. Thanks again."

He stood and walked Marid to the door where they shook hands.

"When will this be published?" the young man asked.

"Probably three or four weeks. It's not up to me."

"Okay. I'll look for it."

"Great. And Marid, take care of yourself. One thing I can tell you for sure is that your mother loves you very much."

"Yeh. I know." Without so much as a hint of a smile, he turned and headed for the elevators. Brady watched him for just a second and then closed the door. He'd hoped he would be able to give Nyla a call to poo-poo the idea that her son had a terrorist act in mind. He wouldn't be making that call.

*****

Derek stood off to the side of the lobby, behind the exit from the elevators. As soon as Marid came down from his interview with Brady, Derek followed at a cautious distance. One of the problems with being a midget was that he couldn't really blend in with the crowd. Even a quick glance could reveal his presence. But he was used to it, and knew how to remain as invisible as someone of his stature could be.

His phone vibrated before he even left the building.

"How'd it go?" he asked, having seen James' caller ID.

"Not great. The kid's very cool, but it's clear he has some kind of chip on his shoulder. The way he deflected questions makes me think he may have received training in counter-interrogation methods."

"That doesn't sound good."

"No, it doesn't. Keep an eye on him. I'd like to know if he contacts anyone."

"We'll do our best."

Even as he turned his cell off, he watched Marid stop and punch some numbers into his phone. He talked very briefly and then continued on his way. Derek scanned the street to see if anyone might be watching the kid; when he saw nothing out of the ordinary, he hurried to catch up with him.

The route Marid took was neither quick nor direct. In fact, his zigging and zagging – down Wilson, across to

Clarendon, and then back past Wilson again – soon had the PI agreeing with his friend's assessment: something wasn't quite right there. Several times he'd had to duck into a shop doorway or hide behind a street vendor or parked car when the kid had stopped and 'casually' glanced behind him. If he hadn't been trained in surveillance detection, he certainly had a natural gift.

Eventually, though, he made his way to The Delta Bakery, a small coffee shop on a side street. Derek found a comfortable spot at the entrance to a large old Victorian house across the street where he could look into the shop through large front windows. The café was too small to chance entering – in such a tiny space he would definitely be noticed. But from where he stood behind nice thick shrubbery that encircled the lawn, he could look through the telephoto lens of his Canon and see every table and every face as if he were standing next to them.

He watched Marid take a seat at a table in the back corner, as far from the front door as he could manage. He chatted briefly with the waitress, and then pulled out his cellphone and apparently checked texts or emails. In any case, it was only about five minutes later when a man about 40 years old entered the shop and made his way directly to Marid's table. The man was about 5'8", maybe 150 pounds, wearing a dark business suit and tie. Perhaps the only distinguishing characteristic that hit Derek at first glance, other than his olive, Middle Eastern skin, was the black, close-cropped beard. It didn't cry out Muslim Radical, but it did whisper the descriptor loudly in the PI's inner ear.

It was clear from their greeting, kisses on both cheeks, that the men knew each other. Derek was so intent on firing off a series of headshots that he didn't hear the light footsteps come up behind him.

"May I help you?" an older woman's voice asked with a decided edge. Derek nearly dropped the camera.

"Uh, no, no. I was just photographing some of the local architecture," he said as he turned quickly, hoping she couldn't hear his pounding heart.

"From behind my shrubs?"

The PI knew he was standing there like an idiot, but nothing leapt to mind. "I...don't like to intrude into their space," he finally said, trying to sound as artsy-fartsy as he could manage. "It changes the reality."

The woman, probably in her mid-80's but very well-dressed and still obviously on the ball, stared at him as if unable to decide if he were some kind of artistic weirdo or a bald-faced liar. "Oh," she offered, apparently having decided to give the strange little man the benefit of the doubt, "I see."

"I'm sorry if I intruded on your privacy – I didn't think anyone was home." He smiled.

"No, no, no. Not a problem. Just wondered what was going on out here."

"Just me. Nothing to worry about."

"All right then. Carry on," the woman said. She stood and watched for a minute or two as Derek snapped a few more photos. When he didn't show any signs of continuing the conversation, she eventually left. The PI waited for a short while and then packed up his camera and moved down the street to a falafel joint with some outside tables. He ordered a kabob wrap and waited. *Might as well be comfortable'* he mused as he bit into the tasty concoction. It might be a while.

In fact, it was about thirty minutes later when the bearded businessman left the coffee shop, alone. Derek had to make a quick decision whether to follow the newcomer, or stay with Marid. Figuring that they had the kid's cellphone tapped, he decided to see what he could learn about the businessman. He kept an eye on the man from the opposite side of the street, moving when he moved, stopping more or less when he stopped. He tried not to be obvious by mirroring his moves too closely. He always walked a half-block or so after the stranger stopped to glance casually left and right, and tried to keep close to small groups of people who could shield him from view. The very fact that the man stopped frequently and changed direction seemingly without reason made the PI very uncomfortable. It looked much too much like the same tactics Marid had used just an hour earlier.

Eventually, after walking all the way to Key Blvd and then back across both Clarendon and Wilson on Danville, the man made his way to the shopping complex in The Market Common. Derek had to cross the street in a hurry, nearly becoming a hood ornament on an Audi A6 driven by a 20's-something young woman who was too busy reading texts to bother looking down to the PI's level as he jaywalked to the Common. Screeching tires and a blaring honk of the horn were not the way Derek had wanted to keep his anonymity, but he dismissed it all with a shrug and smile, and waddled off at full speed without so much as an apology to the momentarily nonplussed driver.

As he was dodging the Audi Derek lost sight of his target, but just a few seconds later he spotted the beard bobbing among hordes of shoppers a few hundred feet ahead. The businessman seemed in no rush, and so Derek was able to close the distance between them despite his stunted legs. He was panting heavily, however, by the time he got to the parking garage where Mr. Beard was already clicking the remote to open his car. Derek leaned against a black pickup truck to catch his breath as the stranger unlocked a silver Mercedes and backed out of his space. It was all the PI could manage to grab his camera and snap a couple of photos of the car's license plate as it slid past. The PI was cursing his physical conditioning and promising to cut back on the beers when he noticed that the car immediately in front of the Mercedes at the cashier's booth was taking an inordinate amount of time to pay. Was it worth the risk? He made a snap decision and hurried to where the Mercedes was idling.

Just as the car pulled up to pay, Derek slipped across to the opposite wide of the car from the driver and cashier and casually put his hand up under the rear wheel well of the Mercedes, just seconds before Mr. Beard gunned the S600 sedan out into the whirl of activity in the Common yard. Derek smiled with satisfaction. The PI had brought a GPS tracker with him just in case Marid rendezvoused with anyone, and now it was beeping merrily on his handheld monitor as the Mercedes travelled unawares toward the District. Derek was parked a few blocks away, but this time he didn't rush. The GPS would operate for days, if not weeks. There was no hurry. Sometimes brains – and luck – were better than brawn.

*****

Brady expected the call, but he wasn't looking forward to it. He probably should have called Nyla earlier, but just couldn't bring himself to deliver the bad news.

"Mr. James?" Nyla's voice asked when he answered the phone.

"Yeh, it's me, Nyla. How are you doing?"

"Not good. Not good at all." She sounded nervous, almost hysterical.

"What is it? What happened?"

"Marid has not come home for lunch. And he hasn't called!"

Brady rolled his eyes in spite of his best efforts to control himself. "I'm sure he's just gotten delayed."

"He always calls!" she said plaintively.

He glanced at his watch: 2:15. "I wouldn't worry too much, Nyla. He'll probably walk in any time now."

"I hope so," she finally agreed. "But I am just so nervous with all that is happening. What of your talk? Did you learn something?"

"Nothing for certain."

"But you have your ideas?"

Brady paused. "Well, yes. But until we can gather more information, they're just ideas."

"You think he is mixed-up with bad people?"

He decided to tell her the truth. "He might be. We have a lot more checking to do, but he might be involved with some bad characters."

"I knew it," Nyla said, her voice small and defeated. "I knew something was wrong."

"Well don't get too upset just yet. We may be completely wrong, or we may be able to stop him before he does anything stupid."

"Do you think so?" she asked, her voice once again animated.

"Of course. At this point he's just reading some dangerous material. That's not illegal."

"Oh thank you, Mr. James, thank you. He is a good boy. He is not like this."

"I'm sure he is, Nyla. Now let me get back to work and I'll let you know when we have anything more to tell."

"You are a good man, Mr. James."

As soon as Brady hung up the phone he dialed Derek.

"Where you at?" he asked the PI.

"The District. Just came across the Key Bridge and we're headed up Wisconsin Ave."

"We?"

"I followed a guy who met with Marid at a coffee shop in Clarendon and have been tailing him ever since."

"Where's Marid?"

"You tell me. You've got the phone tracking software on the laptop. Just sign-in and check it out."

"We can see where he is?" Brady had assumed they'd just be able to eavesdrop on his conversations.

"There's a GPS in most decent cellphones these days," the PI explained patiently. "Maybe not the little piece of crap you carry, but most real phones. And with that software we can pinpoint his location, listen-in to calls, see who he calls and who calls him, read his text messages, you name it. If it passes through that phone, we can see or hear it."

Brady was both amazed and repulsed. Amazed that something so cheap and easy to install could do so much, but repulsed as a journalist and champion of free rights that it was so easy to spy on someone. In this instance his revulsion was trumped by his need.

He put the phone down on the table and cranked up the laptop. A couple of clicks of the mouse and there was Marid's phone data, ordered by date, time, phone number called or called by, and his exact GPS coordinates. He clicked on the coordinates and a map of Clarendon was superimposed over a blinking green light. The light was located at the exact address of the coffee shop.

He picked up the phone. "He's still at the coffee shop."

"Hmm. Maybe he's been told to stay there until his buddy gets to wherever he's headed."

"Maybe he likes the coffee. Or the waitress."

"Maybe. But whatever the reason, keep an eye on him. As soon as I find out where this guy is headed, I'll give you a call. If he's still at the café, I'll swing by and see if I can re-establish my surveillance."

"You got it. And Derek, take care with that guy you're following. I'm starting to get a bad feeling about this kid."

"10-4."

Brady shook his head as he hung up.

*****

Derek followed the Mercedes up Wisconsin until it turned left on Volta, right on 34th, and then right again on Q St. He drove on narrow tree-lined roads, past chichi brick townhouses decorated in the Colonial tradition. The Mercedes definitely wasn't out of place in this neighborhood, though the PI's old Caddy would probably be considered an eyesore by some of the locals. Finally the Benz pulled over and parked in front of a row of nearly identical brick homes, each a model of conservative elegance.

'*So what's this guy doing here?*' Derek wondered. Of course, he could live there, but then again, maybe he was visiting another friend like Marid. The PI parked about a half-block west of the Mercedes and pulled out his Canon just in case he got a glimpse of a wife, or friend, or even a maid inside. But the bearded businessman pulled out a set of keys and opened the front door unassisted. Derek watched for another couple of minutes, then called Brady to report that he was on his way back to Clarendon to check on Marid.

There was no way for him to know that just moments after his Cadillac passed the unidentified businessman's house, the man reappeared, scanned the street quickly, and hopped back into his Mercedes. In seconds, he was gone.

*****

By the time Derek snaked his way through the heavy afternoon traffic all the way back to the coffee shop, it was after three. He parked the Caddy just a block from the shop and walked the rest of the way. When he got to his favorite vantage point across the street from the Bakery, he scanned the house behind him to help ensure that he wouldn't be surprised again, and then lifted the Canon to his eye to see what Marid was up to inside. But there was no one seated at the table. He panned from one end of the small café to the other. No sign of the kid. He quickly dialed James.

"Hey, why didn't you tell me the kid left the coffee shop?" he berated his friend. "I just spent a half hour fighting my way through traffic to get here."

"What? Hang on a second," Brady answered. Less than a minute later he was back. "The GPS says he's still in there."

"Well then he's taking the longest crap in history," the PI grumbled. "I've been standing here for five minutes, and no sign of him. I'll give him another couple of minutes, and then I'm going in." Brady stayed on the phone as his friend first gave him a more detailed rundown of his time tailing the bearded stranger, and then continued with a running commentary as he first crossed the street and then went into the Bakery.

"Still don't see him," he reported as he stepped inside. "I'll go check out the rest rooms." Brady heard a voice greet the PI and ask him if he wanted a table. "Just need to take a whiz," the little man growled, and apparently the waitress decided not to challenge him. The next time Derek spoke, Brady could hear his words echoing off the rest room walls. "No one in here. Hang on." A minute later he was back. "The kid left his phone on a chair at his table. He's long gone."

"Do you think he left it on purpose, or just spaced?"

"I'll sit and have a nice latte and see if he comes back. But if your vibe is right, I have a feeling he spotted me, or just decided to dump the phone. I mean, who leaves a phone accidentally on a chair? The tabletop, sure. But a chair?"

He was right of course. Somehow the kid had known that they were following him and had ditched the GPS. The whole affair was looking worse and worse by the minute.

If he had seen the silver Mercedes parked on a side street less than a block from the coffee shop, he might have understood how the kid had known about the tail. And he might have guessed that the jaunt over to Georgetown had been just a ruse to allow Marid time to get away. And he would have been much, much more worried.

CHAPTER 6

Brady waited until eight o'clock to call Nyla again.

"Is he back yet?"

"No! And now I am very worried. He always calls if he's coming home late."

"Well, don't get too upset," Brady reassured, even though he was increasingly convinced that she had every reason to worry. "I'm sure he'll turn up any time now."

"What does your software that I put on his phone say?" she asked. "Doesn't it tell you where he is?"

Brady had hoped she'd forgotten the software. "Actually, he left his phone in a coffee shop."

"What?! Marid would never do that! He always has his phone with him."

"I can't explain it, but my associate found the phone."

Her long silence spoke more tellingly than her words.

"Is he okay?" she asked softly.

"I'm sure he is. We just need to track him down." In fact Brady had no idea where the kid was or if he was okay. But he wouldn't tell her that.

By the time he hung up the phone he knew they had moved into a new phase. He was so lost in thought that he started when he felt Anne's hand come down gently on his shoulder.

"How's she handling it?" she asked.

"Not great. She thinks something's wrong, and to be honest, I agree with her. Too much smoke without a fire burning."

"So you think the kid's a terrorist?"

"I don't know. I really don't know what to think at this point."

"Are you going to call the FBI?"

"Not yet. I don't want to get the kid on some list that'll ruin his life until we're pretty sure there's good reason. But here, could you have Danny take a look at this?" He handed her Marid's phone, which Derek had dropped off on his way home. "Any incoming or outgoing phone numbers, texts, anything he can find."

"I'll give it to him first thing in the morning."

"Thanks. And I think I'll call Chez first thing as well. This is a little out of my area of expertise. Maybe he has some ideas how to find Marid."

Anne patted him on the shoulder. It would not be a restful night.

*****

As planned, Brady called his DC cop buddy at 8:30 in the morning and made arrangements to meet with him at a nearby hole in the wall restaurant for lunch. He didn't tell him any details, assuming that the police station phones were all recorded, but he told enough to catch Chesley's interest.

The Golden Dragon was Brady's favorite Chinese-Vietnamese restaurant in Arlington. It was small, not the least flashy, but authentic and out of the way. It wasn't one of the places in DC or Crystal City where people went more to be seen than to eat. In fact, if you didn't know the place, the odds were you'd never even find it in the aging strip mall in the Seven Corners area, where many Vietnamese immigrants had landed after the War.

He arrived right at 1, but – as usual – Chez was already there, seated at a table in a back corner of the tiny room.

"Mr. James, good to see you. Looks like conjugal bliss is sitting well with you," the DC detective said with a smile.

"Can't complain. Though what that beautiful lady sees in me I really can't fathom."

"That was my line. But hey, there's no accounting for taste."

"Thank goodness for that. How's life on the thin blue line?"

"Thinner than ever with all the budget problems. But we're still keeping the streets safe and secure for good citizens, and people like you."

Brady smiled. "Glad to hear it. I'm afraid I may need a bit of help."

"I gathered that from your message. What's this about a possible terrorist plot?"

Brady quickly outlined the situation.

"And now the kid's gone missing?" Chez asked.

"According to his mother, he never misses a meal without calling. Yesterday, after that meeting with the bearded guy in the coffee shop, he missed two meals. Never called. And left his prized cellphone on a chair in the café."

"Well that's a pretty good reason for not calling, if you don't have a phone."

"Everyone has a phone these days. The only reason for not calling is if you don't want to be found."

"That's a bit of a reach. But let's say you're right. What do you want from me?"

Brady passed him a handful of photos that Derek had snapped the day before. "This is the bearded mystery man from the Bakery. Can you run him through your face recognition system to see if it comes up with a match?"

"Sure. No problem. But how about the FBI's system? They've got a whole lot more faces in their database."

"Would we have to explain why?"

"Not really. I suppose we could just say 'wanted for questioning.' Why?"

Brady shrugged. "We're still not entirely sure what's going on here. Whether it's youthful rebellion or something a lot worse. For now we'd like to keep this close to the vest, if possible."

"If possible," the DC cop reiterated. "Okay. For now it's all routine inquiry."

"Great, thanks. And here," he continued, pulling another photo out of the pile, "is a shot of the license plate on a Mercedes he was driving. I doubt it's registered in his name, but you never know."

"Okay, I'll run it. Anything else?"

Brady hesitated, and then passed him one final shot. "This is the kid, Marid. See if you can find him on any of your surveillance cameras. I'd like to know if he's still in the area."

"You got any leads on him?"

"Actually, I've got Danny – the computer geek over at the Hart Office Building – looking at the kid's cellphone to see if he can salvage any info from it. If he can't come up with anything, think your guys can take a look?"

"Of course, no problem."

The two old friends continued their conversation over lunch, though the topics veered far afield from Marid: everything from some particularly nasty cases Chez was working on to the state of the Nationals. It was mid-afternoon by the time they went their respective ways.

Brady was in his car on the way home when his cellphone rang.

"Brady, it's me," Anne announced, "I think Danny has something."

"Enough for me to swing by?"

"I'd say so. Actually, it's a little bit odd."

Brady's interest was piqued. "I'll be there in twenty minutes."

After the death of Anne's previous boss, Senator Blayton Wainwright, she'd considered leaving her longtime work as a Congressional secretary. But after a short – and not particularly satisfying – stint with the interim replacement, the fall election had brought a new face to the Capitol, Senator Jeffrey Bolls, and she'd found herself back in the political swirl by the end of November. Her young colleague, Danny, was the one bright spot in an otherwise dismal tech support office. He was bright, affable, and after his fifteen minutes of fame from the Hoch case, was more eager than ever to help Anne and Brady in their pursuit of the truth about Marid.

So it was no surprise when Brady made his way up to Anne's office in the Hart Senate Office Building and found the twenty-something geek bouncing off the walls with excitement.

"Brady! Looks like we've got another great story in the works, eh?" he blurted as he came over to shake James' hand as soon as the older man had kissed Anne.

"Don't know yet," Brady said, "I suppose that depends to some degree on what you're going to tell me."

A satisfied smile crossed the young techie's face. "Well, somebody tried their best to wipe the memory clean, but they didn't count on old Danny boy getting ahold of it."

"Modesty is the best policy," Anne reminded with a shake of her head.

"Funny, I'd always heard honesty was the best policy. And I'm just being honest when I say I'm damn good."

"Can we get on with this?" Brady growled.

"Yeh, sure. No problem. Anyhow, as I was saying, looks like someone tried to wipe the memory clean."

"I guess that rules out Marid leaving the phone in the Bakery by mistake."

"Unless he walked through a magnetic field strong enough to pull the fillings out of his mouth it does. This was pretty definitely done on purpose. But I was able to recreate a call log dating back over a month."

"And?" Danny always had a bit of a problem getting to the point.

"And, most of the calls were to and from local numbers. Some I traced easily using the online reverse directory, some you'll have to track down yourself."

"Anne said there was something a bit strange about the calls?" He was hoping there was more to it than that.

"Well, yeh. I had four weeks of calls, right? So every Friday night, at 11 pm on the dot, he called a number in Nevada. They were the only out-of-area calls he made, and he made each one at exactly the same time each week. Strange, huh?"

Brady nodded slowly. It *was* strange. He'd have to contact Nyla to find out if she knew of any friends or acquaintances her son might have out west.

"Could you pin down the location of the calls any better than just the state?"

Danny gave him his best 'are you kidding?' look. "It wasn't easy, but I think I've got a town. At least one of a few towns in the same area."

"And that is…?"

"Boulder City. It's a little town about twenty miles southeast of Vegas that bills itself as the gateway to the Hoover Dam and Lake Mead."

"Another gambling mecca in the middle of nowhere?"

"No, that's the strange thing about this place – they don't have any gambling. One of two cities in the whole state that prohibit gaming."

It was probably nothing. But Brady's immediate thought was how coincidental it seemed that a young guy who had apparently turned to radical Islam just happened to be calling someone in one of the only two towns in Nevada without gaming. The kind of thing they'd call a longshot in Vegas.

"Well done, Danny. I don't know if those calls mean anything, but I agree it seems a bit unusual."

"What are you going to do now, Brady?" Anne asked.

"Well, first of all I'll check the tracking software Nyla placed on her son's cellphone. See if there's anything there beyond what Danny was able to recover. And then? Then I suppose we play it by ear. I'm still hoping that the kid calls his Mom to let her know where he is. But I'm not counting on it."

They chatted a bit more about Marid and what might be behind his recent activities, and then Brady kissed Anne goodbye and headed to her apartment to continue his investigation.

It was easy enough to bring up the tracking software on his laptop, but it took him a few swipes of the mouse to locate the data he was seeking. He compared Danny's reconstruction of the cellphone memory with the calls recorded since Nyla had installed the tracker. No deviation. No calls from Nevada, and nothing Danny had missed. Brady sighed. He hadn't really expected to find a smoking gun, but he had hoped to find something of value. He almost closed the program right then and there, but his sixth-sense told him to persevere. He checked the texts sent and received: nothing. He reviewed the GPS log to see where Marid had gone other than home and to the coffee shop, but nothing looked out of place. Then, almost as an afterthought, he clicked the Messenger IM widget. He didn't really know anything about IM. Never used it himself. But he knew enough to realize that kids were enamored of the service.

And there it was. A single word transmitted at 2:37 pm the previous day, at exactly the time Derek was following the Mercedes back to DC.

"GO!"

He doubted that they'd be able to track the sender back to his or her computer, but it was worth a try. He called Danny and gave him all the info recorded by the software.

"Give me an hour. I'll get right back to you," the young techie promised, "unless one of my supervisors walks in, in which case it might take a little longer."

Brady thanked him and hung up. He thought back wistfully to his days at the Post when he actually had a dedicated staff to help him research a story. But then he remembered everything else that went with full-time employment and decided he was perfectly happy as he was, thank you very much.

It was just over forty minutes later that the phone rang.

"Brady, it's me, Danny. I might be able to get a better fix with time, but I can tell you right now that it came from a relatively small provider in the southwest named Bright Star. They service parts of Arizona, Utah, California, and…Nevada."

"Nice work. When you get a chance, see if you can pin it down to a town, or at least a state. But Danny?"

"Yeh?"

"Don't get yourself fired. Do your real work first."

He heard the youngster chuckle. "Don't worry. I've got enough free time to do a little freelancing on the side. I'll let you know when I find something."

As soon as he hung up he dialed his travel agent to see if she could find him a cheap flight to Vegas. He had a funny feeling he'd be headed that way in the very near future.

*****

"Vegas! Now we're cooking!" Derek said when Brady informed him of Danny's finding. "When do we leave?"

"Well, I don't know if we can afford for the two of us to go jetting off to Sin City," Brady said, trying to disguise a smile.

"Oh sure. If we need some digging in Redneckville I get the call. But a trip to Vegas to interview some 6'4" showgirl? That's a drudgery you keep to yourself."

The little guy's pout brought Brady's grin out in full force. "Don't get your shorts in a knot. I'm not even certain we need to go out there."

"But it's a possibility."

"It is. A pretty good one, at this point. But unless Danny can get us more details on the location of the person who sent that IM, it's not worth a trip."

"Then that little geek had better get his butt in motion."

"He's on it. But he might take more kindly to honey than vinegar, if you get my meaning."

"I'm not making a goddamn salad dressing!" the PI barked. "But yeh, I get the point."

It was nearly an hour later, at 6:20, when the phone rang. Derek beat Brady to it.

"Hello?"

"Derek, it's Danny."

"Oh, Danny," the PI said, pointing energetically at the receiver to let Brady know who was calling. "Funny you should call. Brady and I were just saying what a great little computer whiz you were." Derek stuck his fingers down his throat to mime gagging himself.

"Oh, well, great," the young geek stammered. "In fact, I'm here at the Hart Building working away on that cellphone memory even as we speak."

Derek glanced at his watch. It was 6:15. "Kind of late to still be at your desk, isn't it?" He rolled his eyes.

"Not so late. I just wanted to let you guys know that I'm closing in on the location of the provider. If all goes well, I'll have it either tonight or first thing tomorrow."

"Well that's just great!" the PI said, pumping his fist up and down above his crotch while staring wide-eyed at the ceiling. "What would we do without you?"

"I, ah, I don't know. It's actually a lot of fun working on this kind of stuff."

"That it is, that it is. Anything else I can pass on to Brady?"

"No, that's about it."

"Okay then. Get back to work and track that provider back to his hole!"

Derek hung up with a flourish. "Is that enough honey for you?" he asked his friend, who was shaking his head in disbelief.

"A good start. As long as you don't give the kid diabetes."

"Speaking of which. I just had an idea." The energized midget punched some info into the laptop.

"Now what? A massage?" James asked.

"He's still at work. I'm going to send over a pizza. He must be hungry by now."

Brady made a mental note to watch what he said to the PI. The repercussions could be unpredictable.

*****

"You think you may be going <u>where</u>?!" Anne asked with raised eyebrows when Brady told her about their new discovery.

"Vegas. Or actually some little burg just outside of Vegas. Boulder City."

"Do you think that's a good idea – you and Derek going to Vegas, together?"

"What, should we go separately? Of course it's a good idea. I can keep an eye on him."

"And who's going to keep an eye on you?" Her smile didn't quite reach her eyes.

"What, are you telling me you're jealous? Think I'm going to hook up with some showgirl and blow my life savings?" He grabbed her by the waist and pulled her close. "Is that what you think of me?"

Her eyes finally softened. "Shouldn't I?"

"There's only one showgirl I give a damn about," he said. "And I see that show for free every night."

She put her arms around his neck. "They've got some pretty good-looking dancers out there, I hear."

"I never had any interest in dating an Amazon. I like to look my girl straight in the eyes, not the navel."

She laughed, just before she kissed him.

*****

Danny called back at 10:30. Derek was stretched out on his sofa watching the Nationals get slammed by a team that was 22 games out of first. He'd just finished crushing an empty beer can against his forehead after a National had overrun third base and been tagged out.

"Derek, it's Danny!" the familiar voice said with way too much cheer for the PI's current mood.

"I would never have guessed. What's up? Did you find out anything more from that IM?"

"It took a while. I had to call in a couple of favors, and even then it wasn't easy tracing it back through the system…"

"Hey, you're a prince and a technical wizard," Derek cut him off. "But let's cut to the chase: what did you find?"

"Boulder City. Again."

The little guy chuckled. "I knew it. LV, here we come!"

"You're going out there?"

"I'm guessing we will."

"Need any help?"

"Dude, the budget on this story is pretty much the same as on all Brady's stories: zero. The Big Goose-egg. I'll be lucky if he pays my airfare. Forget the salary."

"Oh." The kid sounded crestfallen.

"But hey, don't get too upset. Boulder City is no Vegas. They don't even have gambling there!"

"What?!"

"That's what the Big Guy told me. He says their only draw is a dam."

"A dam?"

"Apparently it's a big dam."

"Yeh, well, good luck with that. And Derek, thanks for the pizza."

"My pleasure, kid. Good work tracking the provider. You're our secret weapon, you know?"

"Really? You think so?"

Derek was on the verge of answering the enthusiasm in the kid's voice with his usual sarcasm, but the PI caught himself at the last second.

"Yeh. You did good. I'm sure Brady will tell you the same thing when he talks to you."

"Wow. Cool. Thanks."

As he hung up the phone, Derek could almost feel the honey dripping from his lips.

*****

Brady was still trying to decide whether to travel to Nevada or to wait until they had more information to go on, when Chesley called.

"Your young friend has been hanging out with some strange folks," the cop said before Brady could say anything more than hello. "That bearded guy – the one with the Mercedes you had me check on? It looks like he's one Joseph Samuel Alietto, convicted of larceny, interstate mail fraud – and this one is especially interesting – firearms charges. And guess where he was last busted?"

"Vegas?"

"Bingo! We have another lucky winner."

"So the guy's not Middle Eastern?"

"Italian as Gambino. Looks like he could be from Iraq, but he's from our own made-in-the-USA desert. Just for you, we're keeping an eye on him. And one more thing."

"You've got me on the edge of my chair."

"The firearms charges? They were from a sting operation six years ago in which Alietto tried to buy a rocket launcher from an FBI undercover agent. And the trial linked him to some nut group out there in Nevada –

The Southern Nevada Desert Militia. Real craze-o, end of the world, New World Order types."

"Could they be working with Islamic terrorists?" Brady asked.

Chesley chuckled. "About as much chance of that as the Israelis working with Iran."

"So what's the link?"

"Hey, you're the famous investigative reporter. I'm just a little ol' DC cop. But I do have a transcript from the trial. I could fax it over. Talks about a number of his 'associates'."

"Yeh, thanks, that'd be real helpful," the reporter said distractedly. "What the heck is that kid doing with Alietto?" James mumbled, more to himself than to his friend.

"Oh, hey, that reminds me," Chez said, "we got a hit on the kid's photo as well."

Instantaneously, Brady was back in focus. "Nice of you to mention it. Where was he?"

"Dulles. We've got a great shot of him boarding a Southwest jet Thursday night."

"Let me guess: to Vegas?"

"Man, you ought'a buy a lottery ticket today. You're on fire."

"Right. Maybe I should play some blackjack, instead."

"Give my regards to Caesars Palace."

"Somehow I don't think that's where we'll be headed."

CHAPTER 7

McCarron International Airport in Las Vegas is essentially a casino with runways.

Even as Brady and Derek walked down the jetway from their Southwest flight out of Dulles, they heard the sounds of slot machines before they ever saw them.

"We're not in Kansas anymore," Brady muttered as they made their way down to the baggage area.

"Thank God," the diminutive PI answered, a smile on his lips and a hop in his step.

Even the baggage area did not fail to impress. A small single engine plane hung from the rafters over the carrousels. Bright lights reflected off the polished aluminum ceiling. Passengers walked a gauntlet through enticing slots just to get out the door.

"I feel like I died and went to heaven," Derek said as they wheeled their luggage out of the terminal to board the transport to the off-site rental car area.

"Died and went somewhere, that's for sure," Brady grumbled.

The ride was short, probably only 3 miles or so, through a desert vista dotted with large warehouses, stunted trees, and the omnipresent billboards touting everything from casino shows and slots to wedding and divorce services. Brady had the feeling that Derek would've stood up on the bench seats to see out the windows more easily if it hadn't been for the one other passenger, an older woman seated just a few feet away from him. He glared at her with ill-disguised displeasure from time to time, but she was oblivious.

By the time they got their rental, a silver Ford Fusion, it was nearly dinner time. Brady hopped on the Beltway and then took U.S. 515 to 93 and Boulder City. It didn't take long for the glitter of Vegas to transform into the dusty desert landscape that is the true look of the southern Nevada countryside. Derek looked longingly out the side window at the fast-fading lights of the Strip in the distance, balanced on an inflatable pillow that lifted him up high enough to see past the black vinyl door liner.

"We will get to spend a little time in the city, won't we?" he asked with so much pathos that Brady almost laughed out loud.

"If we can work it into our agenda, sure," he said, not wanting to promise too much and take the PI's focus away from the real reason for their visit.

The little guy was silent for most of the rest of the trip, only once voicing his thoughts after twenty minutes of barren desert vistas.

"Damn. It's like Mad Max out here," he mumbled. Brady just smiled.

He took the Colorado Street exit to Avenue B to Arizona Street, passing by the Boulder Brewing Company on the way. It was the first time that Derek had perked up since they'd left Vegas in the rearview mirror.

By the time they pulled into the parking lot of the Hoover Dam Hotel, they were tired, hungry, and ready to stop moving.

"Jesus, I feel like we just drove into 'Gone with the Wind'," Derek cracked as they first saw the historic old building. Brady couldn't argue with him. Complete with towering pillars and a genteel Old South feel, the big white hotel could have just as easily been located in South Carolina or Georgia. Of course Brady was more interested in the free breakfast, wireless Internet and handy location, all for $65. The Old West quasi-antique furnishings were just an added bonus.

Although they would have preferred two separate rooms, the budget was already straining under the expense of the airfare and so they shared a room with two double beds. Brady knew he was asking for sleepless nights, having been exposed to his friend's buzz-saw snoring from time to time in the past, but he hoped the new-fangled ear plugs he'd purchased back at Dulles would do the trick.

Although they were dog-tired and had hoped to just stumble into the Hotel restaurant for a quick feed, it turned out the place only served breakfast and lunch so they had to look elsewhere for dinner. The closest joint recommended by the desk clerk was called Merkle's Cellar, a small homey-looking place just down the street. The Cellar had tables and chairs on the front porch, and to their great delight, had a decent menu that included a kick-ass Reuben sandwich and barbecued pulled-pork that could have been smuggled in from Texas. More importantly, they featured Boulder Brewery beers including Powder Monkey Pilsner and Hell's Hole Hefeweizen. Both men sampled freely.

By the time they stumbled back to the hotel it was 11 pm their time, and they were more than ready for sleep.

The next morning, after breakfast, the two of them made their way to a small strip mall just down the street from Merkle's, where they had pre-arranged a meeting with the editor of the Boulder City News, a weekly with a circulation of around 2000. Just the kind of local paper where the staff would know everything and everybody in the city.

Linda Heinemann was a bleached-blond, chain-smoking, gravel-voiced veteran of southern Nevada journalism who had wandered out to Boulder City when her longtime gig at the Review Journal had run its course. Her weathered face showed the furrows and valleys of too much sun, too much smoke and drink, and too many late nights. But her eyes were a brilliant blue and showed a glint that warned Brady against taking the woman lightly.

"So what's a big-shot journalist from DC doing out here in our neck of the cactus?" she asked as soon as they'd settled into well-worn kitchen chairs stationed in front of her scarred wooden desk. The office reeked of tobacco and a cigarette burned in an ashtray close by her right hand.

"Well, as I told you when I called, we're doing a story about home-grown terrorists and wanted to take a look at the Southern Nevada Militia," Brady said. "We were hoping to talk to some of their members."

"Watch what you wish for."

"Meaning?" Derek joined in.

Linda pushed a teetering pile of paper off to one side so that she could see the small PI nearly hidden beneath the edge of her desk.

"Meaning that they're a nasty bunch. 'Don't take kindly to outsiders poking around,'" she added with a tone-perfect desert rat accent.

"But you know who they are?" Brady pressed.

"Everyone out here knows who they are. At least some of them. They don't hide. In fact, I'd say they're proud of their affiliation." She took a drag on the cigarette.

"Have you done any stories on them?"

The woman exhaled a massive cloud of smoke. Brady wondered when the last time was he'd been in an office with someone smoking.

"Bet you don't get many flying insects around here," Derek sniped as he waved the smoke away from his face.

She only smiled. "This isn't DC, gentlemen. As you'll learn if you go out there asking questions blindly about the SNM. To answer your question, no we haven't really done much reporting on them. We live here. We need the support of the community if we're going to survive. And more to the point, we need offices."

"They have a lot of financial clout?"

"You'd be surprised. But I wasn't talking about their financial clout. I was talking about the firebomb that destroyed the apartment of a reporter in Vegas who wrote about them a couple of years back. Totaled his place. Sent a pretty strong message."

"Really. Is he still working out here?" Brady had a sore spot for apartment burnings.

"Fool that he is, yes. But no more stories on the militia."

"Can you put us in touch with him?

"I can give you his name. Don't know him, myself."

"I'd appreciate it. How about militia members? Any contact info for them?"

The editor shook her head. "You're not listening too closely, are you? We stay away from those people. But I can steer you to someone who doesn't."

"And who would that be?"

"Jesse, Jesse Winthrop. He's an old-timer who's got no use for any of those crazies. Runs a little in-house non-profit called The Desert Rights Alliance. He tracks them."

"Sounds like a brave man."

"Brave, or maybe a little nuts. I'll let you decide."

"Fair enough. Hey, speaking of crazies, you haven't heard anything about any radical Islamic terrorist groups out this way, have you?" Despite trying to keep the question off-handed, he knew it came across as a bit out of the blue.

Linda narrowed her eyes. "Muslims? Out here? Better chance of finding aliens."

"But there are people from the Middle East working in the casinos, aren't there?" Derek asked.

She shrugged. "Some. Not many. And those that do keep a pretty low profile. Like I said, this isn't the East Coast. Anyone who's different can have a hard time of it in the desert."

The PI tried to push away the sensation that her words were directed specifically at him.

"Just wondering," Brady interjected to dispel the awkwardness of the moment.

"You seem to have something in mind," she said. "Something more than just the SNM. No?"

Brady realized that his initial impression of the woman had been right-on. She was no fool.

"Might be. Don't really know yet. But we wouldn't want anything getting out about that angle just yet…"

She picked up on his hint. "Of course not. We report on news, not newsmen. But if you come up with something, how about sharing a little bit with us? We could use a scoop – to build the subscriber base, if nothing else."

James smiled. He had heard the same line from his own Post editors on more than one occasion. "We'll see what we can do. Maybe simultaneous publication, or a shared by-line?"

He saw the last suggestion register on her face. "In the Post?" she asked.

"Possible."

"You've got my attention."

"I was hoping we might."

Brady persuaded Linda to call Winthrop; a familiar voice would hopefully grease the skids. As it turned out, he wasn't home, or wasn't picking up the phone, and so she left a voicemail introducing the two DC visitors. After she'd provided them with the name of the R-J reporter, they made their goodbyes.

"I probably don't need to say this, you two being big-city boys and all," she said as she walked them to the door, "but watch your backsides. These boys don't have much of a sense of humor."

"Neither do we," Derek piped up, and the editor shot him a look that was either surprise or disdain.

As soon they piled into the rental car, Brady called the Vegas newspaper to try to locate Eric Jacobs, the reporter whose apartment had mysteriously burst into flames just as he was investigating the SNM. At first he was less than forthcoming, but when Brady mentioned the Post he loosened up a bit.

"Post, huh? I applied for a job there once," he said with a hint of lingering bitterness.

"Well, DC is no Vegas," Brady joked.

"And the R-J is no Post," the reporter answered somberly. "But what the hell, sure, let's get together. How about lunch? You boys on an expense account?"

"I think we can manage to treat you to a burger," Brady side-stepped the question. "Where?"

Brady had half-expected the reporter to suggest one of the chichi burger bars that overpopulate the Strip hotels, but to his surprise he suggested Five Guys in Henderson, a chain burger joint that had apparently only been open for a year or so.

"Less chance of bumping into one of our *friends*," he explained. "How will we recognize each other?"

"I don't think you'll have a problem picking us out," James said. "I'll be the big guy, and my associate will be the smaller one."

On the half-hour ride from Boulder City to Henderson, Brady and Derek discussed the turn of events that had taken them into the shadowy world of state militias. Neither of them were particularly well-versed about such ubiquitous bands of armed fanatics, but they both knew about the occasional FBI raids and of course they remembered the Oklahoma City bombing all too well.

"I don't know if I feel better or worse that the kid might be tied up with militiamen instead of Islamic terrorists," Derek said. "Kind of pick your poison."

"Out of the frying pan…" Brady began. He didn't have to finish the sentence.

*****

Henderson is a pleasant little town that grew into the second largest city in the state as its immediate neighbor to the north, Las Vegas, exploded during the 1980's and 90's. In some ways it became the Vegans' Vegas, with enough deals for the locals at the innumerable casinos and golf courses to keep the town growing and prospering. More than a few places shut their doors during the turbulent times of the Great Recession of 2008-11, however, and it was just such economic downturns that fed the anti-government sentiment that fostered militia movements.

As they drove into town, Brady and Derek could still see the scars of the recession in the boarded-up mini-mall stores, foreclosed houses and a stunning array of 99 cent breakfast specials that had just about disappeared before the crash.

"My kind of place," the PI rhapsodized, "booze, broads and breakfasts."

"Such simple needs," Brady jabbed as they turned off route 146 onto S. Eastern Ave.

The burger joint was jumping.

"Man, are they giving them away or what?" Derek asked as he waddled across the parking lot and into the crowded, boisterous Five Guys.

"I hope so. Our 'expense account' is running pretty damn low."

Derek's entry caused the usual ripple of comments and even a single teenage girl's laugh, but he was accustomed to that kind of reaction and ignored it studiously. Both men scanned the crowd for their reporter contact.

"You must be Brady," a voice from behind announced quietly.

Brady turned slowly, while Derek spun like a top.

"How'd you know it was us?" the petite PI asked sarcastically.

A man of about 35, short brown hair, pleasant though anxious face and rimless glasses, smiled. "Lucky guess."

"Mr. Jacobs? I'm Brady James, and this is my associate, Derek DiLaurain. Thanks for meeting with us."

"Hey, you know us reporters, we'd drive an hour for a free lunch," Jacobs answered as they all shook hands.

"Is it always like this? You'd think they were giving the food away for free," Brady said, stealing his friend's line and earning a dirty look for his efforts.

"Most of the time. I'm something of a regular myself, so I actually got here a few minutes ago and staked out that table over there," he explained, pointing to a tiny tabletop off to one side of the crowded room. "Probably be best if one of us parked there before one of these kids tries to rip it."

"Tough town," Derek muttered.

"You go. We'll get you something," Brady said. "What'll it be?"

Jacobs ordered one of their trademark burgers, fries and a soda.

"Cheap date," Derek said.

"I'm watching my waistline," the extremely trim reporter answered without missing a beat.

As he pushed his way through the crowd to their table, Brady and Derek exchanged sotto-voce opinions as they stood in line.

"Seems okay, for a reporter," the PI began.

"Faint praise… But yeh, he'll do. Maybe we can even get some legwork out of him."

"Probably cost you a double cheeseburger."

"What the hell. You only live once."

It was a good fifteen minutes later when they finally carried their hard-won burgers over to where Jacobs fiddled with a smartphone as he waited.

"So, tell us a little about yourself," Brady started-in before the fries were even out of the bag. Derek was already well into devouring a burger that was nearly as big as he was. "How long have you been here in Vegas?"

Jacobs smiled to himself. "About seven years now. Went to grad school at Columbia – Missouri that is. Worked in the Midwest for two years, and then got the bug to come out west and landed a gig at the R-J – the Review Journal. The 'paper of record' out these ways."

"I'm guessing the people over at the Sun dispute that claim."

Jacobs raised his eyebrows. "Been doing your homework. Impressive."

Brady nodded at the compliment. "We've heard you're pretty well-known around here for doing your homework as well. Especially about the SNM."

The reporter's relaxed demeanor disappeared as he glanced around unconsciously at the tables that surrounded them. "Sons of bitches. Nasty pieces of work."

"Tell us about them. How'd you get involved?"

He hesitated a moment, probably trying to decide just how to present himself. "Well, I was a typical young hotshot, new to town, wanted to make my mark. I sure did that…" he began with a wry smile and shake of the head. "Anyhow, I decided that I'd reveal the Militia in all its malevolent glory, so I started asking around. Everyone knows they're out here. I'm guessing twenty per cent of the folks hereabouts know someone who's involved, or certainly know someone who knows someone."

"You're not going to tell us about Kevin Bacon, are you?" Derek cracked.

Brady glared at his friend and took a deep breath, but Jacobs wasn't deterred.

"No, but it's the same idea. So I asked some people, who asked some people, and before long I get contacted by some people from the SNM who think it'd be a good idea if they get some publicity. Probably thought it would help with recruiting or something. I don't know. But we met."

"Where?"

"A little bar on the outskirts of town. Jack's, off of East Stewart just as it's about to disappear into the desert. Probably more bikes in the parking lot than cars, and certainly more pickups."

"Sounds like a warm and welcoming spot for an interview."

"It's crazed. Jukebox blaring, stock cars roaring on the TVs – at first I thought 'no way,' but they had made arrangements for us to meet in a small office in back. Not exactly Caesars, but at least I could hear myself think."

"How many of them?"

"Just two. Eddie was the main talker, about 40, maybe 42, five-ten, 160 or so, balding, tattoos on both arms

– and from the looks, down his back as well. Jake was younger, probably late 20's, maybe 30. Long brown hair, pulled back in a ponytail. Big guy, maybe six-two, 225. Also liked the skin art."

"No disguises? No masks or kerchiefs?"

"Are you kidding? These guys are proud of who and what they are. They think they're untouchable."

"So you interviewed them."

"For over an hour. They were eager to let the world know that they thought the Federal government was a piece of crap and when the day came – as they were sure it would – that the Feds came asking them to turn over their guns, they were going to do something about it."

"Anything specific?"

"Not about reprisals, no. Just a lot of posing and generic threats. But they did tell me all about their beliefs in the essential independence of man, and how the Constitution had been corrupted by politicians over the years. The usual militia bs. They claimed they had nearly fifty members, automatic weapons, and said they trained regularly out in the desert someplace."

"You weren't invited?"

"I asked. Jake said, 'We'd have to kill you if you knew where we trained.' He didn't smile."

"What then?"

"Then, I went back to the office and they went wherever they go. I wrote my story, and it appeared on August 9, 2008. On August 10, my apartment *spontaneously* burst into flames. Total loss. The apartments on both sides went too. A real mess. Investigators called it arson."

"Big surprise. I take it they didn't like the article?"

"Like I said, I thought I was hot stuff. I basically called them nutcases playing games in the desert. They apparently didn't like the tone."

"Anything else? I mean, did they send you anything, or call you?"

The reporter opened the small leather briefcase he carried and pulled out a folded piece of paper. "This was stuck under my windshield wipers. The cops couldn't find any prints, and they never even arrested a suspect."

Brady took the paper and gently unfolded it. 'Any more stories like the last one, and it'll be you that goes up in flames,' it read in block letters. Below the message was a crudely drawn cross with a stick figure crucified and covered in flames. He showed it to Derek.

"We can assume they're not art students."

"Don't assume anything," the reporter said with surprising vehemence. "These bastards aren't stupid. Just mean, *very* mean."

The three men continued to talk for another 20 minutes or so, until Jacobs made his apologies.

"Some of us still work," he jabbed. "Got to get back to the office and knock out a piece for tonight."

"Well thanks for all that," Brady said, standing as Jacobs did. "You've been a big help. Have time for one more quick question?"

"Shoot."

"Ever hear anything about Islamic terrorists out here?"

The quizzical look on Jacob's face answered the question even before he spoke. "You mean Al-Qaeda or something like that?"

"Something like that."

"Nah. These people hate Catholics, let alone Jews or Muslims. Why?" Brady heard the natural inquisitiveness of a reporter kicking-in.

He squelched it. "No reason. Just looking in all directions."

The R-J reporter didn't say anything, but his eyes were not convinced.

"Yeh, well anyway, if there's anything else I can help you with, just give me a call. But, do me a favor, will you?"

"Sure. What do you need?"

"Don't go using my name in your investigation. I'm just now getting to the point where I get in the car without popping the hood, and looking to see if there's anything attached to the underside of the frame."

"No problem. We never even met you."

"Great. Thanks. Take care." He started to go, but turned back. "I know you're both big boys…"

"Watch it," Derek grumbled good-naturedly.

"…but be careful. If you start asking questions about the SNM, they're going to know, and sooner than you might expect. This may look like a big city, but take my word for it, it's a small cow-town. And I mean *small*."

"We'll watch our step," Brady said.

As they watched the reporter walk out to his car, both men wondered just what they'd gotten themselves involved in. Suddenly the bright lights seemed a whole lot dimmer than when they'd arrived.

*****

Brady checked his cellphone as soon as they got back out to the car.

"Got a voicemail," he said to Derek as the PI scrambled up on his seat riser.

"Winthrop?"

"Could be."

Sure enough, the Desert Rights Director had listened to his voicemail and had been intrigued enough to call. Brady dialed him immediately.

After Brady had introduced himself, he started to ask when they could meet. Winthrop interrupted him.

"Sorry to sound a bit…paranoid, but how do I know you're actually who you say you are? I know Lin vouches for you, but she's not the most astute judge of character I've ever met."

Brady was momentarily nonplussed. "Well, I guess you could call my old editor at the Washington Post."

"What's his name?"

"Jimmy Ogden. He's the crime beat editor. I can probably give you his direct number…" he continued as he scrolled down his cellphone's contact list.

"Nope. I'll find the number myself, thank you. You gonna be somewhere I can reach you in a couple of minutes?"

"Sure. Right here in the Five Guys parking lot, waiting to hear back from you."

"Get yourself a cold drink. I'll call once I've talked to this Ogden fellow."

The phone went dead.

"Whoa. Some real hubnuts we've got ourselves involved with," Brady said with a shake of his head.

"What now?"

"The guy thinks we might be imposters. He's going to call Jimmy at the Post."

"Hey, they know these militia freaks better than we do. Another reminder to watch our backsides."

"You can watch mine a lot easier than I can watch yours," James jibed with a smile.

"Great. We're chasing after assholes who threaten to crucify anyone they don't get along with, and you're making short jokes. And *they're* the hubnuts?"

"You either laugh or cry with this kind of story. And I don't feel like crying."

The PI harrumphed as Brady turned on the radio; they sat and chatted for a few minutes before his cellphone rang again.

"Okay, let's talk," was the first thing out of Winthrop's mouth. He told them where he was living, and started to give directions.

"Don't worry about that," Brady said. "We've got a GPS. We'll find you."

"They can track those things, you know," the Alliance Director said. "And not just the cops."

"We'll get the directions and then turn it off. How's that?" James said, all the while pursing his lips and twirling his finger by the side of his head.

"That'll do. See you in a while."

"What now?" the PI asked when he'd hung up.

"The guy is afraid someone is going to track us using our GPS."

"It's not that far-fetched."

"Nobody even knows we're out here."

"It's a small town, remember?"

"Yah, whatever." He punched in the address and then scrolled ahead to see the turn by turn directions. When he was satisfied that they could find the place, he turned off the GPS.

"And our cellphones?" Derek asked.

"What, are you a wiseass too?"

"They have a GPS receiver in them. That's how those cops were tracking the bad guys illegally."

Brady sighed and hung his head in defeat. "Fine." He held the off button on his phone until the familiar musical sign-off sounded. "Happy now?"

The PI took his friend's phone and removed the battery.

"Completely," Derek said smugly as he performed a battery-ectomy on his phone as well. "Shall we go a-calling?"

CHAPTER 8

Most visitors to Vegas see only the Strip, or maybe Downtown; very few trudge out as far as Lake Mead and the Hoover Dam. Brady figured that nobody visiting Sin City ever drove out to where Winthrop lived, unless it was by mistake. A big mistake.

They drove north on 95, past Indian Springs, to a dirt road turnoff that looked to lead straight into reddish brown mountains in the distance.

"You sure this is it?" Derek asked as they bumped and heaved along the rutted road, huge clouds of dust swirling in their wake.

"Of course I'm not sure," Brady snapped. "Do you think I spend a lot of time out here in this godforsaken desert?"

Derek recoiled at the comeback and held his tongue even as he held on for dear life.

It was a good fifteen minutes later, when the only thing they could see was cactus and tumbleweed, that they came to an even smaller road to their left.

"This should be it," Brady said, half to himself.

"My fingers are crossed," the PI said quietly, only half in jest.

After about a mile of potholes and loose stone, Brady was just about to stop and call Winthrop when the dust cleared long enough for Derek to spot a ramshackle old ranch about a half-mile ahead on the right.

"Eureka!" he called out loud enough to be heard over the crashes and bangs of the roadway.

The 'ranch', if that's what it could be called, was little more than a mini-oasis with a half-dozen thinly-leaved trees surrounding a single story home that might once have been a double-wide. The wooden fence that encircled the property might have been white once upon a time, and might have been unbroken, but as they pulled up in front of the house it was no longer either.

"Like this guy's style," Brady said as he evaluated the property, waiting for the dust cloud that had followed them to settle out of the air.

"Is absence of style a style?"

Before Brady could answer, two mixed-breed mutts came running out of the house, barking wildly and making a beeline for their car.

"Oh, great. What's next, trained scorpions?" Derek grumbled.

But before the dogs could even reach the car, a rail-thin, sunbaked older man wearing a cowboy hat, warm-up pants and flip flops, emerged from the house carrying a twelve-gauge shotgun.

"You shut the hell up!" he yelled in a crusty high-pitched voice that spoke of tobacco and booze.

Amazingly, the dogs did as they were told, leaving Brady and Derek to sit anxiously in the car while the man walked slowly in their direction. It was quiet in the desert, they both realized. Very quiet.

"What if this guy turns out to be a loony tune and just blows us away without even saying howdy-do?" the PI whispered, snuggling down in his seat so that his head barely cleared the bottom of the window.

"Then I guess this rental car's gonna come back late," Brady said softly.

Without waiting for direction or invitation, Brady opened his door to get out.

"What the hell are you doing?!" Derek asked through tightened lips.

"Getting out."

"But…"

Derek's protests were cut off by the slam of the car door. He waited a second, his hand resting on the 9mm secured in his hip holster. He watched the old man approach, saw Brady greet him, and saw the barrel of the 12 gauge slide slowly toward the ground as they shook hands. The PI exhaled and opened his door.

"And this is my associate, Derek DiLaurain," he heard James announce as he slid out of the car and landed on the dusty roadway. If Winthrop was surprised or startled to see the little man appear before him, he didn't show it.

"Mr. DiLaurain," he said, reaching down to shake his hand. "Hope the dogs didn't spook ya."

"Nah. Just had to get myself in order," the PI fudged.

"Well, glad you could find the place. Some folks call two or three times before they finally get here."

"Just lucky I guess," Derek said.

Winthrop nodded. "Good. You'll need to be if you're gonna be writing about the SNM. Come on, let's get out of this heat."

He turned and led them back to the house, the two dogs walking on either side of their guests. Brady heard the hum of a diesel generator coming from behind the building, and only then realized that no power lines led to the house. As they stepped through the front door, Brady felt the cool humid caress of a swamp cooler. Made sense. A/C would require too much electricity out in the middle of nowhere like that.

"Make yourselves at home," the Alliance Director suggested with a wave of his hand in the general direction of a sofa and easy chair in the small, cluttered living room. "Can I get you something to drink?"

"A cold beer would be great," Derek answered before Brady's could flash the irritated expression he knew was coming.

"Water, thanks," the retired reporter said.

"Coming right up."

As the older man disappeared back into what Brady assumed was the kitchen, he looked around the tiny desert home. Piles of paper in envelopes and manila folders covered almost every available surface. Two deer heads peered down at them from the wall opposite the front door. A wedding photo of a much younger version of the man who'd welcomed them smiling happily beside an attractive young brunette sat on a side table. He picked the photo up to examine it more closely, just as Winthrop came back into the room carrying a glass of water and a bottle of Bud.

"Don't have any chilled mugs, but you can have a glass if you want one," he said, and then noticed Brady looking at the photo. "Beautiful wasn't she?"

"She was," Brady answered. "You two cut quite the scene."

"That was a while back."

He handed Derek his beer. "Glass?"

The PI shook his head. "Nah. Just another thing to clean. Beer tastes just as good straight from the source."

"That's how I used to drink it myself, back when I still drank. But I had to give it up. Living by yourself out here in the middle of nowhere it's a bit too easy to suck down a cold one whenever a piece of dust floats down your throat. Before you know it, you're putting away a case a week and your gut's out to here and nothing's getting done."

"I can understand."

"So," Winthrop continued, flopping down heavily on the well-worn easy chair. "We're doing a story on the Southern Nevada Militia, are we? Got your insurance all paid up?" He didn't smile.

"It is, but we're hoping folks like you might be able to guide us in the right direction so we don't need to make a claim," Brady said.

"Might do. What's the angle? Why the SNM, and why now?"

Brady was impressed. Cut straight to the heart of the matter. "Part of a larger story about home grown craze-o's," he dissimulated. "We were looking into some gangs back in northern Virginia and we came up with a possible link to your boys out here."

Winthrop's eyes narrowed ever so briefly, but Brady saw the questioning look and knew that their host hadn't bought the explanation. He considered embellishing, but thought the better of it. Unless ol' Jesse asked, he was sticking to that story.

"Okay," the Alliance Director said unconvincingly. "So what can I do for you?"

"We'd like to talk with them. Give them an opportunity to make their case."

Winthrop smiled. "Don't underestimate them, Mr. James. Just because they live out here in the desert, doesn't make them fools." Brady got the distinct impression that Jesse was referring to himself as well. "They're not gonna believe that a reporter from a big-shot east coast newspaper is going to be doing them any favors. They'll know what to expect."

"Will that be a problem?"

"Maybe, maybe not. They haven't had much press lately. They might be looking for a new recruitment tool."

"No such thing as bad publicity if they spell your name right?" Derek suggested.

"That's about it. Folks that don't think the same way they do won't dislike them any more than they already do, and the handful of 'craze-os' out there who are just waiting for a chance to sign up may just do that."

"So can you help us out?"

"I can pass the word to someone who knows someone – that sort of thing."

"Good enough for us."

"Who else have you talked to?"

"Just Linda at the Boulder City paper and Eric Jacobs at the R-J."

"They're ok. You might still be under the radar. Eric's experience didn't put you off?"

"Put me *way* off," Derek said, "but this wack-job won't take no for an answer." He bobbed his chin toward Brady.

"If I gave up every time some tough guy threatened me, I'd have quit a *long* time ago," his friend said.

"I just want to stay alive long enough to be able to quit."

"We'll see what we can do about that," Brady said with a frown. "But for now, why don't we let Jesse here tell us a bit more about this Militia everyone seems so intimidated by."

It quickly became clear just how much time and thought the Director had put into the SNM. He began with the origins of the group some 40 years earlier, when a small number of local Vietnam vets came back to the desert to recharge and forget. They were joined by young locals who never served but held strong opinions about the federal government, nearly all of them negative. The locals provided the philosophy and the property to hold their trainings on, while the vets provided the know-how and experience to turn the petty griping into action. There were a couple of bank robberies, a break-in at an armory, intimidation against anyone who asked too many questions – a low-key but dangerous movement that looked like it might be headed toward a bloody showdown with the authorities. "But they screwed up," Jesse explained. "An FBI agent came around asking questions when they hit a federally chartered bank, and the SNM sniffed him out and made him disappear. That was the beginning of the end – the first time. The Feds got someone inside and busted the entire militia. Put all the senior officers behind bars and scared the crap out of the hangers-on who had thought the whole thing was way too cool."

"When was that?"

"'88, '89. And for ten years or so everything calmed down quite a bit."

"And then?"

"Then some of 'em got out of jail and persuaded a handful of young kids who didn't know any better that the Militia was the way to prove their manhood."

Brady flipped through some notes. "Were Jake and Eddie two of the older guys or the newer ones?"

Jesse nodded. "I see Eric was pretty forthcoming. He must have liked you. Usually he won't say ten words about those times."

"We found his weakness," the PI said.

Jesse looked askance. "And what was that?"

"Five Guys' burgers and fries."

Winthrop laughed. "He's not alone on that one. When that place opened, the lines curled around the block."

"Food's okay," Brady commented drily. "But what about those two SNM members – Jake and Eddie?"

Jesse glanced at Derek. "I see what you mean about perseverance." He turned back to Brady. "They were both pretty high up in the organization."

"But not at the top?"

"Not sure. Might have been, but those guys don't really advertise their internal workings. We know that when they went away the group assumed a much lower profile."

"So if we wanted to talk with someone in the SNM, they'd be likely prospects?"

"As good as any."

"Either one a better interview than the other?"

Jesse chuckled. "Eddie's the only one who'll talk to you, other than maybe a word or two from Jake. But you'll probably get the two of them."

"The more the merrier," Derek said. "How do we get ahold of them?"

"Like I said, I'll pass the word to someone who knows someone."

"How long will that take?" Brady asked, thinking of his fragile budget rapidly dwindling to nothing.

"Hard to say. If they're around and want to talk, maybe no more than a day. If they're not…Who knows?"

Brady gave him their contact information and the three men continued their conversation another half-hour, with the last ten minutes or so dedicated to Jesse explaining to two perplexed easterners why anyone in their right mind would live out there in the desert like that.

"It gets in your blood," was the best the older man could muster. "There's something about the desert that grows on you."

'Like a fungus,' was the retort Derek wanted to use, but he wasn't sure the veteran desert rat would find the quip humorous.

As they drove away from the weather-beaten old house, they waved to Jesse standing at his front gate, his two dogs sitting peacefully beside him.

"Couldn't pay me enough to live way out here in the middle of nowhere," Derek said as soon as they were ten feet down the dirt road.

"To each their own. He'd probably find DC way too crowded and noisy."

"He'd probably find Boulder City way too crowded and noisy." The two men laughed.

They'd driven another couple of miles through the empty landscape, chit-chatting about the story and in particular about what Marid might be doing, when a particularly nasty pothole sent Derek flying toward the dashboard. He was just about to lambaste Brady for not watching where he was going, when the side window just inches from his head disintegrated into fragments, followed almost immediately by an echoing explosion.

"Incoming!" the PI yelled as he reached for his 9mm. "Step on it!"

What had been a bumpy ride turned immediately into a bucking, scraping, roaring dash through clouds of dust. Brady held onto the steering wheel for dear life as each pothole, rock and rut tried its best to tear the wheel from his grasp. They rocketed out of their seats with each jolt, only their seatbelts keeping them from flying out of the vehicle. For once Brady wished that he were as small as his friend, as his head pounded into the roof repeatedly leaving him with a throbbing skull and a sore neck. He chanced a quick glance over at Derek, who had ducked down behind the support column between windows and held his pistol at eye level as he struggled to see through the thick dust that enveloped the car. Brady noticed blood dripping down the side of his face, but the little guy seemed as scrappy and ready for action as ever.

"Gutless bastards!" he roared after a few seconds had passed. "They're gonna wish they never picked on this little s.o.b.!"

Both men braced for more shots, but they never came. After about three or four minutes, Derek put his hand on Brady's arm.

"You can slow down now!' he yelled to be heard over the roar of the engine and the repeated concussions with the roadbed. "You're more likely to kill us than they are!"

Slowly, his heart still pounding in his ears, Brady let up on the gas pedal and the battered Fusion slowed to a crawl and then stopped. He turned off the ignition. For several seconds the two men sat in complete silence, watching a thick beige cloud of dust settle all around them.

"What the hell was that?!" Derek finally asked.

"Looks like someone isn't thrilled we're asking questions about the SNM." Brady motioned to the side of his face. "You're bleeding."

The PI winced as he touched his temple. "Now they really have me pissed," he mumbled.

"Are we sure it was a bullet?" Brady suddenly interjected, realizing that with all the flying stones and debris it might have been something else.

Derek stared at him as if he were crazy, but then quickly examined the opposite side of the car just to humor his friend. Less than a foot directly behind Brady's head he could see the bright blue of the Nevada sky through a half-inch hole. "One hell of a pebble," he said, indicating the hole with a nod of his chin. "I'd say a 30.06 or so from the looks of that crater."

Brady twisted around to take a look. "One hell of a pebble."

"Whoever it was, they weren't screwing around. That thing could stop a tank."

"Which raises a question: if they were trying to kill us, why would they shoot at us while we were in a moving car in the middle of nowhere?"

The PI was about to answer with his usual sarcastic wit, when he stopped. "Good question. They could have just as easily knocked us off in the parking lot of our hotel, or coming out of Jacob's house, or a million other places. So what are you thinking – just sending a message?"

"Might well be."

"Well consider the message delivered. I say we head straight to the local FBI office and tell them what we know."

"Which is?"

"Well, we know we've been asking questions about the SNM and someone put a bullet through our side window. Isn't that enough?"

"When they ask us why we've been talking to people about the SNM, what are we going to say without hanging Marid out to dry? And if they ask us why we think it's the SNM, what proof do we have?"

"Well…I mean…" Derek stumbled.

"It's too early. If we're going to help the kid we need to know what this is all about before we call in the Marines. We need to figure out what an Islamic terrorist in Virginia has to do with a militia here in the desert. And most importantly, what Marid has in common with either one."

Derek sighed. "All right. I suppose we can wait a little longer. But the next time a bullet whizzes past my head I'm either calling in the authorities or catching the next flight back to DC. I like the kid alright, but not enough to die for him."

"Nobody's going to die," Brady said. But even as the words left his lips he wondered how true they were.

He turned the ignition key and headed back toward the airport.

CHAPTER 9

"They what?!" Anne shouted through the phone when Brady told her about the ambush. "Brady James, you get on the next plane out of that place and come back here to DC!"

Brady smiled. It had been a long time since anyone, especially an attractive lady friend, had cared enough to boss him around. Not that he intended to take her advice.

"I'd like nothing better," he began, hoping to calm his girlfriend's fears. "But we haven't done what we came out here to do. Still don't know what the story is with Marid."

"No story is worth a bullet through your head!"

"They weren't trying to hit us. Just scare us."

"And how do you know that?" she answered, her tone a bit more under control. "Did they send you a letter?"

"They could've gotten to us anywhere. If they wanted us dead, I wouldn't be talking to you right now."

"How reassuring."

"Look, Anne, I know it seems a bit crazy, but I promised the kid's mom I'd try to get him out of whatever he's involved in, and I'm not going to give up just 'cause some idiot shot out one of our windows."

"And what if next time they miss – the window I mean? Besides, maybe this whole affair is much to do about nothing. Maybe his Mom's just overly protective. You said so yourself."

"Maybe she is. But until I know for sure, I'm gonna keep at it."

"Brady James…" Anne began.

"Anne, I'll be back there as soon as I can. I promise. You know I'd rather be there than stuck here in the middle of this desert."

"Even with all those showgirls?" She made it sound like she was joking, but Brady thought he detected a twinge of jealousy. Or maybe he was just hoping.

"Oh, are there showgirls out here?" he asked. "All I've seen are cactus and tumbleweed."

"Good. Keep you motivated to get back here sooner rather than later."

"I'll be back there as soon as I can. I promise."

"You'd better." Her anger had been transformed into a pouty insistence. He liked it.

"I'll call you tomorrow."

"You'd better. And Brady, be careful."

"I will. Sleep well."

"Say hi to the little guy."

As he hung up he asked himself, not for the first time, what he was doing out there.

He shrugged, ignoring the voice that whispered in his ear that his gallantry could get them killed.

CHAPTER 10

The car rental agency wasn't happy.

"So where were you again when this happened?" the 20-something agent asked as she inspected the filthy, battered car with a look of abject horror.

"North. A small subdivision near the air base," Brady said.

"You know, if you wanted to go off-road, you should have rented an SUV."

"We weren't off-road. The road had a street sign. It just wasn't paved."

"I can see that."

Derek shrugged. He and Brady just wanted another car and they'd be on their way. They'd already decided to stiff the local cops on this one, since they really had no proof of who'd shot at them, and no physical proof whatsoever. But now this airhead young woman was taking so long with the paperwork...

The short blast of a police siren reverberated through the parking lot.

"Well they sure took their sweet old time," the young agent muttered to herself as she headed over to intercept the officers in the car.

"Oh great," Brady said as the two cops, a man and a woman, climbed out of their black and white.

He and Derek watched as the agent talked to the cops, gesturing animatedly.

"What do you think she's saying?" Brady asked his smallish friend.

"Probably wondering who the stud is with the fat old guy," Derek answered without any sign of sarcasm. Before Brady could respond, the confab broke up and the two cops and the agent headed their way.

"Gentlemen," the male cop said by way of introduction. "I understand you had a little problem with your rental vehicle."

'*Oh crap*,' Brady thought instantly. '*The airhead agent thinks we were trying to run out without paying for the damage.*'

"You could say that," he said aloud noncommittally.

"Miss Harrison here seems to think it was a bullet that broke your side window."

Brady was trying to think of a way to justify not having reported the incident when the female officer called over to her partner.

"Burt, come take a look at this." She was standing on the other side of the Fusion, just about where the bullet hole was located.

"Don't go anywhere," Burt said to Brady and Derek as he turned to inspect the car.

"Don't go anywhere?" Derek whispered to Brady as soon as the cop was out of earshot. "The guy watches too much CSI."

Brady couldn't even manage a smile. A moment later the two cops were back, accompanied by the cocky rental agent.

"Wanna tell us what happened?" Burt asked, pulling out a pocket notebook.

Brady decided on the spot not to tell the whole story, but just enough to get them off the hook. He explained that they were researching a story, "about militias" he added when prompted by Burt's partner, and so had driven out to the desert to talk with a local expert. It was while they were driving back that the window suddenly exploded.

"That's it?" Burt asked, skepticism as evident in his tone as his expression.

"That's it."

Burt scratched a few words in the notebook. "If I'm lining up the trajectory of that bullet correctly, it must have passed within a few inches of your heads. But it seems you didn't think it was worth reporting to the police. Why's that?"

"We didn't know it was a bullet at first," Brady said, shading the truth as closely as he dared. "We didn't find the hole in the roof until we got back here."

"They didn't tell me anything about it either!" the agent huffed.

"I can't really see up that high very well," Derek said innocently.

"And you?" Burt said, turning to Brady. "Do you have some kind of vision problem too?"

"Hey, we thought it was a stone. You don't look for a bullet hole if you think a stone broke your window." Brady tried to look indignant.

Burt gave his partner a look as if to say, 'This sounds like a bunch of bs to me, how about you?' She shrugged.

"All right, so you didn't know it was a bullet. Any reason someone would want to take a shot at you?"

"Not really. I mean, we haven't written anything yet. Heck, only a handful of people even know we're here. You know, maybe it wasn't someone shooting at us at all. I understand all kinds of people go out to the desert to shoot rabbits or just plunk tin cans. Maybe a shot got away."

The cop stared at Brady intently. "You're doing a story on the SNM and a bullet nearly takes your head off, and you don't think there *might* be a link?"

"Might be," Brady grudgingly admitted. "But it's just as likely that it's just a wrong place, wrong time kind of thing."

Burt turned to Derek. "Is he always this naïve?"

"We call him Forrest sometimes." He waited a second and then added, "As in Gump." He saw the cop's eyebrows shoot up in understanding.

"Yeh. Well they're gonna be calling the two of you Missing Persons if you don't watch yourselves. These are *not* nice people."

"We appreciate the advice," Brady cut in. "And we'll be careful. But this is our job. This is what we do for a living."

"Breathing is what you do for living," Burt said solemnly. "I suggest you keep on doing it. Maybe back in DC?"

"Are you running us out of town?" Derek asked.

The cop smiled. "Those days are long gone."

"Unfortunately," his partner grumbled.

"We'll be careful. I promise," Brady vowed, eager to end the conversation. "And if we learn anything more about the shooting, we'll be sure to let you know."

Burt eyed the two of them as if trying to make up his mind. "Not much we can do about it, I suppose. But I would surely make me sad to read your obits in the local papers."

"That makes three of us," Derek said.

The two cops talked a little further with the car agent and then headed back out on their beat. The agent came over to them looking completely frazzled.

"We will be contacting your insurance company," she said as soon as she was close enough to talk without shouting.

"Fair enough. Now, do you have an SUV we could rent?"

The agent looked at him as if he'd just sprouted antlers. "Rent? Another car? I…ah…I don't think we have anything available just now. Why don't you check back with us in another day or two."

Derek indicated the adjoining lot, where it appeared that a dozen cars – including a nice white Ford Escape – awaited renters. "Those aren't available?"

The woman glanced over at the cars. "Reserved."

"All of them?"

"Big convention."

The PI was just about to launch into a diatribe when Brady reached down and patted him on the shoulder. "I'm sure we can find another agency that has something available. Sorry about the accident."

The agent looked relieved to see them walk away.

An hour later they had managed to rent a Dodge Durango and were on their way back to Boulder City.

They had been riding in silence, the events of the day repeating in their minds, when suddenly Derek asked, "what are the odds that the shot was an accident?"

Brady glanced over at his friend. "Oh, I'd say ten per cent, at the most. You know how I feel about coincidences."

The PI did know. Brady didn't believe in coincidences. At all. "Yeh, that's what I was thinking too. So if someone is already trying to kill us…"

"We already went through this. It was probably just a warning shot."

"Warnings usually lead to something more."

"We'll see."

For the rest of the trip back to their hotel they didn't say two words. Brady was trying to envision a plot line in which Marid could be stopped before he did something stupid or ended up in jail. Derek was trying to envision an ending to their visit that didn't culminate with one or both of them in the morgue. Neither man had a great deal of confidence in his vision.

By the time they got back to their hotel, the sun was already low in the sky and food was the primary subject of discussion. They were still debating which of the neighborhood haute cuisine establishments they should frequent when Derek opened the door to their room. He stopped in mid-sentence.

"Damn it!"

Brady looked over his friend's head and saw their room in shambles. Someone had gone through their suitcases, all the drawers, even the refrigerator, and had dumped everything on the floor.

"Housekeeping here sucks," Derek said quietly.

Brady turned around with a grimace. "Having spent some time in your apartment, I'm surprised you even noticed."

"Flattery will get you nowhere," the little guy said as he shut the door behind him. He gently nudged a broken glass out of the center of the room with his booted toe. "Still think we should keep the cops out of this?"

This time James hesitated a fraction of a second. "If I can find that kid and get him out of whatever he's mixed-up in without getting him a five year jail sentence, I'm going to do it."

Derek knew that tone of voice. He didn't even argue.

*****

Chez called at 10 to give them some more bad news.

"Your buddy Alietto?" the cop began without even saying hello. "He's disappeared."

"I thought your guys were keeping an eye on him," Brady said before he could catch himself.

"They were. Now they're not."

Brady didn't pursue it any further. He knew Chez had probably already read his guys the riot act and so just thanked the cop for letting them know before filling him in on the day's activities.

"You need to talk to the local cops. Maybe even the FBI," Chez answered as soon as he heard about the shooting and the room.

"No can do. I want the story, but I also want to try to keep the kid out of trouble."

"And you're going to risk your life, and Short-stuff's, just to save the county some room and board? How do you even know the kid wants to be saved? Maybe he's the one who's driving this thing."

"Don't think so. There's something really odd about this link between Middle Eastern terrorists and the SNM. Something doesn't smell right."

"You know what happens to good little journalists who stick their noses where they don't belong?"

"Been doing it for 25 years. Still in one piece."

"Listen Brady, don't push your luck, Vegas or no Vegas. I asked Homeland Security for a read-out on your desert rats – just for background, I told them. They are not nice men."

"I know. We'll be careful."

"Yeh, well you do that. And keep me informed." They ended the conversation by agreeing to disagree.

The phone barely hit its cradle before starting to ring again.

"What now? Did you forget to kiss me goodnight?" Brady started in without even saying hello.

"Mr. James?" an unknown man's voice said.

Brady stiffened, drawing Derek's attention. "Yeh, this is James," he answered, motioning to the PI.

"Jesse Winthrop says you're looking to talk to some Militiamen."

"That's right. We're working on a story for the Washington Post."

"You're a long ways from home." Something in the way he said it made Brady's skin crawl.

"Not so long by plane," he answered, trying to keep his voice calm.

"No, I suppose not. So, when can we meet?"

"Tomorrow's good. 8:30 ok with you? I hear it gets pretty warm out here in the desert as the day goes on."

"Fine. Where will we meet?"

"We'll give you a call at 8 o'clock to give you the directions."

"Sounds good. Can we bring a camera?"

"No pictures. No recorders. And Mr. James, no cops."

"We're reporters, not police officers." He tried to sound indignant.

"I hope so, for your sake." He paused for a moment and Brady almost hung up, thinking the conversation was over. But then he continued. "Don't suppose you'll be driving that Ford," he said, and then chuckled.

"You know, you could have killed us with that stunt."

"What makes you think we weren't trying to do just that?"

"I'm told you boys have some skill with weapons. I'm guessing you just wanted us to feel at home."

The caller chuckled again. "You could say that. More to the point, we wanted you to know that we know everything that goes on around here. No secrets from the SNM."

"Kind of gives you a warm, fuzzy feeling, don't it?" Brady said, unable to control his sarcasm.

But the caller just laughed. "You know, we might just enjoy our little talk tomorrow. Provided, of course, you obey our rules. Otherwise, we'll have to waste another couple of cartridges, and we hate to waste ammo."

"We'll do what we can to save you unnecessary effort."

"You do that, Mr. James. You do that. And tell the little fellow hi from us. We'll see you both tomorrow." The phone went dead.

"The Militia?" Derek asked as soon as Brady hung up the phone.

"The one and only."

"We're meeting with them tomorrow, I take it?"

"Eight-thirty."

"What'd they say about the Ford?"

"Just making us feel welcome."

Derek took a big swig of beer. "You sure this is a good idea?" It was clear the PI had his doubts.

"Nope. But it's necessary."

Derek started to say something, but then just sighed. Once Brady James had his mind made up, you couldn't change it with a crowbar.

*****

At 8 a.m. sharp the phone rang in their hotel room. The familiar voice on the other end told Brady not only where to meet the SNM members, but a very specific route to get there.

"We'll be watching," the voice said. "You deviate from the route, the interview is over."

Brady agreed.

"Now what?" Derek asked as he saw his friend hang up with a concerned look on his face.

"He's telling us exactly how to go to the meeting. Not just where, but the exact route."

"Setting us up? For what? They want publicity and without us they don't get any."

"If, that is, they aren't somehow involved with Marid's bomb plot."

"Do you really think those desert rats would ever link-up with Middle Eastern towelheads? I can't see it."

"Maybe not, but something is going on here. And I'm not at all sure they want us to find out about it."

"So what are you going to do, ask them?"

Brady lifted his hands in indecision. "I don't know. I just might."

The PI's smirk faded to a frown.

*****

The route was convoluted, to say the least. They took highway 95 all the way to the Strip, and then headed west past all the glitter and glamor of Vegas.

"Man, we've got to spend some time here before we leave," Derek said, his head hanging over the ledge of the passenger-side window like a mesmerized cocker spaniel. "See a show or two, play a little blackjack…"

"Chat up a showgirl or two…" Brady added.

"Hey, there's nothing wrong with being sociable," the little man argued defensively.

"Is that what you call it?"

West Sahara took them under interstate 15, past older homes surrounded by seeming oceans of green grass kept alive by nightly sprinkler intervention. Brady wondered what the people who lived downstream on the Colorado River thought about Las Vegans taking so much water to grow grass in a desert. He bet they weren't thrilled.

At S. Buffalo they turned right to W. Ann Street, and then left to the end of 'civilized' Vegas and the beginning of the desert as it had existed before all the construction. Right on Lansford, left on LaMancha, to a dirt road that just led off into the cactus and sand. All during the drive Brady kept glancing into the rearview mirror to see if anyone was following them. He couldn't be sure, but he hadn't seen anything suspicious.

"You sure this is the right way?" Derek asked as the dust whirled around their tires and the road became more concept than reality.

"It's what they told me."

"Great. And if they told you to drive off a bridge?" the PI mumbled, more to himself than his friend, who he knew would ignore him. As he did.

After 15 minutes of nothing but barren desert, off to their left a small stand of trees appeared, a stunning swatch of green in an ocean of tan.

"That's their meeting spot?" the PI asked as Brady slowed.

"I think so. Let's go take a look."

He turned into what appeared to be a wash, the rocky remains of a fast-moving stream that had sprung into life during one of the infrequent downpours that doused the desert once or twice a year and disappeared hours later. They rocked and rolled for a hundred yards or so, until they came to the fringes of the small stand. Sitting in an opening among the trees that had been invisible from the road, two dusty motorcycles clearly announced that someone had arrived before them. Derek reached automatically for his holster.

"Do you see anyone?" Brady asked, his voice unnaturally low as they sat eying the trees and the small pool of water they surrounded.

The PI swept the scene from left to right, but no one came forward to welcome them.

"Not very hospitable."

Brady opened his door.

"Where do you think you're going?" Derek asked.

"Anybody home?!" James shouted.

The sound echoed off the rocks and boulders. Nothing.

The PI was just about to suggest that they head back to town, when a voice from just to the side and behind him made him jump.

"You always this noisy?" a familiar voice asked calmly.

Derek grabbed for his gun and turned to face the unexpected intruder, when his door swung open and he felt the barrel of a shotgun press against the back of his neck.

"Now, now. Let's not get off on the wrong foot. I think it'd be best if you hand me that little pea-shooter."

Derek looked to Brady, only to see him frozen in place, a pistol aimed at the side of his head. "The man's got a point," the ex-reporter said with no obvious nervousness.

"That he does," the little man said, lifting his 9 mm from its place by two fingers and handing it delicately to what turned out to be a wiry thin man, maybe 40, with tattoos on both arms.

"Now why don't the two of you get out of that hot, dusty car and come on over to our...office, where we can have our little talk."

As Brady did as he was told, he found himself face to face with a big man, maybe 6'2", 225 pounds, mid-twenties, hair pulled back into a ponytail. He didn't say a word, but motioned with the barrel of his gun for the reporter to head toward the trees. Brady did as he was directed and was relieved when the militiaman lowered his gun and walked along casually next to him.

"Have any trouble finding us?" the shorter man asked.

"Not really. Your directions were good."

"Thought this would be a little more private than some office or restaurant."

"Very nice. I didn't realize there were little oases out here like this."

"Oases?" the shorter man said with a laugh. "More like a watering hole. And there's dozens of 'em out here."

"Do you guys spend a lot of time here in the desert?" Derek asked. "I mean, do you live out here, or in the city?"

"What do you think, we live in caves or under rocks?" Mr. Tattoos asked pointedly.

"Under rocks," his bigger friend repeated with a chuckle.

"You tell me," the PI said.

"We live in houses, just like you and your buddy. We work normal jobs, have families, and sometimes even vote. Does that surprise you?

"A little. I guess."

"How about you – do you live in a normal house, or a little Munchkin house?"

DiLaurain was about to snap at him with one of his well-worn comebacks, when he saw the guy's broad grin.

"Bet mine's bigger than yours," was all he said instead.

Both militiamen burst out laughing.

"Funny little shit," the big guy said.

"I bet you've gotten your ass kicked a lot over the years," the other one added.

"Some folks have tried," Derek said, a little more seriously than he'd intended.

"But that's not what we're here to talk about," Brady interrupted. "You boys ready to answer some questions?"

"Might be. Let's hear what you want to know about."

For a half hour Brady asked a series of plausible but largely uninteresting questions about the origins, makeup and goals of the Southern Nevada Militia, sounding just tough enough to approximate a real interview but just soft enough to win-over his two subjects. The older militiaman, Eddie, did most of the talking. The younger, Jake, largely kept his eyes scanning the surroundings as if expecting an FBI raid at any moment.

When Brady finally felt that he'd gained enough of their trust to move on to more pertinent questions, he began to zero-in on his real interest.

"I think our readers might be interested to know how you and your organization reacted to 9/11," he said by way of a lead-in. "Were you outraged? Or…what?"

"What? You think we're some kind of homegrown terrorists so we must have cheered when the Twin Towers went down? Is that it?"

"You tell me." Brady had learned long ago that answering questions was the short route to a bad interview. He called his technique the Shrink Method – never commit, never give an opinion, always probe for unspoken or purposely hidden information – just like a psychiatrist.

"If we could have gotten ahold of some of those rugheads we would have shown you just how we felt about those gutless assholes," Eddie spat. "In a war you go after the soldiers on either side. Sure, there may be collateral damage, but only cowards go after civilians as their target."

"So there's no way you'd work with al-Queda or any other Middle Eastern terrorist group, even if they were going to help you here in the States?"

"Do you think we need the help of a pack of illiterate rugheads?!" Eddie answered, his face growing redder by the second. "If we decide to take action against a corrupt and interfering federal government, we're more than capable of doing it ourselves. And if we did need any help, we could find it right here in the US of A – not in some camel corral."

Out of the corner of his eyes, Brady saw Derek's eyebrows shoot up appraisingly.

Brady weighed his next question carefully. Only the overpowering evidence of the SNM's distaste for all things Arab convinced him to go on.

"Ever hear of someone named Joseph Alietto?" The moment the words left his lips, his little friend's head jerked around to stare in disbelief.

But DiLaurain's reaction was nothing compared to Eddie and Jake's.

"What?! How the hell do you know about Alietto?" Eddie barked.

"His name came up in some research we did."

"Research into what, goat-diddling and bullshitting?"

Jake chuckled humorlessly at his friend's question.

"So you do know the guy?"

"Yeh, we know him. A real piece of work. He was one of our members for 3-4 years. Then took off on his own when we were too... what did he call us, Jake?"

The bigger man didn't hesitate. "Candy-ass. Afraid to go after the big guys in the government."

"Yeh, candy-ass. That was it," Eddie continued. "The little peckerhead thought he could do better than us. When the members didn't put him into my spot, he quit and ran. Just like the greaseball little faggot he is."

"So you haven't had any communication with him lately?"

The militiaman's eyes narrowed. "What is this? I thought you were reporters."

James had done enough interviews with dangerous psychopaths to realize he was on shaky ground. He needed to tread carefully. Very carefully.

"We are. But we've got a lead that this Alietto guy might be working with a terrorist network, maybe from the Middle East."

Derek's eyes shot open wide even as the tension eased a bit in the militiaman's shoulders. "Wouldn't surprise me. The scumbag has no honor, no class. He'd cut a deal with the devil himself if he thought it'd get him his way."

"So he's for real?"

"Yeh, he's for real. A real nutcase. But don't put him in our story. He's not SNM and we don't want the association."

"No problem. Have any idea if he still has any friends out this way?"

"Nah. A friend of his wouldn't want to hang with us." Jake's deep throated sneer from the shadows was more frightening than Eddie's angry stare.

"Nobody he knew when he was with you guys? Maybe somebody outside the SNM?"

Eddie nodded as he stopped to think. "Well, there was one broad he used to plunk every now and then. What was her name, Jake?"

"Doris, or something like that?"

"Yeh, Doreen I think. Doreen Wallace. Bartender over at Play Misty's. Don't know if she's still around."

"We'll see if we can track her down."

"So when is this going to appear in the Post?" Eddie asked.

"Depends when we finish our research. I'd guess in 3-4 weeks."

"Anything else you need from us?"

"Nope. That should do it. Oh, one thing – if you happen to run into Mr. Alietto, do you think you could give us a call?"

"I don't think that's going to happen, but if it does, sure. Why not?"

"Great. Thanks for your time."

The goodbyes were brief. Eddie reminded Brady that they expected the story to be fair and unbiased, "not like that piece of shit that the R-J reporter did a few years back. We didn't like that one."

"So we've heard," Brady said.

"Then we're on the same wavelength."

With that, the two SNM members hopped on their bikes and roared off into the desert.

"Charming," was all Derek could say as they watched the dust explode all around the two bikes as they disappeared into the distance.

"I guess we should swing by Misty's," Brady mused. "Feel like a beer?"

"Thought you'd never ask."

*****

As the two men drove back through the desert using the GPS on Derek's smartphone to guide them to the bar, the PI couldn't help but ask about the way the interview had unfolded.

"Hey, I know the Q&A is your thing, but why the hell did you ask them about Alietto? What if they're still a lot friendlier than they let on?"

Brady shrugged. "A hunch. I just got the feeling that they hadn't parted the best of friends. We'll see what Miss Wallace says about all that."

Derek had worked enough stories with James to know that his hunches were most often right-on, but he still felt uneasy that the one person they were pretty certain was connected to Marid's bomb plot might learn that they were hot on his trail. He'd just have to keep his fingers crossed.

Play Misty For Me was a much bigger bar than Brady had expected. Located on North 3rd Street in the 'less savory' section of Downtown, the bar covered half a city block and must have had 50 motorcycles of every size and shape imaginable parked outside.

"Oh great," the diminutive PI groaned as they pulled up outside the bar. "Just my kind of joint."

"You can stay out here while I go in. Should only take a couple of minutes," Brady offered.

"No way. Who's gonna protect you from all the greasers?"

Brady shook his head but knew better than to try to talk his friend out of coming. The two of them got out of the car and made it to the front door without encountering any of the establishment's patrons. Once they stepped through the front door, however, it was a different story.

Heads always turned when Derek came into a room, but in this place the added attention came with voiced welcomes.

"Hey little man, Circus Circus is out on the Strip!" one very large, very bearded, very drunk redneck said as they walked toward the bar.

"Anybody up for midget bowling?" another yelled, to be met by hoots and hollers of laughter.

"Just try," the PI muttered through a clenched jaw, just loud enough for Brady to hear.

The ex-reporter didn't even break stride or acknowledge the cat-calls. He marched straight to the bar where an attractive young bleached blond, probably in her mid-twenties, spun bottles and slid glasses like the pro she undoubtedly was. The tattoo on her shoulder and the bare-midriff blouse were the only visible clues to her chosen profession.

"What can I get you two gentlemen?" she asked with a pleasant-enough smile.

"The little guy could use a highchair," a long-haired biker quipped from the stool just next to where they stood.

"Keep flapping your gums and you'll be needing dentures," Derek growled, "if you don't already."

The biker's friends howled with laughter, but for just a second it seemed like the biker might take offence. Then Derek smiled his most winning 'got ya' grin and the biker succumbed.

"Get the little man something to drink," he slurred. "He's too damn ornery when he's sober."

Everyone laughed again, including Derek and Brady – though anyone who knew them would have quickly realized that their laughter was forced. But, of course, no one knew them there.

When the bartender brought them each a beer, Brady casually asked, "Is Doreen working today?"

The young woman looked confused. "Do you mean Darlene?"

"Wallace?"

"You're not bill collectors, are you?"

Derek laughed loudly. "Not hardly."

"Reporters. Working on a story."

Her face brightened. "Oh, that's cool. What about?"

"Bartenders. In particular, woman bartenders," Brady ad-libbed.

"And you want to interview Darlene?"

"We do. Heard she's been working bar here for years."

"Twenty-two, or something like that.'

"She must've seen it all."

"We see it all every night. Hey, I don't suppose you'd want to interview a younger woman, maybe compare and contrast?"

"You?"

"I've been here for almost three years."

"I might be interested," Derek said with his closest approximation of an ingratiating smile.

"Are you a reporter too?"

"Was the Pope a Nazi?"

The young woman made a face. "That's pretty rough."

"Journalism is a tough business."

She hesitated. "Not you?" she asked Brady.

James saw Derek turn to him with a look that was half pleading and half insisting.

"We'll see what my associate comes up with. If it's something that helps our story, maybe."

"We're kind of jammed-out just now," Derek cut in immediately. "And you look busy too. You working tomorrow?"

"Night shift. 8-4."

"How about I meet you here at 6 and we can talk - over some food?"

"How about we meet at a place where the food is actually edible."

"Ooh, that's pretty rough too."

"Bartending is a tough business." She smiled.

They finally agreed on a place. After a few more minutes of chit-chat and repeated hints, Brady had to pull his little friend by the arm to get him to leave.

As soon as the bar door closed behind them, it began. "I wonder how she's going to react when she finds out you have trouble typing your name without making three typos," Brady said tauntingly. "Maybe she'd like to rethink that dinner."

"You're just pissed she made the offer to me. If it had been you…" He stopped in mid-sentence, as he noticed Brady's eyes focused on an R-J newspaper machine on the sidewalk next to the door.

"President to Visit Las Vegas!" A headline screamed. Brady grabbed a quarter from his pocket and stuffed it into the machine.

"What's up?" Derek asked.

Brady began to read aloud. "As announced by the White House last February, President Wexler will visit Las

Vegas on August 19th to attend a fund-raising dinner. The President is expected to stay overnight at Caesars, before heading to Los Angeles for a series of fundraisers. Blah, blah, blah."

"That's next Tuesday! We gotta call the Secret Service," the PI said immediately. "No way we can keep this quiet any longer."

Brady nodded thoughtfully. "I wish we could – for Nyla's sake. But having Alietto and Marid out here just as the President is about to visit is too coincidental for me. I don't know if they're going to think we're nuts or legit informants, but it's out of our hands. Let's go."

CHAPTER 11

Brady had expected to catch an earful from the Secret Service, and they didn't disappoint him.

"Who the hell do you think you are, running around like some vigilantes, endangering the President and maybe a lot of other people as well?!" agent Steven Lyle screamed when he heard their story, a vein in his neck bulging menacingly.

"We were researching a story," James answered, keeping his voice calm. "We weren't sure there was a threat. Still aren't, really. But with the two of them out here and the President about to arrive…"

"You better pray we find those two before they can cause any harm, or you may just find yourself charged with obstruction of justice!"

"That's why we're here," Derek said. "So you can find them."

"Yeh, well thank heaven for small favors," Lyle said, his anger somewhat tempered. "Where are you two staying?"

"We're out at the Hoover Dam Hotel in Boulder City," Brady answered. "But we're almost at the end of our budget and planned to leave day after tomorrow."

"Reschedule that. As long as those two are running around out here and you can identify them, we want you to stay put."

"Would love to, but we're freelancing so there's no expense account."

The agent made a face and mumbled to himself. "All right. We'll put you up in a hotel here in the city. But we'll want you to keep yourselves available." He wasn't pleased.

"I think we could arrange that," Brady said, sounding as if it would require a Herculean effort. Derek shot him a dirty look.

"Good. You can play some slots, stroll through the casinos. But keep your goddamn noses out of this investigation, you hear me? You've already jeopardized the President's visit. Don't make it any worse."

"They might cancel his visit?"

"That's what I'm thinking of recommending. We'll see what they decide. Not up to me."

"What hotel?" the PI asked, unable to restrain his curiosity one minute longer.

The agent smiled wickedly. "Well it won't be Caesars Palace, if that's what you were thinking."

Derek looked crestfallen.

*****

The Redrock Motel was definitely not Caesars Palace. Located in sunny North Vegas, miles from the Strip and a pretty good taxi ride from Downtown, the place looked like Bugsy Siegel himself might have stayed there when he first came to the city in the mid 1940's. Two-story, pale green stucco, with a wing-like entrance overhang that must have looked cool to Frank Sinatra and the Rat Pack. Now, it just looked seedy.

"Hey, at least they're paying for it," Brady offered as they pulled up in front of the motel.

"Who's gonna' pay for the flea bath afterwards?" Derek replied.

"We can always move somewhere else if you want to pay out of pocket…"

"Nah, I won't melt," the PI answered quickly. "Let's see if it's any better inside."

It wasn't. Not only were the walls painted in the Caribbean pale greens and pinks of another era, it looked like the last time they were painted was when the colors were hip.

"From the Service, huh?" the desk clerk asked as he checked their reservation. "What is it – witness protection?"

"We were sentenced to 25 to life," Derek sneered. "And this is their idea of hard time."

"Funny," the clerk said, but he didn't smile. "Room 202, up the stairs and to your right."

"Where's the elevator?" Derek asked.

"It's temporarily out of service."

"Since when – 1950?"

The clerk stared at him. "We have amateur comedy night on Tuesdays. You should give it a try."

"I just may do that," Derek muttered as he headed for the stairs.

"It's his time of the month," Brady whispered to the clerk.

"I heard that!" the PI yelled back over his shoulder.

The room was actually a pleasant surprise. Oldish and none too fashionable, at least it had been freshened-up sometime in the last 10 years. And it was large. The size of a suite in most modern hotels.

"At least we won't be bumping into each other," Brady tried to make the best of it.

"Great. Just what I need – lots of space." The tiny PI looked like a pimple on the butt of an offensive linesman in the huge room, all red-faced and puffed-up.

"Take it easy. It's only for a couple of days. Besides, we'll be out and about chasing down Marid and Alietto most of the time anyway."

"I thought our buddy Lyle told us to sit tight."

"He said to keep our noses out of the investigation. We're working a story. I don't know bupkis about their investigation."

DiLaurain shook his head. "I should'a known."

*****

Brady called Eric Jacobs later that night.

"Eric, sorry to bother you, but I just wanted to know if you'd ever run into an SNM member named Joseph Alietto."

"Alietto…Alietto. Sounds familiar. Where would I know him from?"

"He apparently had a falling-out with your buddy Eddie a few years back and left the group."

"Ah, yeh, I remember the guy. Real intense. Thought that the foreigners were taking over the world, and wanted the SNM to do something about it. Eddie realized they were being watched by the FBI, among others, and insisted they take it easy. When it came down to it, more members backed Eddie and Alietto left town."

"Would you say he's dangerous?"

A pause. "I think he could be, given the right circumstances. He didn't seem like the bravest guy in the world but he's probably one of the most rabid. Why? Is he back?"

"He is. Any idea how to find him?"

"Nah. I only met the guy once. Maybe Eddie would know."

"Eddie thinks Alietto will keep his distance. They're not exactly on friendly terms."

"Yeh, I suppose that would be the case. Sorry, can't help you. Hey, what did you think of Eddie?"

"Not as dumb as I expected, and not as dumb as he lets people think."

"Oh, he's not dumb," Eric said quickly, "but he *is* dangerous, and don't forget it even for a minute."

"Don't worry, we won't." He thanked the R-J reporter and hung up.

"Any luck?" Derek asked.

"He didn't know the guy. Only talked to him once. Said he's a real true-believer."

"Radical Muslim?"

"I don't think so. He supposedly hated foreigners."

"Wonder how he'll like little people."

"I understand he prefers them with ketchup."

Derek rolled his eyes. "Every time I think you can't stoop any lower…"

"You realize I'm still taller than you. Come on, let's go take a look at Caesars. See if we can get some idea of what Alietto might be planning."

"Give me a couple of minutes."

"For what?"

"If I'm going to be cruising the Strip, I want to look the part."

Brady was tempted to stick it to his friend once again, but decided to just take it easy and see what the little guy had in mind. Ten minutes later, he found out. Derek reappeared from the bathroom wearing a white sports jacket, black satin shirt open to the middle of his chest, black slacks, and stunning black alligator boots with what Brady could swear were lifts in them.

"Voila!" the PI announced upon his entrance, pirouetting to show Brady his new gear. "Look out showgirls, here I come."

"I'm sure they're all aflutter. Can we go now, or do you intend to have your hair styled too?"

"No improving upon perfection. Let's roll."

Brady followed his friend out the door, a smile creeping to his lips. This might be fun after all.

*****

From their motel it was just a ten minute ride to the Strip, although it might have been light years for the change in surroundings and traffic. From their rundown North Vegas neighborhood they moved first through the Downtown district, with its closely packed casinos and tourist junk shops, before cruising down Las Vegas Boulevard South, aka The Strip. It was already 10 pm and the Strip was jumping. Tens of thousands of computer controlled lights, signs and special effects catering mostly to the small town tourists. The big time players were inside the massive hotel casinos that lined both sides of the Boulevard. Fifteen of the top 25 largest hotels in the world are located on that four mile long stretch of asphalt, including Caesars Palace – for decades the crème de la crème of the legal gaming industry.

As the two men drove slowly down the Strip, they eyed the impossible diversity of people crowding the sidewalks, flowing from one hotel to another. Ma and Pa Kettle from Bumpkinville, USA rubbed shoulders with some of the most expensive hookers in the country (the most expensive never actually strode the streets but responded to summons from casino execs to service the 'whales' that might drop $250,000 in a single hand.) Every race, color and creed were represented in the tidal waves of people who pushed and shoved to get into casinos whose sole reason for existing was to fleece as many willing participants as possible.

"Man, I done died and gone to heaven," Derek said as he stared, hypnotized, out the front and side windows.

"Somehow I doubt heaven uses the same decorator as these guys," Brady said, trying to keep his eyes on the cars in front of and to the sides of theirs, knowing that more than half of the drivers were either drunk, high, or so bedazzled by the lights and glitz that they were just as likely to drive through the car ahead of them as stop when brake lights flashed.

Caesars wasn't too far down the road. With all the columns, statues, fountains, and mock cypress trees lining the entrance, the place looked to Brady like the kind of place where Caligula would feel right at home.

"Tastefully understated," he muttered as they approached the gaping maw of the sybaritic pleasure palace.

"Home sweet home," the PI countered.

They had barely rolled to a stop when a self-important valet parker strolled to the driver's side door, and a smiling greeter opened Derek's.

"Welcome to Caesars Palace, S..." the greeter stopped in mid-sentence as Derek scrambled down from the car seat.

"Must be a bitch to be so tall," Derek muttered as he walked past the flustered five-foot nine bellboy.

Brady soon appeared at his side, and together the two men entered the upscale adult carnival that is Caesars. If they hadn't been working, James knew that his smallish friend would have wandered the interior for hours. The lights, the tables and machines, the beautiful women, the towering ceilings, the Romanesque statues, the statuesque women, the women, the women... all of it kept him mesmerized. As it was, he had to literally steer the PI through the main casino and off to the Events Center, where they'd learned the President was scheduled to make a short speech before breaking bread with several hundred of his close personal campaign donors.

As they approached the Center, a security guard appeared out of nowhere to intercept them.

"No activities in there today," he said jovially, but with enough emphasis in his voice that Brady knew the room was off-limits.

"Can we just take a little peek?" he asked.

"I'll take a very little peek," DiLaurain added, hoping to disarm the guard with humor.

It didn't work. "I'm afraid they're setting up inside for a program on Tuesday. Only employees are permitted in there."

"The President's visit?" Brady offered, hoping to pick up some in-house scuttlebutt.

"Could be."

"So he'll stay here then? I've heard that sometimes he stays at private homes."

"Don't know. Haven't seen a ton of Secret Service, but you never know."

"How much are tickets?"

"You know what they say: if you have to ask, you can't afford it."

Brady surrendered. "Not much doubt about that. Well, thanks anyway. Hope all goes well, for whatever it is."

The guard smiled, but watched them until they had left the area.

"Not very helpful," Derek complained as they made their way back into the casino.

"He's not their PR guy. I'm sure he has his orders."

"I'd like to order one of those," the PI perked-up as a long-legged cocktail waitress drifted past.

"You'd need a step ladder."

"I could make two trips."

It was obvious that they weren't going to discover anything more that night, so Brady cut his friend loose to prowl the Palace.

"Be back before midnight or catch a taxi," he warned Derek.

"Yes, oh evil stepfather."

To kill time, he found one of the myriad smaller lounges and sat to sip a Bud and watch a moderately talented singer warble every sappy melodic hit of the past 20 years, with the occasional Sinatra classic thrown in for color.

Derek, on the other hand, found the liveliest lounge in the casino and ensconced himself in a booth big enough for five full-sized men. He had persuaded a young lady of dubious character to allow him to buy her a drink, and was deep in discussions with her over their future together, when out of the corner of his eye he saw something that made him stop in mid-proposition. He wasn't certain, he might have been seeing things, but he had to know for sure.

"Hold that thought," he told his attractive young friend even as he scrambled out of the booth. "I'll be right back."

The woman looked confused, but quickly acclimated to the empty booth and stretched out with her drink to watch the band. Derek, on the other hand, scurried as fast as his little legs could carry him in the direction of the young, blond-haired man the PI had glimpsed moments earlier. His path took him past a long line of tables, through the slots at the very back of the casino, to an unmarked metal door. He quickly turned and scanned the casino floor, hoping against hope that the man was still lingering somewhere nearby. But he was nowhere to be found. The door was the only way out.

He pushed on the panic bar and found himself in a service hallway – painted concrete, fluorescent lights, a stark contrast to the seductive opulence just a few feet away. At the end of the corridor, perhaps thirty feet away, a similar metal door was just clicking shut. Breaking all his personal rules, the PI broke into a quick jog. Maybe he was wrong. Maybe it was just someone who looked like the kid. But he could've sworn it was Marid.

He was moving along at a pretty good clip when he hit the door with both hands. Even as it swung open the thought crossed his mind that maybe he should've called Brady, and maybe he should've taken it a bit slower. But it was too late now.

He'd taken one step out into a darkened loading area when he felt more than saw a movement to his right. As he turned to see what was going on, a hard, heavy club exploded on the back of his head. He felt excruciating pain, saw stars, and then…nothing.

*****

Brady glanced at his watch. 12:15.

"Randy little twerp," he muttered, leaving a modest tip and setting off to find his friend and get home while it was still a reasonable hour. He headed straight for the loudest, most boisterous bar he could find, but to his surprise, Derek was nowhere to be found. He was about to try another of the seemingly endless lounges, when he decided to take a longshot and ask the bartender if he'd seen the little man.

"Yeh, I saw a midget in here. Maybe an hour ago?" the twenty-something Latino said.

"Did you happen to see where he went?"

The bartender indicated a booth off to the left with a jab of his chin. "He was visiting with Melanie last time I saw him."

Brady thanked him and made his way to the booth, which by this time was occupied by a good-looking brunette and a not-so-good-looking 50-ish hayseed who seemed to be thoroughly soused.

"Excuse me," James interrupted.

"Yeh?" the drunken tourist slurred.

"Miss," he continued, ignoring the intoxicated rube, "I was wondering if you might have seen a little person in here a short while ago."

"Does he owe you money?"

"He's a friend. So he was here?"

"Hey, go find your own girl," her companion complained.

"Put a sock in it, Ralph," the girl ordered. "Yeh, he was here. Lots of talk, but no action."

"Did you happen to see where he went?"

"Over that way," she pointed. "Said he was coming back."

"When was that?"

"Oh, must have been an hour ago."

"Well, if he does come back, tell him to wait right here, would you?"

She smiled. "And if he doesn't, will *you* be coming back?"

"Thought you had a 'friend'." He nodded at the overweight party boy who was slowly sinking down into the booth cushions.

"I'd have to drag him to a room, he's so smashed."

"We'll see. Don't wait up." He started in the direction she'd indicated.

"You don't know what you're missing!" she called after him.

"Oh yes I do," he muttered as he wove his way through the crowds of inebriated players.

He hadn't quite passed the last of the slots when he saw the metal service door in the back corner of the casino. He glanced around to make sure Derek wasn't tucked away behind a bank of machines, deeply involved in trying to hit a jackpot, and then headed straight to the door. He pushed on the panic bar gently, hoping it wasn't alarmed, stepping through quickly when it opened without a sound. He walked briskly down the short stark corridor, trying the two door handles that he passed but finding them locked.

As he opened the door at the end of the hall he braced for whatever might be waiting for him on the other side. There was nothing. Just a typical loading area, a few empty pallets, and a vacant driveway. He put a piece of cardboard in the door jamb to keep it from locking and walked down four concrete steps to the asphalt. He checked both left and right for anything out of the ordinary. Nothing.

He had all but given up and was already opening the door to re-enter the building, when a few drops of red on the cement beneath his feet caught his attention. He knelt down and wiped at the stain with his finger. He already knew what it was before he held his finger to his nose and smelled the distinct iron odor. Blood. And recent.

He didn't know it was Derek's. His friend could be romping with a new playmate even at that moment. But his instincts told Brady that wasn't the case. He knew in his heart that something had happened. It was time to call Lyle.

*****

Brady was relieved when the Secret Service agent answered the phone on the first ring. Even more so when he didn't bite his head off for calling at that hour.

"Mr. James. A little late for an interview, isn't it?"

"I'm sorry, Steve, but I think we have a problem."

Lyle listened, asking short, pertinent questions.

"Stay where you are. I'll call some people I know at Caesars security, and I'll be over there in 15 minutes."

Brady paced nervously, walking the entire perimeter of the casino as he waited – just to be sure the PI wasn't anywhere to be found. He'd just completed the circuit when a man in a gray business suit, wearing an earpiece, approached him.

"Mr. James?"

"Yes."

"Draymond Eslow. Steve Lyle asked me to find you. Would you please come with me?"

"Don't you want to see what I found?" He sounded desperate even to himself.

"When Steve gets here."

Part of Brady wanted to object, to demand that the security officer begin an investigation immediately. But the part that had witnessed dozens of crime scenes went along willingly. He knew there was a procedure. Eslow led him up a back stairway to some offices on the second floor. He offered Brady a cup of coffee, which he accepted thankfully. The initial rush of adrenaline had faded, leaving him feeling exhausted and anxious. Just a few minutes later, a surprisingly alert Steve Lyle appeared in the casino security office.

"Dray, I owe you one," he said with a nod to the agent. "So, what's this with the little guy?"

Brady reiterated the circumstances so that both Steve and Dray could get all the details.

"Think it's connected to those two desert rats you told us about?" the Secret Service agent asked, followed by a quick rehash of the history for his friend's sake.

"What else? Derek's not a gambler, and as far as I know he doesn't know anybody out here. It's got to be them, or…maybe Alietto."

"The guy impersonating a Middle-Eastern terrorist back in DC?"

"Like we told you, he has links to the SNM out here."

"I thought they were on the outs."

"They were. Are. But that doesn't mean he's not involved. Maybe on his own."

Lyle nodded. "Okay, let's go take a look at this loading dock."

It didn't take long for them to come to the same conclusion as Brady: *something* bad had happened out there, and if Derek was involved he might be in real trouble. Lyle called in a team to collect clues and analyze the blood drips from the cement steps. Then he asked Dray for access to the casino's security tapes.

The recording was none too clear, but what *was* clear was that a short person had stepped out of the rear casino door at 1 am and had promptly been clocked by a much bigger guy who had been waiting for him. They could see a third guy, who Brady had to admit bore a resemblance to Marid, appear from just out of camera range and help drag the PI back off-camera. A check with another camera revealed a black van speeding out from behind the building five minutes later.

"Any chance you can clean the video up so we can make out faces or the license plate?" Brady asked.

Lyle shook his head. "Don't think so. Maybe in daylight, but with the lighting they have out there at night, the chances are minimal. We'll give it a try, though."

"How about the van?"

"A black Econoline in Vegas? Must be a couple thousand of them out there. I'll ask the local cops to see what they can dig up."

"So? What now then?" Brady asked, his sense of frustration showing.

"Now, you and I go back to bed and get some sleep so we can focus on all this in the morning."

CHAPTER 12

Marid felt ashamed.

He had no problem taking revenge against the enemies of Islam, but the little private investigator had never shown him or his mother anything other than professional courtesy. And now this.

He didn't know how al-Zahiri knew the little guy would be there, but he knew. He seemed to know a lot. Things he couldn't possibly know. But that was how these groups worked, he'd decided. They had lots of friends out in the community, people that did nothing but give the al-Zahiris of the world information. "Information is power," al-Zahiri had told him. "Information is survival."

He'd seen the PI notice him out of the corner of his eye as he'd crossed the slots area just where al-Zahiri had told him to. He and Trevor had waited outside. Just as al-Zahiri had said. But then Trevor had knocked the little man unconscious and they'd tied him up and brought him out to the camp. It didn't seem right. Oh sure, they had to protect the brotherhood. They had to keep outsiders away. But still...

Marid knew that his Mom suspected something, and that the midget and his reporter friend probably knew something was happening as well. But they couldn't possibly know what. Or when. So why had they kidnapped the PI? Why had they hurt him? Al-Zahiri would tell him he needed to grow up, to get stronger. He'd tell him that it was a war, a battle of corrupt western governments and ideas against Islam. He'd heard it all before. Many times. They didn't know what he felt inside his heart. They didn't know the strength of his faith. When the time came, he'd show al-Zahiri how strong he'd become. He'd show them all.

CHAPTER 13

Derek awoke to a splitting headache and the overpowering smell of horse shit. He fought against puking as the room spun slowly, finally settling with a thud. For a few long seconds he had no idea what had happened to him.

'What the…?'

He tried to open his eyes, only to discover that they were taped shut. The tape was heavy, stiff – probably duct tape, he decided. He wanted desperately to tear it off, but his hands were bound tightly behind his back – more tape. His feet were tied to the bed, or whatever he was lying on. He struggled to sit up before falling back with a groan.

'Damn it!' he thought as the room began to spin once again.

He lay quietly until his head settled, listening. In the distance he though he heard a cow bellow, but he wasn't sure. From the stench he was pretty certain he was out in the country somewhere, maybe in a barn. He struggled to overcome a wave of panic.

'If they'd wanted me dead, I'd already be there,' he told himself, his pounding heart confirming the premise.

He was still trying to get a grip when he suddenly heard a door squeak, followed by soft footsteps. He automatically turned his head in the direction of the steps.

"I thought I heard something," a man's voice announced from a short distance away. "How's the head?"

Derek berated himself for not having kept still. "It feels like some asshole tried to use it for a baseball," he finally said.

The man snickered. "You got a big head for a little guy. And hard."

"Sorry, I'm spoken for."

This time the man laughed out loud. "Din't know you midgets were so funny."

"You ought'a see me dance. I'll show you if you undo my feet."

Just a snort. "Sorry, no can do. Bossman says you're gonna be our guest for a while."

"And who's your Bossman? Anyone I know?"

"Couldn't say."

"Couldn't say who he is, or whether I know him?"

"Not neither. Got my instructions – no conversing with the midget."

Derek thought for a second. "How about something to eat? You feed your guests, don't you?"

"I guess we do. Bossman will have to decide that."

"And what am I supposed to do about a toilet? What if I have to pee?"

"I guess you hold it for now, or piss in your pants."

"Not very hospitable," the PI said.

"I got my instructions."

"And do you always follow your instructions?"

The voice hesitated a beat. "Most always."

"Why? You afraid of the Bossman?"

"I ain't afraid of nothing," the voice answered, anger coloring his words. "I'm…"

"You're an idiot," a new voice joined in from back where the first man entered. This man sounded older, more authoritative. The Bossman? "Didn't I tell you not to talk to the midget?"

"I…I was just making sure we din't kill him," the flunkie said defensively.

"That's what he was doing all right," Derek chimed in, hoping to win some points with the flunkie. "Just making sure your guest was comfortable."

A long pause. "Get the hell out of here," Bossman finally ordered.

"Be happy to, if you'd just untie me and take off this tape," Derek said. The PI was smiling to himself until a hard poke to the ribs doubled him up.

"I wasn't talking to you, midget. You don't talk unless you're asked a question – you understand?"

"Yeh, got it," Derek wheezed.

"And you," the older man continued to his assistant, "shut the door when you leave, and make sure nobody comes in here for the next little bit."

"Okay, Jo…" He cut off the name as if it burned his lips.

"Get out of here!" the Bossman barked, and Derek could hear the sound of running feet.

"Goddamn moron," the man muttered to himself.

"Hard to get good help?"

Another jab to the ribs, this time harder.

"You don't follow directions too well, do you?"

Derek grimaced, but silenced the groan that struggled to escape.

"You keep that up, your stay with us will be very short, and very unpleasant. You understand?"

"Yeh. Got it."

"Good. So what were you doing in Caesars last night?"

His natural instinct was to reply with a quip, but the ache in his ribs made him think again.

"Looking for some members of the SNM," he said, hoping the lie would pass muster. He braced for another shot to the side in case he was wrong.

"Who?"

"Some asshole named Eddie, and a buddy of his, Jake."

"What business do you have with those faggots?" The venom in Bossman's voice was palpable.

"A friend of mine, Brady James, is researching a story that might involve them."

A single throaty chuckle. "We know all about your Mr. James. We know, for instance, that he spoke with Nyla Jacobson in DC."

"That's right," the PI said, calculating his strategy on the fly. Since this guy already knew about Nyla, he decided to go with the flow. "Her son was in some kind of trouble. Brady thinks the SNM might be involved."

"Really…How?" The PI could tell his inquisitor was intrigued.

"Not sure. That's what we're looking into. The mother thinks that the kid's been brainwashed into some kind of domestic terrorism."

"And James – what does he think?"

"He doesn't know enough yet to decide. We don't even know where the kid is – or at least he doesn't."

"Interesting…"

By now Derek really did need to piss. He decided to risk another jab.

"Hey, now that I've answered your questions, I really need to use a bathroom." He braced, but the only response was verbal.

"Sure. Why not? Helpful midgets earn themselves a break."

Derek wondered how many other midgets this guy had interrogated.

"Hey!" the Bossman yelled, and Derek flinched. The sound of running feet.

"Yeh, boss?"

"Take the little man to the shitter and let him do his thing. But under no circumstances untie him, and I mean not his hands or his feet. Understand?"

"Sure. Let him take a leak but don't untie him. Got it."

"Good. We'll talk more later, Mr. DiLaurain."

The PI listened as the sound of footsteps faded.

"Alright, little man. Up you go!"

A large hand grabbed the PI by the front of his shirt and hauled him to a seated position.

"Hey, take it easy on the fabric!" Derek said. "I paid seventy-five bucks for this shirt."

"You got ripped-off." The rope that connected him to the bed or cot fell free. "Come on, let's go."

The same large hand lifted him from the bed as if he were a sack of flour and landed him on his feet. But the little man almost went to his knees as he tried to take a step.

"Hey! I can barely walk with my feet tied together like this."

"That's the idea."

He was pushed along as fast as his restricted steps would take him. He listened intently as he walked, attempting to pick up any clues about his makeshift prison. There weren't many signs to be had, although the sound of straw crunching beneath his feet reconfirmed his guess that he was in a barn or some other rural building. No more than twenty-five feet later, he was pulled-up short and pushed into a foul-smelling stall.

"The hole's right behind you. I'd sit if I were you, unless you wanna pee all over the place you're gonna be using for a while."

"Yeh. Thanks. But, uh, how about a hand?"

"I'll unbutton your pants, but don't be expecting me to give your thing a shake." The guy sounded offended.

"Don't worry, that was the farthest thing from my mind. In fact, if you'd just untie one of my hands..."

"Ain't gonna happen." The PI felt a tug at his belt buckle and in seconds his pants fell around his ankles. "Jesus, that's some sausage!" his jailer said with a whistle.

"I'm the little guy, not him," Derek said gruffly. He tried to sit on the outhouse seat, but it was a few inches too high for him. He was about to complain when a hand grabbed his arm and literally threw him up on the shitter.

"Oh Lord Jesus, thank you!" the midget sighed as he did his business.

"It weren't Jesus that put you up there, it was me."

"Then thank you too." There were a few seconds of awkward silence. "You the one that hit me over the head back at Caesars?"

"Not supposed to be talking to you."

"What, afraid of a midget taking a piss with his hands and feet tied and his pants pulled down around his ankles? What else scares you – Girl Scouts selling cookies?"

"Ain't afraid. Just not supposed to talk."

"You do everything that other guy tells you?"

"Mostly." He didn't sound thrilled with the admission.

"Were you with the SNM too? I mean, I understand they kicked your friend out when they realized he wasn't too bright."

"Didn't have anything to do with that."

"What then?"

"Some of the others didn't get along with him, that's all."

"From what I've heard, that's pretty much the way it is. Him not getting along with others, I mean. He always so bossy?"

"He's ok."

"So he barks and you jump – is that pretty much the way it is?"

A long pause. "You done with your business yet?"

"Yeh. All done."

Derek knew that he'd pushed as hard as he dared. But he also knew that a man who'd disobey his orders a little would disobey them a lot given the right circumstances. Now it was just a question whether he could arrange the right circumstances – before Bossman decided he was no longer of any value and dumped him in a ditch somewhere.

*****

"And you haven't heard from him since?" Anne asked, her voice tense.

Brady shifted the telephone to his other ear. "Not a word. But we've got the local cops, the FBI, Secret Service, hell probably even the National Guard out looking for him." He tried not to let her feel the doubt he felt. "They'll find him." Was he trying to convince her, or himself?

"Brady, I don't mind telling you that I don't like this, not one little bit. I think you should get on the next plane back here and leave the search to the professionals."

"I can't abandon Derek," he said as gently as he could. The little guy might be a pain in the backside every now and then, but he was his friend. His best friend. He wasn't going anywhere until he knew that the PI was okay.

He heard Anne sigh. "No, I suppose you can't. But you take care of yourself, you hear? No running around taking foolish chances like some super hero."

The concern in her voice made him smile. It'd been a long time since anyone had shown that kind of interest in his well-being. At least a woman.

"Don't worry. Even if I wanted to, the local Secret Service guy has me virtually locked-up in this motel." That wasn't exactly true, but Lyle had warned him to stick close and call him if James was going anywhere further than the restaurant next door.

"Good. At least there's some adult supervision out there."

"What am I, some kind of juvenile delinquent who needs a Big Brother?"

"More like an over-achieving Boy Scout. You know, Brady, you don't have to solve *all* the world's problems."

It was his turn to sigh. "I know, I know. But Nyla Jacobson deserves to know what her son's got himself into."

"You're never going to change, are you?"

He chuckled. "Do you want me to?"

"No, I suppose not. I guess I'm the one who needs her head examined, falling for a big lout like you."

"Ooo, I like it when you talk nasty to me," he said.

"You are incorrigible!"

"I try."

They talked for a few more minutes, about nothing really, just wanting to hear each other's voice. Finally, Anne had to head off to work and Brady needed to get ahold of Lyle. SNM or no, Brady had no intention of hiding in a motel room while his buddy was God-knows where. He'd be careful, but not invisible.

*****

He'd barely hung up the phone when his cellphone rang.

"James," he answered.

"Mr. James, this is Eric Jacobs – from the Review Journal?"

"Yeh, sure, Eric, I remember you. What's up?"

"I just got a disturbing phone call."

"Oh? From who?"

"I don't know. But whoever it was knows that I talked to you, and they told me to pass you a message."

"Go ahead."

"They said if you ever want to see the little guy again, you'll call off the cops – and the feds."

Brady felt his stomach squirm. *How the hell did they know about the feds?'* he wondered. "You don't have any idea who called you?"

"Nah. But I'm betting it was an SNM member, or someone connected with them."

"Yeh, that'd make sense."

Eric waited a few seconds for Brady to explain before taking the initiative. "Hey, would I be prying if I asked what's going on?"

"Don't think it'd be too smart to talk about that."

"That's what I thought you'd say."

"Sorry. Maybe later on," Brady said. "Well, thanks for giving me the message."

"No problem. And Mr. James?"

"Yeh?"

"Take the warning seriously. Like I told you, these guys don't value human life very highly."

"Yeh, I'll do that."

Somehow the warning didn't make Brady feel any better about Derek. He hung up and called Lyle.

*****

Joe Alietto knew that he was taking a risk going ahead with the plan, but there was no way after all his preparation that he was going to give up this close to his goal. Besides, from what he'd been able to learn from the midget, James and the cops didn't really know what was going on. As if the Militia could have arranged all this! Those morons could barely figure out how to plunk a can out in the desert.

It wouldn't be long now, just a few more days until the President came to town. Then all those idiots at SNM would know how badly they screwed-up by kicking him out of their pathetic little organization. *They huff and puff about the towelheads, and the federal government, but what do they actually do about it? Not a damn thing. All their training and websites and marches all boil down to nothing more than a big game. What have they accomplished? Nada. Zip.'*

'*Funny thing is, all of 'em think that what we want to do is kill the President. I really don't give a damn about him. Oh sure, he's not one of us. But he's just another figurehead, another pawn of the east coast liberal elite. One of 'em is pretty much the same as the next.*

'*No, what we're aiming for is something much bigger, more glorious. When the kid explodes that bomb, everyone in this country is going to think the goddamn Muslims did it. And what will happen then? Open season on towelheads! It's gonna be a religious war like we haven't seen around here in ages. And who will be right there to lead the hunt? Well little ol' me and my Desert Warriors. We'll have SNM-ers begging to join us. And not just those pussies. People'll be coming out of the woodwork to smoke those Islamic bastards. It's gonna be PARTY TIME!'*

CHAPTER 14

The next day didn't dawn much brighter than the previous one.

"They've put together a special unit trying to find that van," Lyle explained to Brady over the phone. "It's just a matter of time."

James knew perfectly well the one thing they didn't have was time. He was pretty sure Lyle knew it too.

"What else are they doing?"

"Well, you know, following up on leads: known associates, previous addresses, all that." Translation: nothing much.

He felt like shouting at the Secret Service agent. Reminding him that his friend's life was at stake. Maybe the President's as well. But he knew that yelling wouldn't make him try any harder.

"Keep me updated, will you?" he asked instead.

"Yeh, of course. Look Brady, it's not time to panic yet. We'll find the little guy."

"I've got every confidence in you guys. Just...try to find him soon."

As he hung up, Brady's words echoed hollowly even in his own ears. Sure, the cops might get lucky. He'd seen it many times before back when he'd worked the crime beat at the Post. But he'd also been there when they'd arrived too late. He'd seen the bodies. Maybe even worse, he'd seen the families and friends when they'd found out. He didn't want that to be them.

He picked up the phone and called Jesse Winthrop. "Jesse, it's Brady James."

"Did you find your guys?"

"We did. But now I need your help finding someone else." He explained about Derek, and then, with more than a little trepidation, he told the whole story of Marid.

To his great relief, Winthrop didn't hesitate. "How can I help?"

"You must know where the SNM hangs out – training sites, safe houses, all that. I'm betting that they may have my friend at one of those places."

"Snakes do tend to return to the same holes."

"Exactly. You willing to be my guide?"

"You know, you're one crazy bastard. If they catch us snooping around out there, we might just wind up in worse shape than your friend."

"Could be. We'll just have to not get caught."

The Alliance Director chuckled. "I don't know which of us is crazier. All right, come and get me. We'll see what we can find."

When Brady hung up he didn't know if he was more excited or scared. But he was at peace with having decided to tell Jesse the whole story. If the man was going to risk his life, he deserved to know why.

*****

Brady could feel his pulse racing as he drove back up the dirt road where Jake's friends had ambushed him and Derek just days earlier. He could still hear the sound of bullets ricocheting in his mind. If it hadn't been Derek in the hands of some wack-o he probably wouldn't be found within ten miles of that road. But it *was* Derek.

As he pulled up in front of the familiar ramshackle desert house, he waited for the barking of Jesse's dog to die down before he got out of the car. The man himself appeared only moments later. Brady was half out of his car before he saw another figure emerge from the house. He froze. It was Jake, the SNM big shot.

"What is *he* doing here? Are you okay?" Brady asked, keeping the SUV between him and the two of them.

"I invited him to come along," Jesse said with a smile. "He likes hunting trips."

"Especially for rattlesnakes," Jake added.

"I kind of figured Jake here'd like to see Joe Alietto as far away from Vegas as possible," Jesse explained as the three men met in the walkway.

"What makes you so sure it's Alietto?"

"It's him. This whole thing stinks of him," the SNM leader sneered.

"I thought you boys didn't like the President. I'd 've thought you'd be happy if someone took him out."

"Oh I wouldn't cry too many tears if a stray bullet found that asshole, but we ain't Muslim terrorists. We don't blow ourselves up. And we sure as hell don't want the Feds crawling all over us if Alietto gets lucky and actually blasts the Pres into the next world."

"The SNM? Why would they think you guys were involved?" Brady asked. "As you said, human bombs aren't your thing."

"Do you think they'd give a flyin' fig? They'll use any excuse to screw us around. And they'll need to find someone to pin it on fast. 'Round up the usual suspects,' you know?"

"So Jake has agreed to give us a little tour of some of the places Joe and some others have used in the past," Jesse added.

"Appreciate it," Brady said. "Wasn't your buddy interested in seeing Alietto get his due?"

"Eddie? He's got other things to do, like earning a living. Besides, this is sort of a private matter between Alietto and me. Would prefer that it stays that way, if you know what I mean."

"Fine with me. Never even saw you."

"Good. Now that the introductions are out of the way, what do ya say we get moving?"

At Jake's suggestion the three men piled into his big old pickup truck. "Won't attract as much attention as that fancy new hotrod of yours. And where we're going, I'd just as soon have me at the wheel – nothin' personal."

"Hey, I'm never one to complain when someone who knows what they're doing wants to do it."

As they drove through the bone-dry landscape, dotted with cactus and boulders, the Militia leader explained the origins of his feud with Alietto. "Basically, it came down to a choice between him and me for heading-up the SNM. I wanted us to take it slow and easy, while he was all for the quick hit. Not surprising, I suppose, a good many of the younger guys thought Alietto's way was the way to go. So, instead of stickin' to smaller, local banks – like I'd suggested – we went after a big federally chartered bank in Reno. And sure as hell – bang! The FBI came after us and four of us went to prison."

"Including Alietto?" Brady asked.

Jake spit out the window. "Not hardly. He was never even charged. Some of us thought – still think – he turned state's evidence and cut a deal to save his ass. Whatever the reason, I spent seven and one-half years at Pahrump because of that asshole, and I think it's about time for some payback."

Brady saw Jesse arch an eyebrow as if to say, 'Good enough for you?' It was.

*****

After more than an hour of choking dust and oven-hot temperatures, Brady was wishing to high heavens that they'd taken his air-conditioned SUV instead of Jake's 'classic' pick-up. Rolling down the windows hadn't made it any cooler, just dustier and drier – pretty much like using a hair dryer in a dust storm.

They'd first headed out the Great Basin Highway, and then turned off onto some unmarked dirt road, that led to a dirt path, that led to just plain desert. If Brady hit his head one more time on the roof of the cab as they careened over one big bump after another, he thought he might just get out and walk. Except for the fact that there was nothing but...*nothing* for as far as the eye could see. Jesse had it even rougher, having volunteered to take the narrow rear seat to give Brady and Jake enough room to breathe in the front.

Brady was thinking the Alliance Director was probably ruing his gracious offer right about then.

Conversation was limited as they careened along, both because Brady could think of little to say to the Militia boss that might not piss him off, and because the old truck made so much noise plowing through the desert that they'd be unlikely to hear one another. So it was something of a shock when the pickup slowed suddenly and barely crawled along in near-silence.

"What's up?" Brady asked, trying to keep the nervousness from his voice. The expression on his face was stoic, but the thoughts racing through his head were anything but. He'd only known Jesse for two days, and Jake was a convicted nut case who might very well decide to leave a retired old Post reporter out in the desert, just because.

"Up ahead a half-mile or so is the entrance to an old ranch Joe and some of the others used as a base a few years back," Jake explained. "I'd just as soon they didn't know we were in the neighborhood, if you know what I mean."

"Absolutely."

Ten minutes later they came to a shuddering stop. There was nowhere to hide the truck in the sandy emptiness of the desert, so the militiaman just pulled it up next to a very weathered hand-lettered sign – 'Circle J'. Beneath it, in lettering nearly as worn as the sign itself, someone had scrawled in magic marker: "Trespassers will be shot. Survivors will be shot again."

"Doesn't seem like they want visitors."

"People move to the desert because they want their privacy. They don't want the government, or anyone else, screwing with them," Jake said brusquely.

"Desert folk are good people," Jesse amplified, "but not always the friendliest to folks they don't know."

"I'll keep that in mind," Brady said, all the while thinking about the nice green surrounds of DC and the loving arms of Anne. He promised himself he'd never complain about the capital's traffic and humidity again.

"Follow me. Walk where I walk," Jake said, unholstering a .45 caliber pistol. "There's stickers out there that'll cut you up…"

"And rattlers whose bite'll turn your arm or leg black so fast you'd think you was Lebron James," Jesse added. The two Nevadans laughed softly. Brady could see why the Alliance Director had survived out in such uninviting surroundings for so long. He was one of them, at least partly.

"Here, wear this," Jesse said, handing James a well-worn Mint 400 cap. "It'll keep your brains from frying."

Slowly, carefully, Jake picked a path through the cactus, rocks and ravines, all the while keeping his eyes sweeping the ground ahead for any sign of the venomous creatures that called the desert home – reptile or two-legged. Brady followed close behind, struggling to place each of his steps precisely in the boot prints the militiaman left in the dust ahead of him. Jesse, holding a 12-gauge shotgun, brought up the rear. There was no conversation. The only sounds were the crunching of the rocky soil beneath their feet and the buzz of horse flies and bees looking for a mid-day meal.

It didn't take more than a minute or two before the sweat began to roll down Brady's back, chest and butt-crack; he could literally feel his cheeks flushing red. After a few more minutes the only image he could summon in his frazzled brain was that of a plump chicken spinning slowly on a rotisserie. For the first time, he knew how the chicken felt.

Suddenly Jake held up his hand, signaling for them to stop. Brady was concentrating so intently on the placement of his feet he almost rear-ended him.

"What? What's happening?" Brady panted.

"There, through those bushes," Jake whispered. "The ranch house."

Sure enough, through some spindly bushes (which Jesse informed them were whimsically named Desert Willows), and a few mesquites, Brady could see the dilapidated remains of what must have been the Circle J.

"Doesn't look like anyone's used that place for quite some time," he answered.

"Don't let the looks deceive you," Jesse said. "Sometimes they let the exteriors go to hell just to keep intruders away."

"If we see anyone, hit the ground and let me do the talking," Jake said. "Some of these guys shoot first and then talk – if there's anyone left to talk with."

He motioned for them to move forward. They slowly circled around behind the ranch house, bent nearly double to hide as much as possible behind the scrub that dotted the desert. An old rusted car gave them cover to stop and observe from a distance of less than 100 feet.

"Stay here," Jake ordered after a minute of two of inactivity. Without waiting for an answer, he darted out from behind the car and zigzagged toward the back door.

Brady looked over at Jesse with what could only be described as uncertainty. "Too late to question his intentions now," the Alliance Director said.

'*What the hell am I doing out here?*' Brady asked himself, but he kept his doubts internalized.

A few seconds later the empty silence of the desert was shattered by what Brady's brain registered as an explosion. Reflexively he ducked behind the rusted hulk of a car, his face bare inches from a column of ants marching through the desert sand, his hands held tightly over his head. Only when there was no follow-up, no screams or staccato rattle of gunfire, did he chance a peek through the glassless windshield.

Jake stood in the rear doorway, splintered wood hanging akimbo from the cracked frame. He was putting his pistol back into its holster.

"Clear!" he called out loudly. "Nobody's been here in a long time."

Brady let out a silent sigh of relief. He put his hand on the car frame to push himself up, and pulled it off twice as fast.

"Damn!" he yelled, sucking his burned fingers to try to ease the pain.

Jesse shook his head in sympathy. "You touch metal out here, you may as well add barbeque sauce."

"What's the matter city boy, sting a bit?" Jake teased. "Hold on a second."

The militiaman went out into the desert and pushed and poked at a number of bushes. Finding what he was looking for, he cut off part of the pointy leaf of a squat cactus with a bright orange flower sticking up from the center of the plant. As he approached, Brady could see a thick translucent liquid dripping from the severed leaf.

"Try some of this," Jake announced. "Will help with the burn."

"What do I do with it?" James asked.

"Well, you can stick it up your ass, but with all these spines I don't think you'll enjoy it much. Otherwise, just squeeze some of the liquid onto the burn and spread it around."

He did as he was told, and to his surprise the burn eased considerably.

"Aloe. Indians been using it for centuries," Jesse explained.

"Maybe we're not such dumb schmucks after all," Jake muttered as he walked past them on his way back to the truck.

Brady was tempted to apologize, or explain, but decided to keep his own counsel. After a quick shrug to Jesse, he followed the militiaman back out through the desert. As they walked he couldn't help but wonder where Derek was right then, and what – if anything – he was doing.

*****

The restraint around his ankle had been rubbed raw as the PI tried to work his foot free. He could feel a little slack in the bindings, but still not enough to slip free. It had been one full day since he'd been taken prisoner, and except for the knock on the head he'd been treated ok. Not great, by any means. But okay. In the back of his mind, however, a ticking clock told him that his time was rapidly running out. At the very most, he had until the President arrived. Two days. Maybe much less.

Derek was straining against the blood-stained nylon rope, trying to stretch it enough to pull his ankle through the loop, when he heard footsteps. He immediately pulled his pant cuff down over the ankle with his toes and lay still, feigning acquiescence.

"So, Mr. DiLaurain, I hope the accommodations haven't been too far below your normal standard," the voice of Bossman said from the side of his cot.

"If I had my druthers, I'd like a room with a view," the PI said.

"Still joking. Good. We'll be on our way in just a short while, and you can go back to your 'story.'"

"How long's a 'short while'?"

"That's not important. The only thing you need to know is that if you do as you're told, you'll come out of this not too much the worse for wear."

"I'll try to keep a low profile."

Bossman chuckled. "You do that. It'd be a pity to lose a funny little guy like you."

"I don't disagree."

"I'm sure. By the way, do you happen to know where the President will be speaking during his visit to Vegas?"

The sudden change of topic caught the PI by surprise. "I...ah, I think he's going to be at Caesars."

"And if you were going to try to get to him, get someone close enough to do him in, how would you go about it?"

What was this guy up to? He surely had his plans firmly in place. Why ask Derek? "I suppose I'd try to get someone in the service crew, maybe as a waiter. Take him out with a pistol, like RFK, or maybe a cake bomb."

"A cake bomb!" his jailer said with obvious amusement. "Why didn't we think of that?! Maybe we could have Nicole Kidman pop out of the cake wearing an explosive vest."

"At least she'd look good in it."

"Yes, yes she would. But I don't think we could afford her. Besides, the Secret Service probably sweeps his cakes, don't you think?"

"Don't know. Probably."

"I bet they do. Anyway, you just take it easy and we'll see what unfolds. We'll talk again soon."

"I'll be here."

"Yes, you will."

As the steps faded, Derek tried to imagine why his kidnapper had chatted him up. He finally decided the Bossman was probably playing some mind game, though to what end he wasn't sure. Maybe trying to put him at ease so he didn't make any trouble.

'Good luck with that,' the PI thought, and he pledged to make his move sooner rather than later.

*****

It had been a long day. Brady could smell the acrid stink of his own sweat, and that of his two truckmates. They'd searched three other possible hiding places for Derek, and turned up nothing. Just rusting vehicles, collapsing shacks, and two irritated rattlesnakes.

They had just left the last location when Jesse broached the conclusion all three of them had been thinking.

"Joe may not be the swiftest arrow in the quiver, but he's not an idiot. He probably got a new place to stash your friend."

"So you think we're just wasting our time?" Brady asked.

"I think it's a good possibility. You, Jake?"

"Lookin' that way. That's what I'd do if I was them."

"Yeh, that's what I was thinking too."

Brady stared out the window through the cloud of yellow dust that whirled around the truck. He knew they were probably right. But Derek was out there somewhere! What if it turned out he was being held at the next place they were going to check, and they never went there?

For several long minutes they drove without saying a word, the sounds of the truck echoing the turmoil of their thoughts.

"There are other places…" Jake finally said, but without much conviction.

"Yeh. I mean, we're not sayin' we won't look," Jake added in the same apologetic tone.

Brady let out a breath he didn't realize he'd been holding. "Nah. You've done enough," he said. "Let's get back to town and see if the cops have found anything."

No one argued with him.

The three men fell back into an exhausted silence as they bumped and crashed through the rugged landscape. It had been nearly a day since they'd grabbed Derek. A day that seemed like a week.

Brady couldn't help wondering: how many more days did he have left?

*****

When Brady pulled up at his hotel there was an unmarked gray Ford parked illegally just feet from the front entrance

Brady knew in his gut that they were waiting for him. He parked and got out with his stomach churning.

Seconds later Steve Lyle came bursting out of the hotel.

"Goddamn it James, I told you to stay put!" he yelled loudly enough to draw stares from passersby. "I was about to report you missing as well!"

"Yeh, sorry about that," he struggled to explain. "I had a hunch."

"You're lucky you didn't get a bullet to the back of your skull. Where the hell were you?"

For just an instant Brady thought about inventing a less-damning lie, but in the end decided to come clean. As he explained, Lyle's face went from expectant, to disbelieving, to just plain pissed.

"Are you friggin' nuts?!" the agent screamed. "For all you know, those guys are in on this whole thing. How do you know that Alietto isn't working with them? How do you even know Alietto is the one who grabbed your friend?"

"I don't. But I had to do something," he said, his voice shaky.

Brady saw the steam drain from Lyle's anger. The pulsing vein in his forehead faded from view.

"Yeh, well, I suppose I might have done the same thing," he admitted reluctantly. "Only *I* would've told me what the hell I was up to!"

"I'm sorry."

"Well, don't even think about doing anything that goddamn stupid again. Hear me?"

"I won't, believe me."

"I'm not sure I do, but for now we need to move on. We think we got a lead on the Econoline."

Brady's face lit up.

"What? Where?"

"A security camera out at the Desert Rock air strip captured a shot of a black Econoline passing on Mercury Highway last night around 1 a.m. – just about the right amount of time to drive there from Caesars, if you were lead-footing it."

"So you don't really know if it's the same van?"

Lyle grimaced. "No, not one hundred per cent. But it's the only black Econoline we have moving around the city at that time of night."

"Ok, so now what?" Brady tried to hide his impatience.

"We've already got unmarked cars cruising the area, asking around to see if anyone has seen a van of that description."

"Where is this air strip?"

"It's out to the northwest. On the Test Site."

"You mean like, nuclear test site?"

"The one and only. Over 1000 bomb tests, a hundred of them above ground."

"Not too many people out there, I take it?"

Lyle tilted his head. "Actually, urban legend has it that some locals have been sneaking out there for years to hunt, and just snoop around. They bring their radiation counters and supposedly keep the rads below danger level."

"Be a good place to hide if you didn't want anyone to come looking for you."

"If you were a little crazy."

"Or a lot."

CHAPTER 15

Marid was starting to feel the stress. Stuck in a two-bit fleabag of a motel on the outskirts of town, he felt like a prisoner. Al-Zahiri still hadn't come to give final instructions as he'd promised, and now it was only 48 hours until The Day.

The quiet, and loneliness, were starting to get to him. Sitting there alone day after day, he thought too much. Bad thoughts. He missed his mother. He knew he would see her forever in Jannah. But he needed her now. Needed to talk. Needed her understanding. He knew many people would say what he was doing was wrong. But she would eventually understand. She always understood.

He wasn't afraid. Not really. The idea of leaving this earth and going to Paradise was reassuring. But the idea of killing a man he didn't even know... He tried to focus on what al-Zahiri had told him. *He is not a man, he is the leader of a people who hate Islam, who hate Allah. You are righting the wrongs of centuries. Avenging thousands who have died at the hands of infidels. Women. Children. Killed with no more concern than if they were animals.'*

But the President *was* a man. He'd seen photos of him with his wife and children. He'd read about him, about his childhood, his family. Should he be blamed for what others have done? Could he be blamed?

And what of the martyrs? Yes, they'd given their lives for a holy cause, but they had killed too. They had taken the lives of not only infidels, but believers – women and children as well. How were they any better than the President and his people? How would *he* be any better if he followed their lead?

Marid pressed his hands to his temples. His head throbbed. He couldn't go on like this. He had to talk to someone. He had to be certain.

CHAPTER 16

It was as hot as an oven inside the old barn, for that's what Derek had deduced it was. Probably an old horse stall, from the smell of things. He'd been lying on the straw-stuffed cot for hours, maybe a day or more – it was difficult to keep track of time with his eyes covered. But he'd had time to think, and plan, and prepare. He'd had enough contact with his two principal jailers to realize that his best chance at escape lay with the flunky. Bossman might be taken by surprise, but he doubted it. The other guy, however, didn't seem too swift.

He'd decided that he needed to make his move now. The longer he waited, the more likely he'd end up in a shallow grave out in the desert.

"Hey, anybody out there?!" he yelled. "I gotta take a crap!"

There was no reply.

"Come on, man! Give me a break – I gotta go!"

Nothing. He was about to give up and wait for a while, when he heard the sound of slow-moving steps.

"What's your problem, little man?" It was Flunky.

"I gotta crap."

"This ain't a four star hotel."

"I realize that. But taking a crap isn't exactly the same as lunching on caviar and Dom Perignon."

The flunky didn't laugh. "We don't have none of that neither."

"No, I didn't really think you did. Come on, man, give a guy a break. It's just a crap."

The flunky paused a few seconds and Derek could feel his life slipping from his grip.

"All right. But make it quick. I got other things to do besides taking you to the can."

"You're a real prince."

"Keep the bullshit to yourself. Come on, let's go."

The PI could feel the flunky untying his ankles. He rolled onto his side and sat up on the edge of the bed. His feet didn't touch the floor.

"Hey, a little help here?"

"Jesus Christ, my little niece is bigger than you, and she's only 11," the flunky complained. But he came toward the bed.

Derek knew he'd only have one shot at this; if he failed he'd probably die. With the tape covering his eyes it'd be a crap shoot, but it seemed like his best chance. Maybe his only chance.

He felt Flunky grab him roughly under the shoulder and pull him upright. As he'd rehearsed in his mind, Derek stumbled and his jailer reached out instinctively to balance him. At that instant, the PI ducked his head and threw himself forward with all his strength. He heard the air rush out of the Flunky's gut and a dull groan as he fell to the ground. In a move he'd practiced several times lying on the cot, Derek knelt and painfully dragged his arms down along the dirt floor so that he could step back through them and pull his bound hands free. He felt as if his arms would dislocate, but one advantage of his body type was that his arms were proportionately longer than his legs. 'Normal' people, like Flunky, usually didn't realize that. Their mistake.

He tore off the tape covering his eyes just as Flunky regained enough wind to try to call out. Derek dropped to his knees, directly atop his jailer's solar plexus. Flunky's eyes bulged as he sat bolt upright, just long enough for Derek to slam his forehead into the stunned man's face. There was a sickening thud and for just an instant the PI tottered, dazed. But this wasn't the first time he'd used his pronounced forehead as a battering ram, and it wouldn't be the last.

He rolled off the bigger man and coiled his arms around Flunky's throat in a classic choke hold. He counted to ten, and then held it a couple of seconds longer to be sure. When he finally let go, Flunky's head lolled to one side.

The clock in his head told him he might only have a minute or two to get loose and get moving before someone missed ol' Flunky. He quickly searched the unconscious man and found a long hunting knife in a sheath strapped to his belt.

'Maybe this is my day', he thought as he pulled the knife from the sheath with numb fingers and cut the ropes binding his feet together. Then he sawed furiously at the duct tape securing his wrists. His shirt was drenched with sweat by the time the last strand fell free. He massaged his wrists and ankles furiously, trying to get feeling back into them. As soon as sensation returned, he quickly tied and gagged his former jailer and dragged him up on the cot. A

quick glance might convince the others – if there were others – that the PI was still where they'd left him.

He searched all around the cot for the shoes they'd taken from him, but they were nowhere to be found. In frustration, he pulled off Flunky's boots, stuffed straw into the toes, and pulled on his dirty, worn socks. He laced the boots as tightly as he could, but they still felt like clown shoes on his tiny feet.

And then, hobbling like some stroke victim, he ran.

Much as he'd pictured it in his mind's eye, the dilapidated old barn was lined with horse stalls. He slid to a halt at the shadowed entrance to the barn, listening intently before daring to peek around the corner of the worn red clapboard. He heard no one, and saw nothing moving.

Sucking in a deep breath, he darted across a small open area to a cluster of dry, leafless bushes. He ducked down behind the scraggly branches and surveyed the scene. The barn was set off about thirty feet from an equally dilapidated shack with a partially collapsed roof. The remains of an outhouse stood behind the shack. There was not another person in sight.

When he was certain that no one was pursuing him, he took a moment to get his bearings. From the angle of the sun and the mountains in the distance, he was fairly certain that he was somewhere northwest of Vegas. But where, and how close he was to any outpost of civilization, he had no idea. He was tempted to search the shack to see if there was water in there, but thought better of it. If someone happened to be inside, especially if they happened to be armed, he could find himself back on the cot – or worse. No, better to risk it and head out into the desert, even without drinking water or protection from the sun.

The PI took one last look at the ramshackle ranch and turned to begin his trek. He hadn't taken two steps when, far off to his right, across miles of open desert shimmering under the harsh mid-day sun, he saw a moving coil of dust coming his way. A vehicle? He couldn't be sure at that distance, but he quickened his pace and didn't look back.

CHAPTER 17

It took Brady more than a half-hour to convince Lyle that they needed to go take a look up by the airstrip.

"It'd be like looking for a needle in a haystack," the Secret Service agent had argued.

"I can't just sit here and do nothing," James countered. "Miracles happen. Maybe we'll just stumble over him."

What finally convinced the agent was Brady's pledge to go looking, with or without Lyle.

"You know this is crazy," he said.

"Humor me. Please."

"You know I got the President coming in here tomorrow."

"Even more reason."

"I don't even know that there's any real threat!"

"But you think there might be."

Lyle had had to solicit special permission, but they'd received it. He'd warned Brady that there were hundreds of miles of nothingness out there, but the retired reporter had insisted. And so, there they were, driving up Mercury Highway, past the intersection of Jackass Flats Rd, and out into the Test Site. To the northwest he could see the Spring Mountains in the distance, with Mt. Charleston towering above the others. To the east, nothing but desert as far as the eye could see: rock, sand, cactus and scrub. Not the kind of place you'd want to be spending any time.

"So, where do you wanna look?" Lyle asked his quiet passenger.

"Are there houses anywhere out here?" Brady asked. "Maybe someone saw something?"

"Out here? No chance. Still too much radiation from all the nuclear tests. Might be a security guard shack, or some such."

Brady felt his breath catch. "Can you find one?"

"I can try, but I'm guessing the local police have already been out this way."

"Humor me."

"Hmmph. Who's gonna humor me?" the agent mumbled, but he got on his car radio.

A number of short exchanges followed, most of which ended with a stream of expletives pouring forth from the increasingly short-tempered agent.

"Goddamn it, can't these local yokels do anything right?!" he finally exploded after a Vegas cop – the third one he'd spoken to in ten minutes – explained that they couldn't even supply a list of all the security guards employed by the Department of Energy to keep an eye on the perimeter of the Test Site, let alone any others. "How the hell did they interview all the guards, if they don't even know who or where the guards are?!!"

Changing strategies, Lyle pulled the car over to the side of the road and pulled out his cellphone. This time he called an old friend at DOE.

"Bingo," he said as he closed the phone after a considerably more sociable conversation. "He's SMS-ing me their whole list. Four of them on this stretch of the Site alone. He doesn't think there are any others – private, that is." A few short minutes later, after they'd listened to Eric Church belt out *Springsteen* on the radio, a familiar binging sound announced the arrival of the SMS. "Let's get at it," Lyle said, his temperament greatly improved.

Their first stop was back in the direction of the air strip, at the point where Desert Rock Dr. met Mercury Hwy just outside the airport. Sure enough, as they approached a tiny guardhouse that looked not a heck of a lot bigger than an old phone booth, a tall gangly guy in his mid-40's wearing the distinctive mock-cop uniform of the DOE rent-a-guards, came out and held up his hands, signaling them to stop.

"Let me do the talking," Lyle said as he rolled down his window.

"Gentlemen," the guard said, bending down to look inside the car. "Can I help you?"

Lyle pulled out his ID and flashed it at the guard. "Secret Service. Was hoping you might help us out a bit."

The tension in the guard's shoulders lessened visibly. "Secret Service? What're you doin' out this way? Don't tell me the President is going to fly into this little patch of asphalt."

The agent forced a chuckle. "I'm not sure your runway's big enough to park that big ol' bird of his, let alone land it." The guard returned the chuckle. "No, we were just wondering if you might have seen a black Econoline van driving around out this way."

A look of consternation, or perhaps it was thoughtfulness, came over the guard. "Can't say as I have. Ain't too many cars come out this way. I mean, there's some, but it's not exactly I-15. When would this have been?"

"Over the last few days, and especially late at night, the night before last," Brady answered across Lyle. "Were you working that shift?" The agent glanced at James, but didn't say a word.

"I wasn't, but I can tell you who was, if you can wait a second. Need to take a look at the schedule."

"We'd appreciate that," Lyle said. As the guard returned to his shack, Lyle said softly, "You're not much good at following directions, are you?"

Brady shrugged. "Old habits die hard. I'm used to being the one asking the questions."

Lyle nodded as the guard walked back toward the car carrying a clipboard.

"Looks like it was Jim Essex," he said. "Worked from 11 to 7 in the a.m."

"Got a number for Jim?"

"I do, but we're not allowed to give 'em out. But hang on, let me give him a call. If he's in, maybe you can talk to him right now."

"Appreciate it."

The guard dialed his cellphone and moments later was talking to someone. He handed the phone through the window to Lyle.

"Jim," he said.

When Steve explained that the Secret Service was looking into whether an Econoline had been seen out in that area, the guard was more than happy to help. Only problem was, he wasn't sure.

"You know how it is, late at night. Unless the car approaches the perimeter fence, I don't usually pay it much mind."

"But you might have seen it?"

"Yeh…might have. Seems I do remember a dark van late that night, but I couldn't be sure."

A few more questions only confirmed his uncertainty. By the time the call ended, the agent was exasperated. "Doesn't know what he saw. Maybe something, maybe nothing." He handed the phone back to the guard. "Thanks. Say, if you happen to see a black van in the next day or so, give me a call, would you?" He pulled out a business card and handed it to him.

"Sure thing, Mr…Lyle."

They thanked him and headed back out the highway.

"I was afraid of this," Lyle said. "These guards are protecting the Site, not keeping track of cars passing by."

"Can we just talk to the other three?" Brady asked, a hint of desperation in his voice. "If they can't help, that's that."

Steve weighed the alternatives for just an instant. "Yeh, I suppose we can. But then I've got to get back to the city. As much as I want to help you find your friend, I've got a President coming to town. My people need supervision."

"I understand. And I appreciate it."

Brady slumped down in his seat as they drove through the shimmering heat of the desert. Lyle wasn't the only one running out of time.

*****

Derek winced with each step as his cavernous boots rubbed quarter-sized blisters on his heels and toes. It was nothing compared to the pain when they burst.

He wanted to sit down, pull off the boots and survey the damage. But he knew that he'd be tempted to sit too long, and the sight of his bloody feet would sap some of his resolve. That's all he had now. Resolve. The top of his head, face and arms were burnt raw. His tongue felt like worn shoe leather. He could barely force one foot in front of another. But he did. And he would keep doing it until he found someone or they found him. One way or the other. But he would not stop. He couldn't.

All his life they'd said he wasn't big enough, wasn't fast enough, wasn't…normal enough. They'd made fun of him, taunted him, even beaten him up when he didn't play the fool. But they never broke him. And these bastards wouldn't either.

He glanced up at the white-hot sun and then back at the endless sand and cactus that confronted him. "They won't break me," he muttered through cracked lips. "They won't."

*****

Joe Alietto drove as fast as he dared through the unmarked desert landscape. He followed his own tracks from the day before, but the wind had made the path patchy at best and he wanted to be sure he didn't miss a turn or drive headfirst into a hidden gulley.

'Should have rented an SUV,' he complained to himself as the Lexus bucked and bounced through the hellish backdrop.

He'd tried to call Trevor several times to be sure he had the midget under control. No answer. The kid was no rocket scientist, but he'd always been dependable. At least he'd answered his phone.

Joe had a bad feeling. Something was wrong. Maybe the kid's battery had just died. Maybe he'd lost his phone. But maybe the little shit had found a way to get free. Maybe...

No sense in worrying. Nothing he could do until he got there anyway.

As if he could stop.

*****

It was nearly an hour later when the dust-covered Lexus skidded to a stop in front of the shack and horse barn.

"Trevor!" Alietto yelled out as soon as he stepped from his car. "Where the hell are you?!"

No answer.

Damn it!' he thought as he hurried to the shack and threw open the door. The kid's bedroll lay on the floor, scraps of food and empty soda cans surrounding it. But no Trevor.

His stomach starting to turn. He didn't even bother to shut the door as he pivoted and started toward the barn at a quick jog.

"Trevor!!"

The barn door was open and there was no sign of a problem, but Alietto could sense trouble in his bones. He pulled the 9mm he kept on his belt and moved slowly past the darkened stalls, glancing briefly into each as he went by to be certain they were empty. Sweat ran freely down his back in the stifling stench of the barn, but he barely felt it. He listened intently for any hint of what lay ahead. Finally, when he was less than twenty feet from the stall where they'd been keeping the midget, he heard an animated grunting and guttural moan. It didn't sound like the midget.

His senses on high alert, Alietto dropped into a crouch, scanning every inch of the barn as he moved. When he was as sure as he could be that no one was waiting in the shadows, he stepped around the last divider between stalls to where he could see the cot. What he saw sent a rush of adrenaline through his system. He took one last look behind him and hurried to the cot.

"Goddamn it, Trevor, where's the midget?!" he yelled as he ripped the gray duct tape from his associate's distorted mouth.

"He tricked me!" Trevor croaked, more as a plea than an explanation. "The goddamn midget tricked me!"

"There's a big surprise," Alietto muttered as he holstered his gun and began loosening the tape around Trevor's wrists. "How long ago?"

"I don't know. Maybe a couple of hours. He choked me! Knocked me out!"

"I should've just put a bullet through his head."

"He won't get far out in that desert," Trevor said as he fumbled with the knots at his ankles. "The sun, or the snakes, or the cactus will get to him before he gets far. City boy ain't used to the desert."

"Maybe, but we aren't taking any chances," Alietto said. "Come on, let's go find the little piece of crap."

Alietto started toward the car. When he glanced back to make sure Trevor was keeping up, he saw the younger man limping, bare-footed, in the rocky dirt of the barn floor.

"He stole my boots!" Trevor said before Alietto could say a word.

"Damn shame he didn't steal the rest of you while he was at it. Come on. Serves you right." He left in a hurry.

Alietto was already all buckled into the idling Lexus by the time Trevor scrabbled out to join him.

"Let's go hunt us some midget," the Bossman said through tightened lips.

*****

Far in the distance, in the foothills of the distant mountains, Derek saw the tell-tale dust swirling from a fast-moving vehicle. He didn't know who it was, but he knew he didn't want to meet them on their terms. He scanned the desert all around him, looking for somewhere to hide until they drove past. A few hundred yards ahead he saw a gulley or ravine. That would have to do.

Stumbling from exhaustion and pain, he slowly dragged himself through the rocks and cactus, glancing back every few seconds. The car was gaining on him, coming quickly in his general direction. Had they seen him already? Or had he accidentally wandered closer to their track to the ranch?

He moved as fast as he could, his breath coming in short pants, his heart pounding loudly in his chest. Slowly, painfully, he closed the distance to the gulley. The car had already halved the expanse between them. He had to go faster! Faster! He was just at the edge of the drop-off when his heavy boots caught on some rock or root and set him tumbling head over foot down the steep incline into the ravine. He felt thorns tear his skin and stones bash his body, but he was too exhausted to even try to slow his free-fall.

After what seemed like minutes, he came to a crashing stop in a cloud of dust at the bottom of the gulch. With one last painful roll, his head collided with a large boulder and stars danced in front of his eyes.

The last thing he heard before he passed out was the sound of a child's rattle.

*****

There was no guard at the second shack along the Mercury Highway, so Brady and Lyle continued north into the Test Site to find the third name on their list. They found their man in a guardhouse at the end of a short access road that passed through the chain-link fence and into the Test Site. Older, probably pushing retirement age, his long scraggly beard seemed a strange contrast with his neat uniform.

"Looks like a Civil War reenactor," Brady said as the guard came out to meet them.

"I don't care if he fought at Gettysburg, as long as he's been paying attention to the traffic out here," Lyle said as he lowered his window. This time he held out his ID instead of waiting for a request.

"Afternoon," the guard greeted them.

"Mr. Wesley Heet?" the Secret Service agent asked. "I'm Steven Lyle from the U.S. Secret Service, and this is Mr. Brady James. May we ask you a couple of questions?"

Heet took the ID and examined it closely, his eyes straining to read the tiny print.

"Agent Lyle. Mr. James. To what do I owe this unexpected visit out to the very middle of nowhere?"

Lyle smiled. "We're looking for someone who might have gotten lost out this way. Short little fellow named Derek DiLaurain who might have been riding in a black Econoline van, say late two nights ago?"

"Secret Service looking for lost kids these days?"

"He's not a kid, he's a midget," Brady chimed in.

"Okay. Secret Service looking for lost midgets these days?"

Steve chuckled. "Not often. He's part of an investigation we're working on."

"Have anything to do with the big visit coming up?" He held up his hand as soon as he'd finished his question. "Never mind. None of my business. As to your question, I haven't seen any midgets lately, but the black van may be more familiar."

"You saw it?"

"Can't say whether it was your van, but there's been one that's come by here a few times in the last week or so, including – I think – two nights ago. After midnight?"

"Closer to one in the morning is how we calculate."

"Could have been. Couldn't testify it was an Econoline, but it was black."

"Don't suppose you have any idea where it was headed?"

"Nah. Unless there's gunfire or trespassing, we pretty much let folks go their own way out in these parts."

"Anything else you can tell us? Don't suppose you ever got a glimpse of the driver…"

"Nope. You know, there's not a whole heck of a lot of traffic out this way come midnight. Kind of odd to see anything moving, actually. Oh – one thing: if I'm not mistaken, he was moving like a bat out of Hades. I remember thinking he was going to get himself a ticket if he didn't slow down."

Lyle looked quickly at Brady, who nodded.

"Well thank you very much, Mr. Heet," the agent said as he handed the guard his business card. "Call me if you think of anything else, or if you see the van again."

"Or DiLaurain," Brady added.

"Most certainly will do. Hope your little friend isn't wandering around out here in the desert. This sun'll fry your brains."

"That it will. Thanks again."

The fourth and last guard on their list was only about four miles up the highway, but he was no help at all. He was eager, almost desperate to chat, but he hadn't seen a black van and he certainly hadn't seen the PI.

"Well that wasn't much of a help," Brady said as the guard walked back to his shack examining the business card Lyle had given him.

"I wouldn't be so sure," the agent said as he backed out into the highway to head back towards Vegas. "If we can assume that the lack of traffic out this way would draw attention to anyone driving, and driving fast, at one in the morning, then maybe we can also assume that the black van turned off somewhere between the last guard shack and here."

"But that's four miles!" Brady protested.

"It is. But subtract the mile or so you can see headlights at night out here in the desert, and we might have a strip of a mile or two where the van could've turned off and couldn't be seen by at least one of the two guards."

"Still a lot of territory to check."

"Too much for us today. It'll be dark out here in a couple of hours."

"You heard what Heet said: this sun will fry Derek if we don't get to him soon."

"Sorry. Really am. But I've got to get back to my people."

Brady was about to protest, but suddenly thought of something better. "Do the local police have a helicopter?" he asked.

"Oh no," Lyle said, shaking his head. "We don't control their birds."

"But you could put in a request, couldn't you?"

"I could, but…"

"They'd be likely to look upon a request from a Secret Service agent the day before the President comes to visit pretty favorably, don't you think?"

"Jesus, and I thought criminals were devious," Lyle said, still shaking his head as he drove. "Oh, what the hell. Let's see what they'll say."

Steve was on his cellphone and talking to his contact in the LV Police Department in less than a minute. The conversation was short and to the point.

"Your friend is one lucky guy to have you on his side," the agent said as he closed the phone. "They'll meet you at the airstrip in 20 minutes."

"Thanks, Steve. I appreciate it. You're very persuasive."

"Yeh, well go find the little bugger. Maybe he really does have information about a plot to assassinate the President."

"Sounds good to me," Brady said with a knowing smile.

Seventeen minutes later they were sitting in the airstrip parking lot as a police helicopter kicked up a huge cloud of dust and stones as it landed 50 feet from where they waited.

"Good luck," Lyle said, shaking Brady's hand.

"Thanks. You too."

The copter engine never stopped as the officer in the passenger seat ran over to their car, talked briefly with the agent, and then shepherded Brady back under the whirling blades and into the Hughes 369 H-6. Brady took the helmet that was offered and strapped it on before tightly securing his seatbelt. He wasn't all that fond of helicopters, but this time he'd overlook his qualms.

"All ready?" the pilot spoke to him over the headset in the helmet.

"As ready as I'll ever be," Brady said.

"Then let's get to it. I figure we've got maybe two hours of light left at most. Agent Lyle said you two think your man may be off toward the mountains somewhere between 6-7 miles north of here. Sound about right?"

"If Lyle says so, then that's good enough for me."

"Roger that. Hold on!"

With that the pilot gunned the motor and pulled up in a zero-g climb that left Brady's stomach parked on the landing pad. It only took a minute of two, however, before his focus moved from his gut to the rugged landscape below. They flew low enough that he could see the shack where the bearded guard had last seen the van, and then another minute or so before the pilot banked off to their left.

"This seem about right?" he asked.

Brady nodded before realizing the two cops couldn't see him in the rear seat. "Seems good."

"We're gonna take it low and slow all the way out to the mountains," the pilot said. "Speak up if you see anything."

True to his word, the copter dropped down to less than 100 feet and cruised slowly over the barren expanse. Even at that slow speed, however, Brady found it hard to see anything clearly on the ground.

"Can we go any slower?" he finally asked in frustration. "I can't make out a thing."

"Look out a few hundred yards," the pilot responded. "If you look right next to the copter it's all a blur, but if we slow down much more we'll never cover this whole area by sundown."

"Got it."

Brady scanned from one side of the helicopter to the other as they gradually made their way west toward the mountains in the distance, but except for a few rabbits and what might have been a coyote, he didn't see anything moving. The two cops up front each concentrated on their own side of the copter. Despite the miles of open range Brady still felt some confidence that they'd see Derek – if he was out there.

They'd been flying for about a half-hour and were coming up to the foothills of the Sunrise range when suddenly the cop in the passenger seat pointed to the horizon and called out over the intercom: "What's that up there?! Abandoned ranch?"

Brady squinted into the setting sun in the direction he'd indicated. Sure enough, hidden in a tiny box canyon just a short distance from where the foothills turned vertical, he could just make out the worn and weathered remains of a couple of ramshackle wooden buildings.

"And take a look over there," the pilot added, pointing to a set of tire tracks that snaked through the desert and lead straight to the buildings. "Let's take'er down and have a look."

The pilot found a fairly level spot without too much vegetation and landed in a cloud of sand and dust.

"Rough on the engine and rotors," the other cop said.

"Tell it to the mechanics."

They waited until the blades had stopped turning before getting out. Both officers drew their firearms.

"Stay back here for a second," the pilot ordered Brady. "Don't know what we're likely to find in there."

The two cops fanned out, one moving to the horse barn on the left, the other to the dilapidated shack. They coordinated their approach with hand signals, setting up hold positions by the front entrances to each building.

"Las Vegas Police – come out with your hands up!" the pilot ordered loudly when both were in place.

All three men braced for a confrontation, but there was none. Just a quail flushed from the brush behind the shack.

"I'm going in," the pilot announced. Brady waited anxiously. Fifteen seconds later he was back outside. "Nothing. Looks like there was someone here recently, but they're gone."

He crossed over to his partner, and covered him as he entered the deeply shadowed barn.

"Clear!" the cop's voice echoed moments later from inside the barn. "Come take a look at this."

The pilot waved to Brady. "Come on, if you'd like to see."

By the time Brady made his way inside the structure, the two cops were examining a metal cot covered with straw at the back of the barn.

"Someone was here not long ago," the pilot said as James approached them. "There's blood on the cot."

Seeing the distress in the reporter's face, he quickly added, "Not so much. Probably just a cut – something small."

Brady looked to the spot on the frame and straw mattress the cop indicated. He was right. It didn't look too bad. He'd seen hundreds of crime sites, and as far as those things went, this one was minor. But the blood might be Derek's.

"Any idea when they left?" he asked.

"The tire tracks outside haven't been obliterated by the wind, and the blood is still tacky…I'd say a matter of hours. You Chester?"

The pilot's partner nodded. "Definitely not much more than that." As Brady and the pilot examined the cot, Chester broadened his search to the dirt floor back towards the entrance. "Got a few more drops over here." Brady followed close behind as the two cops followed a meager trail of blood drops and smears out into the yard and off into the bush beyond.

"Looks to me like someone came from the barn out this way, and then headed out into the desert," Chester said.

"Might be your friend."

"If it is, it looks like he's headed off in that direction," Chester added, pointing to the southeast. "Let's go see if we can find him."

*****

Derek's eyes opened slowly, gently cracking the crust of dust and sand that nearly cemented them shut. Moving carefully, he ran through a quick triage of body parts; aside from a sore shoulder and aching feet, he seemed to have survived the fall in one piece.

Until he tried to sit up.

His head exploded with pain and his vision blurred. He gasped from the hurt and settled back down onto the ground, trembling. It took him a few moments to get his bearings and remember what he was doing near the bottom of the ravine. As soon as he did, he remembered the dust cloud moving his way from up in the foothills. He needed to get back up there and see what he could see. The deepening shadows told him it was getting close to sunset. He wasn't sure he wanted to be out there at night.

As gently as he could, he propped himself up on one elbow and took a look at where he had landed. He'd been lucky, sort of. There was a large pile of jagged rocks not twenty feet away that could have left him with broken bones, or worse. As it was, if he could just climb up the fifteen feet or so to the top lip of the ravine, he should be able to get a good look around without attracting notice.

He slowly raised himself into a sitting position, the agonizing throbbing in his head a constant reminder of how close he'd come to disaster. Once he was confident he could stand the pain, he braced his right foot and tried to push off against a small boulder. His foot slipped slightly and a tiny avalanche of stones and dirt cascaded the rest of the way down the slope toward a small undercut cave at the side of the gulley. Immediately he heard a familiar rattling sound. Only this time, he knew exactly what it was.

In the deep shadows of the undercut he saw a nest of rattlesnakes react to his intrusion, with one large defender coiling and sitting up for a strike, its three inch rattles sounding ominously in the desert quiet. Derek froze. He felt a cold sweat well-up on his forehead. He didn't particularly like snakes, and these were even less friendly than most.

He'd read somewhere that eye contact could be seen as a threat to wild animals. He didn't know if that applied to rattlers, but he forced himself to drop his eyes even as the snake kept its glare focused directly on him. After a few seconds the rattling slowed and then stopped. Derek chanced a glance out of the corner of his eye. With all the care he could muster given his tired, bruised body, the PI began to drag himself up the opposite wall of the ravine, slowly, methodically. He felt woozy, sick to his stomach, but he forced himself to crawl, one inch at a time, up the steep incline. Thorns stabbed his fingers and tore at his clothing. Several times he lost his handhold and began to slide back down, but each time he was lucky, or determined enough to stop his fall before it got out of hand.

He didn't know how long it took to get out of that ditch, maybe fifteen minutes, maybe a half hour, but finally he pulled himself up over the edge and collapsed in a sweaty, panting heap on the desert floor. At first all he could hear was his own rasping breaths and the pounding of his heart. He glanced up to see the sky had turned a deep blue, streaked with shades of red and orange. He knew he didn't have long before nightfall.

As each precious minute ticked by, he fought to slow his breathing and ease the pounding in his head. Finally, slower than he'd hoped, he got himself under control, the pain almost manageable. As he raised his head to take a look around, he thought he heard a distant whirring sound, coming closer.

"Now what?" he thought.

*****

They had been flying in a zigzag pattern for nearly a half-hour in the direction they thought Derek – if it was Derek – had taken. As the sun dipped behind the mountains behind them, the shadows lengthened and darkened across the broad expanse below. Brady was increasingly worried that the pilot would call it a night and abandon the search, when suddenly Chester called out from the front seat: "Over there. By that ravine at three o'clock!"

Brady strained to see what he was pointing at. In the dim light, at that distance, he wasn't sure what he saw, but he knew it was something. The helicopter banked abruptly and headed straight for the gash in the desert. At the top edge of the ravine, a mere speck in the vastness of the arid landscape, a tiny body lay very still.

"There's something there all right!" the pilot announced.

It wasn't until they were less than a hundred yards away that Brady allowed himself to believe that it really was Derek. He still couldn't make out many details, but he could see enough that he was willing to hope it was his friend down there. He withheld one small iota of doubt until he could be sure, but even that scintilla was fading fast.

The helicopter landed about 100 feet from the ravine, kicking up so much debris that for several seconds he lost sight of the body. But as the dust slowly settled all around them, he could finally identify the motionless figure.

It was Derek.

Brady tore off his helmet and unsnapped his seat belt.

"Now take it easy, Mr. James," Chester warned from the front, turning to make his point. "Wait until the blades stop turning."

Brady heard the admonition but he was already half out the door. Seeing the course of events, the two officers quickly followed suit. Running in a tuck below the slowly spinning rotors, the three men hurried to the battered PI.

"Derek! Derek! Are you okay?!" Brady asked, kneeling by his friend's side and supporting his head in the crook of his arm.

For a moment the midget's eyes remained closed. Then, with an obvious effort, they fluttered open.

"Jesus. Do you think you could've kicked up any more crap into my face?" he whispered through cracked lips.

And then he smiled.

CHAPTER 18

Marid took a deep breath and then attacked his ragged beard with a pair of scissors. He cut slowly at first, but as the hair fell away he began to chop wildly, frenetically. Minutes later he stared into the mirror at the patchy stubble that remained. His eyes seemed too big for his face. His cheeks too thin.

He reached for the shaving foam and covered his face with the soothing white lather. As the razor slid across his skin, he fought to keep tears from his eyes.

'Forgive me this insult,' he prayed. *'It is for the greater good.'*

When the deed was done, he stepped back to evaluate his work. He'd cut his hair much shorter, died it a dark brown, and combed it over like so many of the kafir he had lived with for so long. He wore a blue knit golf shirt, with a trendy logo. Khaki pants. Sport shoes. Without a beard his pale blue eyes beamed out at him like beacons of determination.

He looked every bit the good, home-grown secular Christian. No one would take a second glance at such a clean-cut, innocuous young man. No one would question his motives, or his intent.

Al-Zahiri had finally called. He wanted one last meeting. Probably to go over his instructions for the hundredth time. But Marid knew what he must do. He still had his doubts, but as Zahiri had explained, even the Prophet had had his moments of confusion. "It is what you ultimately do," he'd explained to Marid, "not how you arrive at that moment."

He glanced down at his hands and grabbed his left with his right to stop the tiny tremors in his fingers. He hadn't slept well for days. He had dreams – troubling dreams. Blood and torn flesh spattered everywhere. His mother crying endlessly in mortal anguish. He himself surrounded by flames, burning, burning!

He took a deep breath as al-Zahiri had instructed and repeated a short prayer in Arabic. Slowly the tremors subsided and his breathing calmed.

He would do this thing! It was his duty, his obligation. Only heretics shied from their religious obligations. Heaven awaited him.

He hoped.

CHAPTER 19

Alietto glanced down at the speedometer and eased up on the gas. It wouldn't do to get stopped by the cops for speeding, now would it?

It was just... just that everything had been proceeding so smoothly. And now? Now, it all teetered on disaster. All because of that damn Post reporter and his midget friend. He'd seen the helicopter land and pick something – or someone – up. If it was the midget, so be it. They'd get theirs. And soon.

But first he had to check-up on the kid. He sounded unsure. Shaky.

Abu al-Zahiri would take care of that, he thought with a smile. He glanced in his rearview mirror at the robe and headpiece sitting on the back seat. Zahiri would play on the kid's insecurities, all the little hurts and insults he'd suffered over the years for having had a rughead mother. It'd gotten them this far, and it would get them the rest of the way. Just one more day...

*****

The Silver Sluice Motel was more than out of the way – it was perilously close to the edge of nowhere. Tucked far off in the southeast corner of Enterprise township, although only a few miles from the Strip it might as well have been in Sparks. The front of the building looked as if it might be condemned; the back looked out over rusted dumpsters at open desert. Not a place you'd want to call home, but exactly the place Alietto had chosen to deposit Marid.

He parked his rented Lexus off to the side of the building, under a scrub oak that provided the only hint of shade in the baking lot. If anyone had been looking out of their room window – if they could see through the years of dust and grime – they would have seen a sight straight out of 'Lawrence of Arabia': a white-robed Arab-type wearing a kufiya – the headdress that earned the desert dwellers their 'towelhead' sobriquet, carrying a leather briefcase and walking quickly across the cracked asphalt in simple leather sandals. Being Vegas, no one would have paid too much attention, but as it was, there was no one there to see.

Alietto, now al-Zahiri, entered the motel through a side door to avoid the desk clerk up front. He'd been to the room once before, and so made his way quickly down the narrow corridor with its worn, stained blue carpeting and flickering fluorescent lights. At room 107 he knocked three times, waited a second, and then knocked twice more. In less time than it took him to straighten his kufiya, the door opened a crack. Alietto saw the blue eyes peering out nervously.

"It is me," he whispered, pushing the door open before Marid could even respond.

What he saw was not reassuring. The kid looked nervous. Real nervous.

"I thought you said you were coming at 9," Marid began at once, his voice a notch higher than it should have been.

"Salam wa aleikum," Alietto said sternly. "I was delayed," he added in his best impression of Arabic-accented English. "There is more to this operation than just you, you know."

The kid took that in and seemed to calm a bit. Probably made him feel better that he wasn't alone.

"Oh. Yeh." He watched as Alietto put his briefcase down on the Formica table, dialed the combination and flipped it open. He pulled out some papers.

"Come here," he ordered, and the kid obeyed silently. As he began to unfold a large hand-drawn diagram, Marid bridled.

"Not again! We've gone over that a hundred times!"

"And we will go over it one more time, to be certain that there is no confusion. To ensure the success of our operation, insha'Allah."

"Insha'Allah," Marid mumbled, but with less heart than usual, Alietto thought.

"Tell me," he said. "Tell me how it will happen."

After Marid had regurgitated his instructions one last time, and Alietto was convinced he knew exactly what he was meant to do, he folded the paper, took it into the tiny bathroom, and held a match to it. He only dropped the burning embers into the bowl when the flames began to lick his fingertips. He flushed the rest away.

When he turned, Marid was pacing.

"Marid, you must not let negative thoughts into your mind," he said softly. "You will do well. You will make the Prophet proud. You will make all true Moslems proud."

"I know," the kid said, his attention seemingly a million miles away. "It's just…"

"We are but the hands of God's will, Allah be praised," he continued, placing one hand on Marid's shoulder. "You should be proud he chose you."

"I am…proud," Marid said softly. "But, to take the lives of innocents…"

"They are heretics! Their country takes the lives of true believers every day! The Koran says 'Life for life.' It is clear."

The young man took a deep breath. "Yes, it is clear."

"Good!" Alietto said, patting Marid's shoulder. "Your name shall live forever."

"Yes."

"We shall not meet again on this earth, but rather in Jannah. Until then"

The two men shook hands, and then Alietto kissed Marid on both cheeks. When the door to the room closed behind him, Alietto felt confident that the kid would follow through on his promise. And then the fun would begin!

*****

Not ten minutes after al-Zahiri had left the motel, Marid went to a payphone in an alcove off the lobby and called a long distance number. The phone rang several times before it was answered.

"Hello?" a familiar voice said. He hesitated, his mouth unwilling to speak.

"Mom?" he finally said, "it's me, Chip." He didn't know why he used the infidel name that he had been given by the non-believers. It just came out.

"Marid! Where are you? Please, come home, my son."

Marid cut her off. "Mom, I'm in kind'of a hurry, so I can't talk long. Just wanted you to know that I'm okay and...I love you."

A moment's silence. "Marid, whatever you are involved with, it will be forgiven. Just come home!"

"I am coming home, Mom. I hope you will understand and be proud of me."

"Marid, do not listen to those crazy people! Marid..."

He hung up, tears streaming down his face.

She didn't understand. She could never understand.

CHAPTER 20

Despite the gauze bandages wrapped around his head and a few cuts and bruises, Derek looked pretty much his old self as he sat up in the hospital bed and chatted with Brady.

"A good night's sleep works wonders," he said. "I'm feeling pretty damn good."

"Your doctor says you need to take it easy for a couple of days. You took a nasty bump to the head."

"Hell, I've felt worse after a good all-night bender. Besides, this is it – D-Day. You need me out there helping to stop Alietto, and the kid."

"What we don't need is you passing out in the middle of Caesars and the rest of us having to take our focus off the kid and put it on you. Stay here; get some rest."

"Come on, Brady, give me a break. What am I going to do here? Tiddlywinks?"

Brady looked at his friend and saw the determination in his face. But the reporter was just as determined. Besides, Anne would give him holy hell if he didn't insist the PI stay put in the hospital. She'd made that pretty clear last night.

"We'll keep you informed every hour," he offered by way of a peace offering. "But for now, I've got to get moving. Lyle is busy with his agents finalizing everything for the President's arrival this evening. So it's up to me and the Las Vegas cop they assigned to help me out. Nice guy – Chester Ashcroft."

"TWO people?! That's all you've got to try to stop these nutcases? Brady, you *need* me."

"We'll just have to do this one ourselves," Brady said with a gentle pat to his knees. "You take care. And leave your cellphone on – I'll be checking in for some feedback."

"Yeh, okay," the deflated PI said. "We'll talk."

Brady nodded and started for the door.

"Hey Brady," Derek added just as James turned the knob, "good luck."

James smiled and nodded to his friend. He'd need it.

*****

Derek waited for several minutes until he was sure that Brady had left the hallway. Then he gently disconnected the IV from the needle in the back of his hand and yanked the needle free with one quick tug. A few drops of blood bubbled up at the site of the insertion, but he wiped that away with a piece of gauze that he held in place for 30 seconds or so.

His head ached slightly as he threw his legs over the edge of the bed and lowered himself to the floor. The room started to spin and his knees trembled, but he grabbed the side of the mattress and held on tight. In a second or two his head cleared and his legs strengthened. He found the plastic bag with his dirty, bloodied clothes in the drawer of the side table next to his bed.

'Couldn't have brought me a change,' he fumed as he slipped back into the filthy duds. He decided he'd have to

swing by the hotel and pick up some clean things before he
did anything else. As if his stature wouldn't draw enough
attention as it was, he sure as heck would draw some stares
with blood stains and rips dotting his shirt and pants.

Glancing around cautiously as he crept towards the
door, he happened to catch sight of himself in a mirror. Not
much he could do about the clothes and bright blue
hospital booties, but the gauze head-wrap would have to go.
He gently unwound the lengths of gauze, wetting a section
at his temple where the clotted blood glued it to his skin.
Pulling precisely from first one side of the wound and then
the other, he finally tugged the bandage free. A small trickle
of blood streaked down his cheek. He wiped it away with
the used gauze and took another peek in the mirror. He
wasn't going to win any beauty contests, but it would do. It
would have to.

He cracked open the door and peered into the
hallway outside. No one to be seen. About ten feet down
the corridor a gurney lay unattended. He knew it would be
hard to get out of the building without someone spotting
him and making a fuss about leaving without an official
discharge. So, he used what was available to him and
crawled under the gurney, pulling the sheets down on either
side to effectively create a tent as he slowly rolled the bed
down the hallway. From outside it must have looked like a
scene from *Ghostbusters* as the seemingly unattended gurney
made its way toward the elevators. Unless, that is, someone
looked close enough to see a pair of blue hospital booties
creeping along in the shadows beneath the bed.

He was almost half-way there when the sound of
several voices coming his way froze him in mid-step. He'd
kept close to the wall as he'd traveled, staying out of the

middle of the corridor, but still he knew that just one overly inquisitive aide or nurse could ruin his day. He held his breath as the voices came closer and closer, until they were right on top of him.

"She looked terrible!" one female voice said emphatically.

"You didn't have to tell her!" the other countered.

"What was I supposed to do?"

"Lie, like everyone else! This is a hospital, not a court of law!"

He braced himself for a quick escape if need be, but the voices and accompanying footsteps passed right by without so much as a comment. He waited until he'd counted to thirty. His patience at an end, Derek trotted the gurney the last 50 feet to the elevators. Breathing heavily from the exertion, he peeked out from under the sheets to see if anyone had noticed his mad dash. No one to be seen.

A short arm topped by plump stubby fingers slowly emerged from beneath the gurney to push the 'Down' button. He waited anxiously, each tick of the clock another threat that he'd be discovered and tossed back in his bed. Just as he was catching his breath, the familiar ding of the floor signal finally sounded and the doors swished open.

He darted out of his hiding place and into the elevator, jabbing furiously at the Close Door button until it finally responded. Three floors. That's all he needed. Three lousy, stinking floors.

"Don't stop, don't stop," the PI chanted to himself, trying to influence the machine with his psychic powers.

Almost immediately the floor bell rang.

"Damn it!" he muttered. "Don't let anyone get on, don't let anyone get on."

The doors swished open and a woman about 30, wearing a very short mini skirt and very tight blouse, stepped into the car. Derek saw her stop, look down at him, and hesitate.

"It's okay," he said with a smile. "I don't bite. Just a bad day."

"Must've been a real bad day," she said, continuing in and hitting the Lobby button that was already lit.

"Until just this moment," he said.

She turned and looked down at him.

"Are you hitting on me?"

"Didn't see a ring on your finger."

She held up her hand to look for herself. "No, you didn't."

"So yeh, I guess I am. Have any plans for, say, day after tomorrow?"

"Is that how long it's going to take you to clean up?"

"Ooo! And I thought you were a sweet young thing."

"Not that sweet," she said, turning to face the elevator doors.

"Your loss," Derek said matter-of-factly. She glanced back once more over her shoulder, either in disbelief or – as the PI chose to believe – to take one last look.

He was still waiting for a change of heart when the floor bell rang and the doors opened on the Lobby.

"Sorry. Gotta run. Maybe next time," he said as he waddled past her, through a half-dozen visitors and nurses who stared and blinked as if witnessing an alien landing, and out the front doors.

"Taxi!" he called out, holding up his hand for emphasis. Before anyone could figure out what was

232 William J. Millman

happening, he'd scrambled up into the cab and was on his way.

The ride back to the hotel only took a few minutes, but it took quite a bit longer for Derek to get himself back into shape for public viewing. First off, he asked the desk clerk to ring his room to make sure Brady hadn't gone back there as well. When he was reasonably sure the room was empty, he made his way upstairs and quickly stripped off his filthy clothes. He had planned on an equally quick shower and a change into clean duds, but whether it was the heat of the water or just everything catching up to him, by the time he'd scraped the worst of the dirt off his skin and hair he barely had the strength to towel himself dry before sinking down on his bed and dropping off to sleep.

It was nearly noon when he awoke with a start from the maid knocking on the door.

"Housekeeping!" a cheery Latina voice called through the door.

"Come back in an hour!" a less-than-cheery PI answered.

When he saw the time he climbed out of bed as quickly as he could, given the mild headache and dizziness that blurred his vision. He knew he should stay in bed. He also knew he wouldn't.

He had roughly five hours to find Marid and prevent what he was confident would be an assassination attempt against the President of the United States. And all the while keep out of Brady's sight.

"Great. Just friggin' great."

*****

Brady had awakened at 7 am, thanks to an insistent alarm clock backed up by a call from the front desk. Blurry-eyed, he dressed and went downstairs for breakfast. He was pleased to see Chester, the Vegas cop who'd ridden shotgun in the copter, waiting for him in the coffee shop.

"Morning. Looking bright-tailed and bushy-eyed," the officer greeted him.

"Hold the sarcasm until after coffee," Brady grumbled, flopping down into the seat across the table.

"Rough night?"

"I was at the hospital until after midnight, and then I just couldn't fall asleep. I kept trying to see any pattern that'd lead us to Alietto, or the kid, before the President lands." What he didn't tell him was that his thoughts veered irrevocably to another President. November 22, 1963. He'd been just a kid, but he'd never forgotten those images. The pain.

It wasn't going to happen again, not if he could help it.

"Any bright ideas?"

Brady scowled as he sipped the stale coffee. "Nothing. I still don't even understand why Alietto is impersonating an Arab, or why he'd want to kill the President. I mean, I know all those guys are anti-Washington, but there's a big leap between that and an assassination. Particularly now that he knows we're closing in on him."

"On that front, I think we might have a lead." The cop pulled a piece of paper out of a manila folder and handed it to James. "We got a call last night from a Wesley Heet, a guard out at the Test Site I think you talked to with Lyle?"

"Yeh. Guy looks like he stepped out of a Matthew Brady photo."

"Whatever. He says he saw a white Lexus speeding down the Mercury Highway late yesterday afternoon. Going so fast he thought 'the Devil was on his tail.' That's a quote. Made him suspicious, so he grabbed his binocs and got a partial on the plate as it flew by. We ran it overnight, and just got ahold of the agency that rented it a few days ago to a man by the name of Jeffrey Hughes."

"Hughes? Who the heck is he, and what's he have to do with anything?"

Chester held up a hand to stop Brady. "The agent gave us a description: 5' 8", maybe 150 pounds, beard…"

"Alietto."

"That's what I'm thinking. Used a fake driver's license and paid cash."

"You can still pay cash for a rental?"

"At little Mom and Pop places like this one – absolutely. You could probably pay with casino chips."

Brady remembered where he was and nodded. "Makes sense. You got'a lead on him?"

"We assume that the address he gave for his local hotel is bogus, but we've got half the force looking for the car, and Lyle has pitched in with some Secret Service help. With any luck, we should get something pretty quick."

"Until then?"

"I'm thinking the kid's probably in some little rental house or out-of-the-way motel nearby. Some place where he wouldn't be seen. I've got a half-dozen staffers calling every real estate agent and motel manager in town with the descriptions of the kid and Alietto. We can just sit back and sip our coffee…" he began.

Brady winced. "Or?"

"Or we can get out there and start showing this mugshot of Alietto and your photo of the kid to every sleazebag motel clerk we can find." He held up a fax with front and side images of a slightly younger Alietto holding a numbered sign in front of his chest.

Brady swallowed a half piece of toast from the cop's plate as he pushed away from the table. "And I've got another idea. Let's go."

Out in the car, Brady pulled out his cellphone and scanned his Contacts list.

"Who you calling?" Chester asked.

"His name's Eddie, an SNM contact. Something tells me that he and his buddies would like to find Alietto nearly as much as we would."

The LV cop smiled. "You're a nasty piece of work, know that?"

"I try."

Sure enough, Eddie was more than willing to help locate his old adversary. Not just for old times' sake either. "Like I said, that SOB will bring the Feds down on us like a ton of bricks," he told Brady. "We'll do what we can." Eddie promised to call if they found anything.

"Now," the reporter said as soon as he hung up, "have you ever heard of a joint named Play Misty For Me?"

"That dump over on North 3rd?"

"That's the place. Can we head over there?"

"A little early to be hitting the sauce."

"Even for me," Brady said. "But there's a bartender over there we should talk to – Alietto's old girlfriend."

"Are they even open at this hour?"

"24 hours. If she's not there, someone will know where to find her."

"Okay. Let's go."

The ride north was a quick one, cutting through the heart of Glitter Gulch. In less than fifteen minutes they pulled into the bar's parking lot.

Brady followed Chester into the bar. It was dark inside and it took a few seconds for their eyes to adjust. When they could see again they scanned the bleak interior. Two old ladies sat at a row of slots, tapping the spin button as if they couldn't lose their Social Security checks fast enough. One kid with long stringy hair sat at the bar nursing a drink. The place smelled of stale beer, cigarettes and body odor.

"I'll do the talking, if you don't mind," Brady whispered.

"Be my guest."

They walked over to the bar, where a middle-aged woman who looked like she'd spent a bit too much time in the sun busied herself straightening up.

"Darlene?" Brady asked. He wasn't surprised to see her working at such an ungodly hour. He was betting the young blond they'd talked to earlier got the prime nighttime shifts.

"Who wants to know?" she answered, her voice bruised from too much booze and too many cigarettes.

"I'm Brady James," he said. "And this is Chester."

"You both cops, or just Chester there?" she asked casually.

"Why Darlene, have you had that much contact with the boys in blue that you can pick us out at 10 feet?" Chester asked with a hard smile. The kid with stringy hair glanced over and quickly drained his drink and headed for the door. "Don't have to leave on my account," the Vegas cop called after him.

"Gotta get to work," the kid said.

"I'm a journalist," Brady continued to the bartender. "Write sometimes for the Washington Post."

A light popped on in Darlene's eyes. "Ah, you're the one who talked to Emma a couple of days ago. Looking for Joe."

"Still are. Have you seen him lately by any chance?"

Darlene glanced at the cop and back to Brady. "Is he in trouble with the law?"

"Not yet," Brady said. "But we have reason to believe he's about to get himself into some big trouble unless we can stop him."

"Like what?"

Brady hesitated, weighing how much to tell her. He decided it was too late in the game to tiptoe around the truth. "Like assassinating the President when he visits this afternoon."

Even in the dim light they could see her eyes widen.

"Kill the President? Joe? I don't think so."

"He's not going to do it himself. He's convinced some young kid that he's an Islamic terrorist and that the kid should blow himself up for his religion, or some such."

Darlene stared at the two of them as if trying to decide if they were crazy or for real. "Wow," she finally said. "That's just crazy enough to be Joe."

"We need to stop him. We need your help."

"Me? I don't know anything about some cockeyed plan to kill anyone," she answered, her hands up in self-defense.

"But you've seen him since he's been back, haven't you?" Brady said softly.

She exhaled deeply. "Yeh, I've seen him a couple of times. But he didn't say anything to me about some plan."

"We're not asking about his plan," Chester cut in. "We just want to know where you met with him. Did you ever go to his motel, or wherever he's staying here?"

"No, he came to my place."

"You never met him for a drink, or dinner?"

She paused. "Just once. He said he was running around and asked me to meet him over at The Steak Out, on Charleston."

"He never mentioned anything about where he was staying...?"

"Nope...But he did say that he'd just barely had time to grab a shower and run over to the restaurant. I assumed he was close by."

"Nothing else?"

"Sorry. Hey look, I don't want to see him go back to prison for the rest of his life. But I don't want to see that asshole in the White House dead either. Defeated, yeh. But not dead."

"If you hear from him, you'll let us know?" Chester said passing her his card. "Without letting on anything's wrong."

She hesitated. "Yeh, I'll give you a call. But don't hold your breath. He's not exactly what you'd call the dependable type."

"We can hope."

They thanked her for her help and left the silver-haired ladies to their slots. As soon as they were back in the car, the cop notified his men to concentrate their search in the area of Charleston and the Beltway, in and around Summerlin.

"It's a longshot, but better than spreading our people all over the city," Chester explained.

"Why don't we head out there and show the mugshot around a bit," Brady suggested.

"Better than sitting here waiting."

Neither man spoke as they drove. They could both see the sun rising higher in the morning sky. Time was running out.

CHAPTER 21

The air conditioning in the Silver Sluice was tepid at best. But that wasn't why Marid was sweating.

To activate the vest he only needed to connect two wires. So why was sweat dripping down his temples?

It was early yet, but he didn't want to wait until the last minute and make a mistake. After locking the door to his room and jamming a chair under the door handle, he'd taken the martyr's vest from where he'd kept it hidden in the back of his closet and opened it up on the bed.

He hadn't looked at it since al-Zahiri had demonstrated to him how it worked. Couldn't. Now, to see it lying there, to see the thin molded blocks of explosives and the telltale lumps from hidden ball bearings, the whole thing seemed so much more real.

Marid tried not to think about the other people who'd be standing nearby when the ball bearings ripped through the crowd. He refused to acknowledge the women and children who would be hurt, or even killed.

'People must be held accountable for their leaders, their government, their society,' he thought. *'If they are righteous, they will go to heaven. If not, they do not deserve to live among the righteous. Sometimes we must take actions that seem to contradict some of our beliefs, in order to uphold the greater good. We must be strong.'*

He knew he was parroting what he'd been told by al-Zahiri, but it was all he had to hang onto. He was frightened, confused. What had all seemed so clear back in DC didn't seem that way at all now that the vest lay on the bed in front of him and the President's plane was scheduled to arrive in less than 3 hours.

He noticed the slight trembling of his hands as he prepared to bring the bomb to life. He'd practiced many times before on an inert vest. This was not the same. Then it had been no more difficult than assembling a jigsaw puzzle. Now his breathing sounded rapid and shallow in the quiet of the room; his heartbeat pounded in his chest. His mouth was inordinately dry. The sweat dripping down his face itched, distracting him. He could not be distracted. Not now. One wrong move and the motel room would be nothing more than splinters of wood and cement.

He ran through his instructions one more time.

'The red wire to the left contact. The black wire to the right.' Simple. Only the more he thought about it, the less sure he was of which went left and which right. He even began to wonder which way the vest needed to be oriented. He took a deep breath and tried to calm himself, repeating his prayers over and over.

"*Alhamdulillaahi rabbil 'aalameen. ArRahmaanir Raheem. Maaliki yawmid deen. Iyyaaka na'budu wa iyyaaka nasta'een. Ihdinassiraatal mustaqeem.*" Guide us to the Path of Righteousness. Guide us.

He wiped the sweat from his brow. He must be strong. He must succeed.

Taking the black wire in his right hand, he exhaled as he gently touched it to the right contact. No explosion. Nothing. He tightened the small screw until he was confident it would hold. Then he took the red wire. 'Red to the left. Red to the left.' He tried to convince himself, but the words began to sound like nonsense syllables as he repeated them over and over. His fingers held firm as he lowered the thin red wire.

He paused a half-inch above the contact. What if he were wrong? What if it was the other way around? What if...? "All glory to Allah," he said aloud, and then he touched the bare wire to the contact.

He half-expected to hear an explosion. Half-expected to feel the blast tear through his body. But the room remained silent.

He stepped back to admire his handiwork.

The bomb was ready.

CHAPTER 22

A shower and change of clothes had made the PI feel almost normal again. True, his head still ached and his knees felt a little shaky, but given all he'd been through he was doing better than he had any reason to hope. As he packed a small knapsack with tools of his trade, he weighed his next moves against the sketchy facts available to him.

Derek was sure that Alietto's conversations with him in the barn must hold some clue to his plans for Marid. In his experience, even the most professional bad guys couldn't help but dangle a snippet of important info when given the opportunity, if only to gloat or try to put their interrogator off on the wrong path. And that's what his gut told him Alietto was doing at the ranch. He talked too much, and too glibly, to be on the up-and-up. He was trying to misdirect them. But how?

He locked the door to his room and headed to the front desk. The pasty young man who'd been working the desk when they'd first arrived had been replaced by a middle-aged woman with doubting eyes.

"May I help you?" she asked in a tone that suggested she'd rather not.

"I'm going out for a little while. The maid can clean up now."

"I'll let her know. Where you headed – over to the airport to see the President come in?"

"I doubt they'll let people get close enough to see much," Derek said absently.

"That's not what the radio is saying. They say he's expected to work the crowds when he arrives. I'd try to get over there myself, if he wasn't a Democrat."

Something clicked in Derek's thinking. "Did the radio say exactly what terminal he's using?"

"I don't think so, but the bigshots always use the VIP lounge."

"Yeh, right…Thank you. Thanks a lot," he said, hurrying out the front door.

Alietto had focused on Caesars. On the speech itself. He wanted Derek to think that's where it would happen. He wanted them to prepare for an attack at that venue, leaving the airport relatively unprepared.

"VIP terminal at McCarran," he told the cab driver. It all made sense. It *had* to. He wouldn't have time for a second guess.

*****

Summerlin is a fashionable suburb to the west of downtown Vegas. Lots of big houses on grass grown unnaturally green by constant soaking with river water 'borrowed' from the Colorado River. The people who live down-river complain mightily about all the water Las Vegas drains off before it can reach them. But without water, Vegas would quickly return to being just another dusty one horse town. With over a million citizens, and fully one-third the total voting population of the state, no politician in his right mind was going to voluntarily give that water back. And so, suburbs like Summerlin blossom all around the city.

Brady and Chester had worked up a list of all the motels located out in that section of the city, and one by one they stopped by to show their photos to the desk clerks. An hour passed. And then two. Nobody had seen anything. Chester checked with his task force. Nothing. It was as if Alietto and the kid had disappeared.

Until they pulled into the Cliffs at Red Rock, a decidedly upscale resort just off West Flamingo.

"Doesn't seem like his kind of place," Chester said when Brady suggested they take a look.

"Maybe that's just what he wants us to think."

"Suppose it can't hurt."

The front desk at the resort looked like something out of Travel & Leisure: lots of polished wood, chrome and brass, and flowers that had never seen the light of day within a thousand miles of Vegas. The lovely young woman behind the counter could have stepped out of a Chanel advertisement.

"Gentlemen – can I help you?" she asked with a blinding smile.

"Las Vegas Police," Chester said brusquely, holding up his badge. "We're looking for this man," he continued, trading the badge for the faxed mugshot of Alietto. "He'd be about seven years older and might be sporting a beard…"

The woman didn't hesitate. "Mr. Hughes? Is there some problem?"

"Hughes, is that how he registered?"

"Why yes, Jeffrey Hughes."

"Have you seen him lately?" Brady cut in.

"As a matter of fact, he just checked out less than an hour ago."

"Did he mention where he was going?"

"No. Not to me, anyway."

"Was he still driving a white Lexus?"

"I'm not too good with car models…"

"A fancy white car?"

"I…don't think so," the clerk said. "I seem to remember the valet bringing a black car to the front door. I can check with him."

"Please do. In fact, ask him to come here if you would," Chester directed.

The woman picked up the phone and relayed the request. In less than a minute a young Latino wearing a red valet's jacket appeared at the desk.

"Juan, these fellows are from the Las Vegas Police," she explained.

"He is," Brady corrected.

"I have my green card," the valet said defensively, reaching for his wallet.

"Keep it. We're not here to hassle illegals," Chester said. "Did you get a car for this guy this morning?" He showed the mugshot of Alietto.

"Mr. Hughes? Sure. Maybe an hour ago."

"What kind of car? White Lexus?"

"No, not today. He say the Lexus not comfortable for long drives. He had a black Lincoln. New, I think."

"Don't suppose you noticed the plates."

"Sorry."

Brady turned back to the desk clerk with a photo of Marid. "Was this man with Mr. Hughes?"

"Nope. Not that I saw. Juan?"

Brady showed the photo to the valet. "No. I never see this man."

"Okay, thanks. If he comes back here by any chance, give me a call." Chester handed her his card.

"I will. Is Mr. Hughes in some kind of trouble?"

"Not yet," Chester said. "Not yet."

As soon as they climbed back into Chester's unmarked car, he grabbed the 2-way radio to send a description of the black Lincoln to the task force.

"He may be headed out of town on the highway," he suggested to his dispatcher. "If anyone sees him, hold him as a material witness."

"Witness to what?" Brady asked with a questioning smile.

"Interstate transportation of explosives. Maybe."

Brady had a very strong feeling it was more than a maybe.

*****

By the time Derek got to the airport, crowds had already begun to gather. He quickly scanned the police barricades, but he saw no familiar faces. The police presence looked impressive, but without wands or magnetometers they were merely window dressing. Anyone who wanted to do the President harm basically had a free hand to do so. They might catch or kill him after the fact, but it'd be too late for the President by then.

He wondered where Brady was and what he was doing, but he knew his friend could take care of himself. Besides, he needed to concentrate on the situation at hand. If he were right, and his gut still told him he was, then either the kid or Alietto or both would be making an appearance sometime before touchdown. The question was, where and in what guise?

He patted the spare 9mm he carried in a holster hidden beneath a thin blue windbreaker. He knew that his DC PI license wouldn't keep the Secret Service from beating the crap out of him if they caught him carrying this close to the President's visit, but he wasn't going to let those two nutcases carry out their plan without some major resistance. Secret Service or no Secret Service.

He waded into the crowd, his eyes alert to anything and anyone that could help him find the kid. It was only moments later that he saw a roving TV news crew recording a few cutaways for the local nightly news. He sidled up to the young, harried woman who he deduced was the field producer.

"Getting anything interesting?" he asked casually.

She looked up from her iPad to see a man standing nearby but looking in the opposite direction.

"Down here," Derek directed.

The woman's face registered the usual surprise as her eyes dipped to his level.

"Oh, sorry. Didn't see you there."

"No problem. Was just wondering if you're getting anything good."

She laughed humorlessly. "Not going to get an Emmy for this piece, that's for sure."

"Maybe you can get the President to say something as he comes by."

"That's why we're here," she said, her attention already shifting back to an interview with a nine year old.

"Think this is the best spot for getting a look at him?" the PI pushed.

She grimaced, but answered. "That's what we've been told. Hey, nice talking to you, but I've really got to knock out these interviews."

"Yeh, sure, no problem." He'd already gotten the information he needed. He'd prowl around a bit, but more than anything he'd just wait. They had to come to him.

If he was right.

*****

The taxi ride to the airport took less than 20 minutes. Marid rubbed the tender pink skin on his cheeks and peeked at his reflection in the rearview mirror. He barely recognized himself without the beard and with short, black hair. The loose-fitting shirt and trousers made him look bigger than he really was. They wouldn't identify him. Allah would shield him from their eyes. But he'd have to find somewhere out of the way to hang out until just before the arrival of Air Force One.

He knew from al-Zahiri that the reporter from the Post was in Las Vegas. He only hoped Mr. James would stay away from the arrival. He knew his mother had involved James because of her concern for him, and he didn't want the reporter to die trying to help. But if he tried to interfere, he would die. On this count James' midget private investigator friend was lucky al-Zahiri had grabbed him and was holding him until after the bombing. That might have saved the PI's life.

Marid looked over the crowd that had begun to assemble just outside the VIP terminal. Just a few hundred people at that point. The TV news had predicted there would be thousands. All the better from his perspective. Al-Zahiri had repeatedly explained that it was easier to hide in a big ocean than a small pond. The crowd here would be plenty large. Besides, who would be looking for a clean-shaven blue-eyed supporter?

If everything worked as planned, he'd be right up front, face to face with the dhimmi leader. And when the President passed by, when he stood next to Marid, it would all be over.

But he didn't want to think about that just yet. He tilted his head skyward to feel the sun's rays on his face and then strolled over to the commercial terminal where he took a seat at Starbuck's. He liked coffee. He'd only just recently discovered the Cinnamon Dolce Latte. He would enjoy one last cup here on earth before ascending to Jannah where he'd have his choice of any coffee he wanted. Funny, so many of the righteous were eager to partake of the 72 virgins promised to all martyrs. He was more interested in a good cup of coffee. Women were too difficult to understand. He didn't think it would be all that different in Jannah. He just wanted some peace and quiet. No more questions. No more debates. No more pain. Just a nice cup of coffee…

*****

Brady and Chester were on their way to LV Police headquarters when Chester's cellphone rang.

"Ashcroft," the LV cop answered.

Brady stared out the side window, wondering what Marid was doing at that moment. Suddenly the tone of

Chester's voice changed and he turned to see what was happening.

"Keep him there!" the cop said into his phone. "We're on our way!" He closed the phone.

"What's going on?" Brady asked before Chester could say a word.

"Alietto. He's at that bar visiting with the bartender, Darlene."

"What?" It didn't sound right. Alietto must know they would be looking for him. What was he doing sitting in a bar, chatting with an old girlfriend?

Chester called in a Code 30 and floored his unmarked police car, hanging a quick u-turn to take them east and then north toward Play Misty For Me. The houses and small businesses flew past as they shot up 515. They exited just after the expressway crossed I-15 and swooped down to North 3rd St.

"What do you think he's up to?" Brady asked.

"Alietto? Who knows? Maybe he changed his mind. Maybe we were wrong all along. Maybe he's just nuts."

"Maybe," Brady said, but he didn't believe it. Not for one minute.

Chester slowed as he pulled into the bar parking lot.

"Look, we don't know if this guy is armed, or what. You stay back a bit when we go inside – okay?"

Brady knew the procedure. He'd been through it a hundred times before. But he simply nodded. "Got it."

Brady didn't know what to expect when they stepped through the bar door, Chester with gun in hand, but to see Alietto sitting at the bar, sipping a beer, chatting with Darlene as if nothing was amiss, was not it.

"Las Vegas Police!" Chester yelled, pointing his gun at Alietto. "Keep your hands where I can see them!"

A woman playing the slots screamed loudly, while two men at a table threw their hands into the air, eyes wide. Alietto held his hands up in front of him, a big smile on his face.

"What's the matter officer, someone report a jaywalker?" he said as calm as calm could be.

Chester was in no mood for stupid jokes. He grabbed Alietto by one wrist, spun him around, and tossed him up against the bar.

"Put both hands on the railing!" he ordered, as he quickly patted-down the still smirking militia leader. "He's not carrying," he said aloud to no one in particular.

"Carrying what, officer? I think this must be some sort of mistake." His voice sounded aggrieved, but his expression never wavered.

"Where is he?" Brady said, unable to keep quiet a moment longer.

"Where's who?"

Brady usually abhorred physical violence, but in that instant he was sorely tempted to rearrange the man's nose. Chester saved him from temptation.

"Don't play games!" he shouted, pulling Alietto around by the shoulder to face them. "Where's the kid – Marid al-Zabaar?"

Alietto feigned confusion. "Al-Zabaar? Sounds like a Middle Eastern name to me. I can't say that I know many people from that neck of the woods."

"You know him, all right, you SOB, and if he goes through with your little plan, we'll be happy to watch them throw the switch on the electric chair to send you to your maker." Brady had seen many a criminal crumble when confronted by the reality of the chair. Not this guy.

"My, my, my, don't we have a vivid imagination. Almost as if you were…oh, I don't know, a writer of some kind."

"Cut the crap Alietto," Chester cut in. "We know all about your plans to kill the President."

At the mention of the President, the small group of barflies – who'd been eavesdropping with undisguised delight – gasped in horror.

"Like I said, this must be some kind of mistake." Brady looked for any sign that Alietto was concerned about their confrontation, but he saw none. *This guy thinks he's got it beat,'* he thought. *'He thinks he's home clean.'*

"We've got your conversations with Marid on his cellphone," Brady said. He wasn't sure if they did, but he was hoping Alietto wasn't sure either.

A flicker of concern showed in the militia man's eyes. "We wouldn't be having this conversation if you had anything more than a wild-ass theory," he finally said. "And it's been my experience that wild-ass theories don't usually stand up in court."

"How do you think we found you here?" Brady pushed. "How do you think we know about your plans?"

"I'd imagine you found me by checking the passenger logs out of DC. And I don't know what plans you're talking about."

"You don't really think you're going to get away with this, do you?"

Alietto smiled. "Let's just say, for the sake of argument mind you, that there was some kind of *plan*. And let's say that this Middle-eastern kid, what was his name –

Marid? – was involved somehow. I'm pretty sure that you can't prove any link between me and this Marid, and I'm just as sure that there won't be any evidence linking us if the plan works out. I mean, here I am, with the two of you as witnesses. As a matter of fact, I bet that if this kid was involved with anyone in a plan to kill the President, it would be another Middle-easterner. Some rughead who wants to undermine these United States and replace our democracy with some Moslem nutball Imam – isn't that what they call them? Can you imagine how the crap will hit the fan if some rughead kills our President? Even the jackass who's in the White House now? Can you imagine how it'll piss off the real Americans, the God-fearing, gun-toting patriots who'll be foaming at the mouth to get out there and hunt down every rughead they can find? And who do you think they'll turn to, at least out here in Nevada, to help lead that hunt? Maybe a militia that has trained for just such a venture?" His eyes gleamed.

"You are absolutely friggin' nuts," Chester said.

"Maybe. Maybe not. You'll just have to wait and see."

Brady glanced up at the bigscreen TV behind the bar to see a local reporter interviewing people at the airport awaiting the President's arrival. He was just about to go back to grilling Alietto, when he saw a familiar little body waddle through the background of the shot.

"Idiot!" he said through clenched teeth.

"What?" Chester asked.

"Derek is out of bed and over at the airport."

"The airport?" Alietto said before he could stop himself. There was something in the way he said it that caught Brady's attention immediately.

"Yeh, the airport," he replied. "Why? Something going on at the airport?"

The militiaman tried to disguise his reaction, but he was only partially successful.

"Nothing I know about."

"You know Alietto, I bet you're a lousy card player."

"Don't know what you're talking about." He sounded defensive, suddenly not at all the cocky hotshot they'd been interviewing moments earlier.

"What's your friend doing over there?" Chester asked Brady. "I thought the focus was on Caesars."

"Apparently he's changed his mind. Maybe he has a lead."

"He's just wasting his time," Alietto muttered.

"Is he? Then why have you become such a meek little mouse all of a sudden? Chester, I think maybe you'd better see if you can get a few extra LV cops over to McCarron, and I'll try to call Steve Lyle. See if the Secret Service can call up some reserves."

"Just spinnin' your wheels," Alietto said, his self-assured smile returning.

"That may be," Brady said, "but then again, maybe you thought you could send us off on a wild-goose chase over at Caesars while you sent Marid over to the airport to meet the President there."

"Like I said, you have a vivid imagination."

"Why don't you handcuff that asshole," Brady said. "I'm calling Lyle."

*****

Eddie, Jake, and a half-dozen of their fellow SNM members had been visiting everyone they knew who'd known Joe Alietto when he lived in Vegas. Perhaps not too surprisingly, given the kind of transient town Vegas was, many of his old buddies had left town. But they'd still located a few of the old gang, none of whom had seen or heard from Joe in years.

They had just finished talking with one such former friend, Ben diBenedetto, when the rail-thin, balding former militiaman tossed off a random thought just as Jake and Eddie were about to climb back on their motorcycles.

"You know, if anyone would know if Joe was back, it'd probably be Trevor - Alison. I wouldn't say they were friends, exactly, but Trevor was always following Joe around like a sick puppy. If he's back here, Trevor might know about it."

"Any idea where he might be living these days?"

"As a matter of fact, I just ran into him a few months back at Albertson's. Said he was living over on West Sahara. I think it was out by Rainbow Blvd. A condo. The Oasis, or something like that?"

Eddie was on his iPhone in seconds. He found the listing and Googled directions.

"Let's go pay Alison a visit," he said to his partner as he gunned his Harley and squealed out of the parking lot.

*****

Trevor was stretched out on his living room sofa, a bag of chipped ice resting uncomfortably on his bruised neck, when the doorbell rang.

"Who the hell is that?" he thought as he got up awkwardly and made his way to the door.

When he opened the door he was more than surprised; he stood motionless, his face a pained questionmark. His expression brought a smile to Eddie's face.

"Why Trevor, we don't hardly see you anymore," he said, pushing past the stunned militiaman into his apartment. "Been too long."

Jake herded his old associate into the living room, closing the door behind him.

"Jake, Eddie," Trevor was finally able to mutter. "What brings you way out here?"

"You got anything to drink?" Eddie answered.

"Sure. What'll it be – a beer? Some water? Juice?" He tried to act calm and relaxed, but his voice shook.

"Beer'd work for me. Jake?"

"Make it two."

"Yeh, sure, I'll go get 'em." Trevor made for the kitchen. Jake followed a step behind, just to be sure their old friend didn't slip out a back door.

"Nice place, Trev. What're you up to these days?" Eddie called after them.

"Oh, not so much. I work at a garage down in Boulder City."

"Mechanic, eh? Stayin' busy?"

"Yeh, sure, pretty busy. You know how it is in the fall: everyone's so happy to see the temperatures drop, they're not really thinking about workin' on their cars so much."

Eddie looked around at the barebones furniture and stained rug. It didn't look like ol' Trev was doing all that well. "Still seeing any of the old SNM gang?"

A long pause. "Not so much," Trevor said, coming back into the living room carrying a beer for Eddie and another for himself. Jake stayed close enough to reach out and touch if need be, sipping from a bottle.

"So you've had a little free time?"

"A little, yeh. Why, what's up?" There was more than a little trepidation in his voice.

"Well, we heard that an old friend of ours was back in town, and wondered if you'd seen him: Joe Alietto?"

Trevor froze. Not for long, but long enough so that both Eddie and Jake both knew they'd hit a nerve.

"Uh, no, no. Didn't know he was back," the wiry 35-year-old said, taking a hard swig from his beer to hide his nervousness.

"Really? That's not what we heard," Eddie said, hoping Trevor was still as fragile as he'd always been in the past. He motioned to Jake, who went over to where Trevor was sitting and just stood behind his chair, not saying a word.

"Hey, what is this?" their host said, trying to get up from his seat. Jake grabbed him roughly by the shoulder and pushed him back down. Eddie got up and went over to stand right in front of him.

"We don't have time to screw around," Eddie said, his voice suddenly harder. "Where's Alietto?"

"Hey, look, I don't know anything about the goddamn midget!" Trevor blurted. "Joe just asked me to babysit for a couple of days."

Eddie backhanded the younger man. "I said we don't have time!" he screamed. "Now I'll only ask you once more: where's Joe?!"

Trevor rubbed his cheek. "I don't know." He sounded like he might cry.

"What about the midget?"

His defenses shattered, the mechanic told them everything about the kidnapping in one non-stop torrent of pleading confession. Eddie listened impatiently, his stare cold and unflinching. When Trevor finally stopped, Eddie leaned in until his face was just inches from Trevor's, a long hunting knife held in plain sight. His voice was low, but unmistakably threatening.

"So where's that bastard Alietto now?"

Trevor's lower lip quivered. "I told you – I don't know! I haven't seen him since yesterday!"

Eddie looked back at Jake, who nodded ever so slightly. He agreed: the little scumbag probably didn't know where Alietto had gone.

He spoke directly to Jake. "Keep an eye on our little buddy. I need to make a phone call."

Eddie stepped into the kitchen and dialed his cell.

"Mr. James, Eddie. Hey, I found someone who's seen Alietto. Even better, he was in on your friend's snatch."

Brady looked over at Alietto, who was engaged in unproductive give and take with Chester. "Do you know where the bar Play Misty For Me is?"

He did. In just minutes a tense and stunned Trevor was on the back of Eddie's Harley, headed north.

CHAPTER 23

Brady wasn't the only person who had a TV within view.

Marid had been staring idly at the big LCD in Starbuck's as he prayed for the strength to carry out his task, when he too saw a familiar little person walk through the background of an interview right there at the airport.

"No!" he muttered aloud. He instinctively scanned the coffee shop and looked out through the windows at the crowd in the distance. The PI was nowhere to be seen, but that only meant he'd be harder to avoid.

Marid gulped the last of his latte and headed for the door. He took a quick glance to be sure the PI wasn't lurking nearby, and then slipped out into the hot mid-day sun. He pulled on a pair of sunglasses and scurried across the street in the opposite direction from the crowd awaiting the President's arrival. He needed to find a place to wait this last hour or so. Some place where the little guy wouldn't find him and ruin everything.

He made his way into the parking garage on the other side of the road leading to the VIP arrival center, and climbed the stairs up to the third floor. From up there he had a good view of the crowd below. He settled down into a small nook behind a row of parked cars, sitting on a concrete barrier as he scanned the hundreds of people congregating just 100 yards away. He wiped a stream of sweat from the side of his face. His racing pulse began to gradually slow. He could see anyone coming his way, with very little likelihood they would see him in the shadowed garage.

He probably wouldn't have felt quite so comfortable if he'd realized that directly above him Secret Service snipers were scanning the same crowd.

But he didn't know.

CHAPTER 24

Joe Alietto showed little sign of breaking. Except for the momentary lapse when he'd learned that Derek was prowling around the airport, he had been as cool as a cucumber during their questioning. For the time being, Chester had left him handcuffed to his barstool while he and Brady discussed their strategy just outside the bar.

"That SOB isn't going to tell us what we need to know," the LV cop said, shaking his head. "I'm thinking I might need to take him into a back room for a little 'private interrogating'."

I bet that wouldn't be the first time,' Brady couldn't help thinking. The LV police force had had some bad press over the years for excessive use of force. The thing that really bothered Brady was that he was tempted to agree. Time was running out.

"Let's see what happens when Eddie gets here with this other sleazeball. Maybe we can use the two of them against each other."

As if summoned, the roar of two big motorcycles echoed across the bar parking lot. Brady could tell at a glance that the passenger seated behind Eddie wasn't having a good day. His sullen look matched the bright red mark on his cheek. *'Looks like the cops aren't the only ones using enhanced interrogation techniques,'* he decided.

"Here he is," Eddie said, reaching back to shove Trevor off the bike. "For what it's worth."

"We really appreciate it, Eddie. Owe you guys one," Brady said.

"Just don't screw us over in your article, if there *is* an article."

James nodded. He'd have to learn to quit underestimating people. "You'll be our knights in shining armor," he said with just a hint of sarcasm.

Eddie looked like he was going to spit. "Don't go overboard. We've got a militia to run." He smiled. "Take it easy. Hope you find the kid before he blows himself up."

Brady noticed Trevor's eyebrows shoot up in alarm as the two motorcycles roared back out onto the road and off into the distance.

"What was he talking about, 'blow himself up'?" Trevor asked. "Joe told us to grab the midget because he was going to make trouble for the Militia."

"Why don't we go inside and ask your old friend Mr. Alietto about that," Brady said. Chester took the wide-eyed militiaman by the arm and pushed him toward the bar.

"Joe, look who dropped by!" Brady said as he walked through the door. Alietto's expression changed from boredom to alarm in less than a second.

"I didn't tell them anything!" Trevor yelled to his friend.

"Except that you and he kidnapped one Derek DiLaurain," Chester said as officiously as he could. "That's life imprisonment here in Nevada."

"I don't know what you're talking about," Alietto growled, but his words sounded hollow.

"You know, the little guy you grabbed at Caesars and held against his will up at that run-down Test Site ranch? Maybe we'll just put the two of you in a room somewhere and let him settle things one on one. What do you say, Officer?"

Chester smiled. "Sounds like poetic justice."

"I'd tear the little asshole apart," Alietto said.

"Somehow I doubt that," Brady said solemnly. "Not only does he have a black belt, but he has one nasty temper. You'd be better off in the can."

"All hot air. I'll take my chances in court."

"What chances? Your buddy here has already admitted to kidnapping DiLaurain."

"If he did, I didn't know a thing about it."

"What are you talkin' about, Joe?!" the younger militiaman cried out. "*You* told us to grab the midget! I'm not going to take the fall for this all by myself!"

"Shut up!" Alietto ordered. "They can't prove a thing. It's all bluff."

"We'll see," Brady said. "If the kid blows himself up, then I guess we'll know that we were right. And you'll know that Joe here has been setting you up for a fall," he added, nodding toward Trevor.

"They're just playing you," Alietto argued, but his words lacked authority. "They're trying to get us to fight among ourselves."

"Did Joe here ever tell you anything about the airport?" Brady pressed. "About killing the President?"

"What?" Trevor looked stunned.

"That's a capital crime," Chester cut in. "You're looking at lethal injection."

"He's just trying to scare you!" Alietto said. "They haven't executed anyone out here in years."

"For killing a sitting President? I'm betting they'd bring back the electric chair for that one. Or maybe hanging."

"I don't know anything about killing anybody," Trevor said with enough emotion to convince Brady that he was telling the truth. But that didn't mean he didn't know anything, even if he didn't realize it.

"Fact is, Joe has conned some young Muslim guy into blowing himself up to kill the President," Chester explained. "We think it's supposed to happen today."

"Don't say a word!" Joe ordered, his face now a purple mask. "They don't know what they're talking about!"

"Keep your friggin' mouth shut or I'll stick a sock in it!" Chester said with a look that meant business.

"This may be your last chance to earn yourself a break with sentencing," Brady said, leaning in close to the young militiaman. "If you know *anything* about what might be going down at the airport, you've got to tell us."

"Trevor…" Alietto began, but one look from Chester and his mouth snapped shut.

"I don't know nothing about no bombing!" Trevor said, his voice trembling.

"Did Joe mention *anything* about the airport? Anything at all?"

Trevor took a deep breath and appeared to be wracking his brain. "Well," he finally said, "it wasn't exactly about the airport, but Joe and me was joking one day up at the ranch and when I told him I'd need a vacation after all

I'd been doing for him, he did tell me not to fly anywhere today. He said it'd be a bad day for traveling."

"Shut up!!" Alietto roared.

Chester had had enough. He pulled a dirty handkerchief out of his pocket and stuffed it in Alietto's mouth.

"When did he tell you this?"

"Couple of days ago. But he didn't say nothin' about no bomb!"

Brady nodded. "I think we've got enough," he said to Chester, ignoring Trevor's unspoken plea. "Let's get these two put away someplace safe and head over to the airport."

"I'll call a black and white to come pick them up," the LV cop answered.

While they waited, Brady stared out the window at the brilliant sunshine outside. *'Funny — so bright out there,'* he thought, *'and yet it seems so dark in here.'*

*****

Derek had been moving through the crowd for more than twenty minutes and he was rapidly losing his cool — literally and figuratively. He could feel a stream of perspiration slide down his back even as his Bluetooth earpiece was slipping out of place; he still had his phone turned off so he didn't have to listen to the diatribe he knew would come if Brady tried to get ahold of him, but he adjusted the earpiece so that he could dial out in an instant if he found Marid.

'Where the hell is that kid?' he thought as he eyed probably his thousandth expectant face. He'd never really thought much about all the people who go to see a President, or other celebrity, in person. It would never cross

his mind to do it himself. He'd supposed that most of them were slobbering idiots, teenyboppers, or old farts with nothing better to do. So he was fairly well amazed to see a much broader spectrum of eager citizens that hot afternoon, all baking in the hot Vegas sun awaiting the imminent arrival of Air Force One. In addition to the three groups he'd expected, there were housewives, military men and women, blue collar worker types, and even a few business execs in their $800 suits and designer ties.

Pretty much a little of everything.

'All to see the Big Guy for just a few seconds. Maybe get an autograph or shake a hand,' he thought. *'Strange.'*

He shook his head. In his mind's eye he couldn't avoid seeing a large number of those people scattered all across the driveway – arms and legs blown every which way, blood flowing down the sidewalks in small rivers, screams filling the air – if the kid succeeded with his plan. He had to find him, and fast.

In the blazing sunshine of that warm Nevada fall, the PI was beginning to feel like a steamed vegetable in his thin windbreaker. Completely lost in his thoughts, he peeled off the jacket to tie it around his waist.

"Gun!" a woman's voice screamed. "He's got a gun!"

It took Derek less than a second to realize that he was the one she was screaming about. He glanced up just in time to see a couple of earpiece types look over in his direction. He needed to do something, and he only had about a heartbeat to do it.

"Secret Service," he said authoritatively to the woman. "Protection detail." He turned his ear toward her and pushed back his hair to reveal the Bluetooth earpiece.

The horrified look on the woman's face turned to puzzlement. A dwarf Secret Service agent?

He didn't wait for further discussion. Moving through the crowd as quickly as he could without appearing to run, he got to the side door of a hanger and slipped into a corridor that led back to some administrative offices. He could see a couple of uniformed LV cops out in the hanger just a few yards away, and from their animated discussion and scanning looks realized a Secret Service alert had probably just gone out. An alert for him.

Part of him wanted to just walk up to the cops and explain what he was doing there. Certainly they'd been advised by the Service that a possible plot against the President had been uncovered. But he'd had more than enough negative interaction with cops in tense situations to know that they'd probably just throw him in handcuffs and wait until after the 747 landed before listening to his story. And by then it would be too late.

He ran.

"There he is!" a voice called out. "Hanger G – by the Admin offices!"

The PI didn't bother to look; he knew that they'd spotted him. He turned a corner and found himself facing an emergency exit. With no time to think, he pushed open the door and then ducked into an open office just to his right. A fire alarm sounded immediately, the ear-splitting wail a welcome distraction.

Derek scanned the small room quickly. Where could he hide?! Then he saw it. Moving quickly, he secreted himself in the one place he hoped they wouldn't check, and then waited.

He heard footsteps, voices. Some came so close he was sure they'd find him. But they didn't. It took them a few minutes, but then the alarm was finally turned off. He held his breath.

"Looks like he exited through a rear emergency door," he heard someone say into a walkie talkie.

"Find the bastard!" an angry voice responded. "Now! The plane's only 30 minutes out!"

The footsteps seemed to be moving away. And then silence.

He counted to a hundred before lifting his head. The papers he'd grabbed off the desk above him showered down onto the floor. He unfolded slowly, trying not to tip over the metal trashcan.

'Sometimes it pays to be small,' he thought with a shaky smile as he stepped out onto the carpet. He picked up the papers and put them back on the desk. No need to draw anyone's attention.

Moving as quietly as he could, he made his way back to the open office door and looked out. He could see the uniformed cops back in the hanger, now accompanied by two dark-suited agent types. Couldn't go that way.

He quickly evaluated the situation. Without the hanger exit, there were only two ways out: the window, and the same emergency door he'd pushed open before. The window might seem safer, but there'd be no doubt that someone would call it in if they saw someone crawling out a window with Air Force One just minutes out. The door was the only answer. He took a deep breath and crossed his fingers that they hadn't been able to reset the fire alarm yet.

'*Here goes,*' he thought as he stepped out of the office into the hallway and gently pushed on the panic bar. The door swung open without a sound.

"Thank you, Jesus!" he said as he slipped out the door. He found himself behind the hanger building, in a parking lot emptied of everything except two big dumpsters. He ducked behind the nearer of the two trash bins and took a second to look around the lot. He knew there had to be a dozen cops and agents running around looking for him, but from his vantage point he couldn't see a single one. His luck was holding, but luck had a way of changing at the worst possible moment.

He needed a plan.

*****

Chester turned off the unmarked car's sirens and lights as they approached the airport.

"No need to make a grand entrance," he said.

They had roared across town at speeds over 80 miles per hour as they made a mad dash to intercept Marid before he could carry-out Alietto's insane plan. They still weren't sure that the airport was their target, but they were sure enough to have argued with Steve Lyle to send additional cops and agents to McCarron.

"If you're wrong about this…" Lyle had said ominously.

"Let's just hope we're right. And in time," Brady had countered.

As they pulled into the airport driveway, he dialed Derek's cellphone number for the third time. He received the same "Not available" recording as the first two times.

"Damn it, Derek," Brady fumed. "Answer the goddamn phone!"

Adding to his frustration, they were stopped twice at police barricades by officers wearing protective vests and carrying automatic weapons. Chester showed his ID both times, but he still had to explain to Secret Service agents what a Vegas cop and a retired journalist were doing at the airport without the proper Presidential visit pins to identify them as cleared participants. Luckily, the agents had believed them. At least enough to have sent them – with a policeman as escort – to a control center inside the airport perimeter.

"I've got a dozen people running around looking for a very short man carrying a gun!" Lyle had barked when he saw them enter the center. "I don't suppose you know anything about that?"

Brady quickly explained all he knew, hypothesizing that Derek had come to the terminal looking for Marid.

"Jesus Christ, that goddamn kid again," Lyle muttered. "How certain are you that he's here? And how certain that he has a vest?"

"Pretty certain," Brady ventured. Lyle pulled the two of them off to the side.

"We've been talking about re-routing the President's plane," the agent said softly. "Do you know how much crap I'll take if this all turns out to be a mother's fantasy?"

"What if we're right?"

Lyle didn't answer right away. "We've got maybe 15 minutes before we have to divert the plane."

"Then let's find him. Contact all your guys who are looking for Derek and tell them to concentrate on Marid,"

Brady suggested. He pulled out a photo of the kid. "Give them all a copy of this."

"They've got his photo." Brady could see the agent's mind whirring. "Okay, but if we don't find him in 15 minutes, I'm pulling the plug."

"He's gotta be close enough to where the President will appear to get there in a matter of minutes. He can't risk being further away. Limit your search perimeter to 100 yards. He's almost got to be inside that."

Lyle stared at the journalist. It was obvious he wasn't used to taking direction from an amateur. But he did. "Pull the men off the search for the midget," he said into a walkie talkie. "Put all unassigned personnel into a 100 yard radius of Hawk's departure route," he said, using the Service's code name for the President. "We're looking for that kid whose photo was distributed this morning."

"He might have changed his appearance," Brady suggested. "Maybe shaved or cut his hair." He'd been involved in so many fugitive searches, he knew how people hoping to avoid capture thought.

"Right." Lyle pushed the 'transmit' button on his radio. "He may be clean-shaven, or with shorter hair. If found, approach with *extreme* caution! He may be wearing a bomb vest." The agent lowered his radio. "Satisfied?"

"Not until we find him. Come on!" Brady ran from the control center with Chester and Lyle in close pursuit.

*****

The people down below looked like a herd of animals from his observation point in the parking garage. Or so he tried to convince himself. Just animals.

Marid looked away from the crowds below and stared intently at the concrete gray wall just inches from his face. He tried to ignore the feelings of doubt and mistrust welling up in his chest. What he was going to do was just and right! He had to protect his faith against the infidels, he had to bring down the Great Satan if Muslims were to ever achieve their birthright of a world dedicated to the teachings of the Prophet!

Try as he might, however, he could not completely rid his mind of the nagging voice, a voice that sounded all too much like his mother's, telling him to reconsider.

"They are just people, like ourselves," the voice reminded him. "They have not sinned, even if their country has. Innocents must not die to redeem the guilty."

He found tears forming in his eyes. "I must follow the fatwa," he repeated over and over. "I must follow the fatwa." And then he began to pray.

*****

Derek hid behind the dumpster just long enough to formulate his next steps. He needed to get to a vantage point where he could scan the arrival scene from above, hoping to at least eliminate sections of the crowd if not identify Marid himself. The only building that he had any hope of gaining entry to was the parking garage directly across the pavement from where he was now hiding. It was about twenty-five feet from where he stood to the closest door to the four-story concrete building. Twenty-five feet. At his fastest, Derek calculated that it would take him at least five seconds to get across and inside. Five seconds during which any wandering eye might see him and report him to the Secret Service agents that dotted the landscape. Or the LV cops. Either way, he'd be out of the game and the kid would have one less impediment to carrying out his plan. He had no choice.

He was scanning the garage one last time, when movement three-quarters of the way up the building caught his attention. It wasn't much, just the smallest of moves, but it stopped him in his tracks. He assumed it was a Secret Service agent, or a cop, looking down on the crowd just as he planned to do. He waited, hoping the person would show themselves again, if only for a second. In less than a minute, his patience was rewarded.

A head popped up from behind a row of parked cars and glanced quickly over the railing at the people below. Derek froze.

'That's not a cop!' he thought. He couldn't be certain, but it looked like the kid!

Taking a deep breath, Derek got ready to dash out from behind the trash bin on his way to the garage. There's no telling if he would've made it, if he would've escaped notice in the endless seconds he was exposed to public scrutiny. But as it happened, luck was on his side. Just as he was debating when to make his move, a scream erupted from the densely packed thousands. Someone had fainted from the intense heat. For just that moment, just that instant, every eye was focused on the downed spectator.

'Now!' he told himself, and he ran. He ran with every bit of strength his middle-aged body possessed. He knew he was no Olympic sprinter. He knew his short, stubby legs were not built for speed. But on that day, in that situation, they were just fast enough.

He slammed against the metal entrance door and fell into the concrete coolness of the garage. He didn't hesitate even a moment. He ducked into a line of parked cars and headed straight to the nearest stairwell. He half-expected to hear a shouted order to stop, or perhaps even a shot. But the only sounds he heard were his own slapping footsteps and the pounding of his heart.

He hesitated at the door to the stairs. He knew that agents or police might be stationed in the stairwell, so he opened the door just a crack, just enough to peek inside. There didn't seem to be anyone there. He stepped through and listened for just a moment before he pulled off his shoes and began to scurry up the stairs as fast as he could. His previous experience with the Secret Service told him that they'd almost certainly have a spotter, and probably a sniper or two, stationed up on the roof. That meant the third floor was as high as he could risk. The third floor it would be.

His stocking feet made very little sound on the concrete steps, so little that he could hear the crackle of radios and the mumble of police officers as he made his way past the second floor landing. From what he could tell, they were all still talking about the ill spectator and paid no attention to the tiny shadow moving quickly on the darkened stairs. He was tempted to pause and eavesdrop to learn if they had any idea where he was, but he thought better of it and moved up quickly to the next landing.

The scene on the third floor was the same as on the second. The security agents and cops had been drawn to the edge of the garage by the arrival of the ambulance below. Derek knew that the situation might change at any moment, so he decided to take his chance right then, no hesitation.

He took a quick glance to be sure no one was keeping an eye on the stairway door, and then crouched low to slip inside behind the closest row of cars.

He scampered on all fours behind the cars until he felt reasonably confident that no one could see him ensconced behind a large delivery van. He peered out just as the congregated police turned away from the scene below and returned to their individual posts.

"Hot enough to fry an egg out there," one LV cop said as he walked past within 15 feet of the PI.

"Surprised we haven't had more pass out," the second replied.

Derek waited until two of them set up surveillance posts at opposite sides of the building. A third, apparently a supervisor, gave final instructions and headed back into the stairwell. Each of the two that remained behind was looking out at the people and vehicles crowding the airport drive directly below, scanning with binoculars every few seconds for a closer look. Neither of them, however, was looking inside the garage. And that gave Derek the chance he needed to get to the side of the building that overlooked the arrival area.

The moment he saw the agent on that side of the garage pick up his binoculars, he made his move. Staying well below the agent's normal level of sight, the PI dashed across the twenty feet of open concrete and into the row of cars about halfway down the wall from where the agent stood guard. He looked over at the agent and was relieved to see that he hadn't heard anything over the hubbub below.

Derek put his head down next to the concrete floor and looked under the cars in the direction he'd seen the movement from below. All the way at the end of the row, opposite from where the cop surveyed the crowd, he saw a small swatch of blue and white behind the long queue of tires. He couldn't be sure it was a person from that angle, but his gut told him it was the kid.

*****

Brady and Chester were moving as quickly as they could through the hundreds of people awaiting the President's imminent arrival.

"This is like trying to find your lost kid in Macy's at Christmastime," Chester complained as they pushed their way through the crowd.

"Just keep moving," Brady said. "Just keep moving."

They saw both uniformed and plainclothes agents doing the same, but without any luck.

'He's got to be here somewhere,' Brady thought as he scanned the endless faces, all turned towards the exit from the VIP building. *'I know Alietto was hiding something when we mentioned the airport.'*

They stopped for a second as a loud argument broke out just a few yards from where they stood. Seems one of the early-arrivals had taken offense that an agent had pushed his way in front of him, assuming that he was trying to get closer to the President. It took the flash of a badge to quiet the scene.

Brady shook his head. Just minutes remained before Lyle would have to advise Air Force One to abort its landing, and there they were, arguing with spectators. He began to feel that maybe it would be for the best to send the President's plane somewhere else. If they couldn't guarantee the security of the airport, he should land somewhere else. He wondered where the nearest landing strip was that could handle a 747.

He was just about to voice his thoughts to Chester, when suddenly a handful of agents went running to the far side of the crowd.

"What's going on?" he asked.

"Don't know. Let me check." He clicked on his walkie-talkie transmit button.

"Outpost One, Outpost One, this is Blue 34. See a number of agents running past the crowd out here. What's going on?"

"They've ID'd the Muslim kid we've been looking for!" an excited voice answered. "In pursuit!"

"Tell them to keep their distance until we get there!" Brady yelled, hoping he might be able to convince Marid to abandon his plan once he knew that Alietto had used him.

"Understood."

"That way!" Brady said, pointing to where the agents had disappeared.

It was tough going, pushing their way through an uncooperative mass of people who were hot, tired, and none too willing to cede an inch of their hard-won viewing turf. But the two men did the best they could and finally burst out into the open. A uniformed LV cop immediately intercepted them.

"This area is off-limits!" he called out loudly before he even made it over to where they stood.

"LV Police!" Chester called out, waving his badge. "We are in pursuit of a suspect!"

The cop looked confused, but then recognized Chester. "Ashcroft! What the hell are you doing running around like a chicken with his head chopped off?"

"We're after that kid the agents just ID'd. James here knows him. He thinks the kid's trying to..."

Brady dug his elbow into the cop's ribs.

"We're not alone here!" Brady said sternly through pinched lips, tipping his head in the direction of the crowd just behind them.

"Right. Sorry," Chester said. And then turning back to his fellow officer added, "We need to get to him – fast!"

The cop hesitated just a second. He could see they didn't have the Secret Service access pins, but he knew Ashcroft. "Go! Go!" he ordered.

And they did. Finally free of the mass of spectators, Brady and Chester ran as if their lives depended on it. Their lives and many more.

*****

Derek inched his way toward the corner of the parking garage where he'd seen someone move just 15 minutes earlier. He glanced repeatedly back toward the cop over in the opposite corner, but his interest was riveted on the crowd below. He never even glanced back inside the garage.

If it were the kid hiding behind the cars, he only hoped that he could talk him out of his insane plan before he decided to push the button and blow himself – and Derek – to kingdom come.

'Be just my friggin' luck,' the PI thought as he moved closer and closer to the final car in the row. *'Save the President but die in the process. Dead hero. Great.'*

The oil-stained concrete felt cool beneath his hands as he crawled silently toward the kid. Two more cars. Then one. He stopped and took a deep breath.

'This is it. Stay cool. Don't spook him.'

"Marid," he whispered. "Marid it's me – Derek DiLaurain, the private investigator you met back in DC? The little guy? Hey, look, I know why you're here, and I know that you think it's for some kind of religious reason. But Marid, this guy, al-Zahiri? He's a *fake*, Marid. He's not even Middle-Eastern. He's a thug from out here in Vegas who's *using* you! Do you hear me, Marid, he's not a real Muslim! He's using you to make it look like Muslims killed the President. He wants to start a religious war here in the U.S.! Marid, I know this is a lot to take on, but you've got to believe me – the guy's a fake! You don't have to do this!"

Derek glanced quickly at the cop across the garage. With all the noise from the spectators below, he hadn't noticed a thing. But the kid wasn't answering. Was that a good thing, or was the PI about to meet his maker?

"Marid? Listen to me. You don't have to do this."

Nothing.

Derek poked his head around the last car parked between him and the kid. Something wasn't right.

The PI crawled as slowly as he could toward the last car in the row.

"Marid, I'm coming over to you," he whispered. "I'm not going to hurt you. I just want to talk."

With each foot he moved forward, his heartbeat seemed to double. Finally he was there, right at the rear bumper of the last car.

"Marid? Can we talk?"

Still nothing. Derek didn't like it, but he couldn't wait any longer.

"I'm coming around the car," he said softly, doing it even as he spoke. He turned the corner of the car and braced for the worst.

It was even worse than he had thought.

The kid wasn't there. Just a pair of khaki pants and a blue shirt.

"Dammit!" he fumed.

His mind whirled. Time was up, and the kid was almost certainly down below somewhere. He'd taken advantage of the diversion by the fainting spectator just as Derek had. Or was it even a real emergency? Maybe the sick person was all part of the plan...

He turned on his cellphone and hit the speed dial.

CHAPTER 25

Brady and Chester approached the cornered youth slowly. A ring of police and agents encircled him, their guns drawn.

"You James?" the agent in charge asked as they came forward.

"Yeh. Give me a second to talk to the kid. I might be able to persuade him to surrender."

"Okay, but take this," he said handing James a hand-held blast barrier. It looked like a high-tech version of the shields that the Crusaders had used thousands of years earlier. Brady just hoped that Marid wouldn't see it that way. "And stay at least 30 feet away from him."

Brady nodded. The agent didn't have to explain why he had to keep his distance.

"Marid!" he called out to the youth, half-hidden behind a column in the VIP terminal luggage area. He could see the back of the kid's hair and part of his shoulder, but not much more. "Marid, it's me, Brady James. Do you remember – I'm the former Washington Post reporter your Mom asked to talk to you back in DC?"

The kid continued to peek out at James from behind the column.

"Tell the police to stop pointing their guns at me!" the youth called out. He sounded afraid. Petrified, actually.

Brady turned to the agent in charge. "Can they holster their guns?"

"I can't chance letting him take some of our guys with him," the agent said. "But I suppose we can lower their aim." He ordered his people to do just that.

"Okay, Marid? They're not pointing their guns at you anymore. Okay?"

A soft voice said, "ok."

"I just want to talk to you. I'm not armed. Is that ok? Can I come closer?"

"Ok."

Brady moved as close as he dared, not stopping until the agent signaled that he was close enough.

"Marid, I know that a man you knew as Abu al-Zahiri convinced you that this would be a good idea. I know this wasn't your plan. But al-Zahiri is a fraud, Marid! He's not a Muslim. He's not even from the Middle-East. He's a militiaman from Nevada who wants to start a religious war here in the United States, Marid! He's just using you to start his war. Don't let him do it, Marid. Don't let him use you." The reporter paused, waiting for some kind of a response. "Do you hear me, Marid?"

For several long seconds the terminal was unnaturally silent.

"What are you talking about?" a shaky voice finally replied.

For the first time Brady noticed the timbre of the young man's voice.

'Oh no,' he thought.

"What's your name?!" he called out loudly.

"Lester, Lester O'Connor!" the kid answered anxiously. "I'm not your *Marid!* A guy just paid me $50 to grow my beard and come here to see the President fly in! I don't know anything about any plan!"

"Step out from behind the column!" Brady ordered. "No one will hurt you."

The youth did as he was told, coming out with hands held high. He was Marid's height and weight, with the same color hair and a long straggly beard that made him look a lot like Marid from a distance. But he was clearly not Marid.

"It's not him!" Brady said urgently to the agent in charge.

"Goddamn," the agent swore. He held his sleeve up to his mouth.

"Camelot, this is Grizzly. Over"

"Read you Griz, what's up? You got that kid under control?"

"It's not him!" the agent said into the hidden mike. "It's a decoy! The kid might still be out there! I repeat, it was a decoy!"

"The plane's on final approach!" the person at the other end answered. "Only Merlin can call him off now," he added, using the code name for the Secret Service agent in charge of the visit: Steve Lyle.

Brady looked through the floor-to-ceiling windows of the terminal waiting room and saw the huge blue and white 747 coming in for a landing in the distance.

*****

At that same moment, Lyle heard the bad news through his earpiece. "Too late now," he replied as calmly as he could manage. "Set up a perimeter around the plane as soon as it stops taxiing. Keep them out on the tarmac. Do NOT direct them to the terminal. I repeat, keep them on the tarmac and set up a perimeter!"

He turned to one of his supporting staff. "The kid they got in the terminal isn't the one they think could be a suicide bomber. The bomber might still be out there in the crowd."

"Jesus!" the younger agent said. "What do you want me to do?"

"Get every cop and agent you can find and go through that crowd once more, person by person! And make it fast!"

The agent ran off immediately, collaring personnel as he went.

Lyle watched him for a moment before turning to watch Air Force One touch down.

The mid-day sun was hot. But that wasn't why he was sweating.

*****

Brady's cellphone rang even as the police were taking young Mr. O'Connor in for further questioning.   He answered on the second ring.

"James," he said, sounding slightly winded.

"Brady, it's me, Derek," he said quietly.

"Derek! Where the hell are you! They had half the agents and cops here at the airport looking for you!"

"You're here too?"

"Yes, I'm here! What do you think you're doing? You should be in bed!"

"I'm fine, don't worry about that. I think the kid is here, James. Marid? I think I saw him."

"Where?"

"In the parking garage across from the VIP terminal. Where are you?"

"I'm in the terminal. We thought we had Marid here too, but it turned out to be a decoy Alietto hired to throw us off his trail."

"Damn that asshole," the PI muttered. "But I'm almost sure I saw the kid about five minutes ago – over here at the garage!"

"Are you sure?"

"Not 100 per cent – if it was him he's cut his beard and dyed his hair black. I only saw his face for just an instant from three floors below, but I'd bet it was him. Worse, I just found a pair of pants and a shirt where I thought I saw him."

Brady didn't answer for several seconds.

"You think he changed clothes?"

"Looks like it. And that most likely means he's wearing something he thinks will get him where he wants to go."

Brady wracked his brain. "What – emergency medical technician? Plane mechanic?"

"Could be," the PI said, trying to picture the young man in his mind's eye. "Or…"

"Or?"

"What if he got his hands on a police uniform? With all the different city and county cops down there, it's likely that any strange face would just be accepted as someone from another jurisdiction."

"A cop?! You think he's dressed as a cop?!"

"It'd give him the greatest access and least suspicion. Besides, just think of the PR value if a uniformed LV cop blew himself up and killed the President."

"Jesus. Yeh, yeh that would make sense. Can you get down here?"

"If the cops'll let me, sure."

"They should. I'll meet you right outside the terminal."

"Be there in two minutes."

Derek glanced over at the cop scanning the crowd below. He hoped that Brady had gotten his info right, 'cause otherwise he was about to get gunned down by the cops or Secret Service if things went south. He crept out to the front of the cars, away from the cop, and tiptoed his way along the row toward the exit door. He was so focused on the cop that he completely missed his counterpart on the other side of the garage, looking over in bemused amazement as he watched a very small man tiptoe through the garage in his stocking feet.

"Hey, I've got a midget strolling through the garage in his socks," was how the cop described it to his control.

"What?"

"The midget we were looking for a few minutes ago – I think he's here in the garage."

There was a pause. "Let him go. Apparently he's no threat."

"I wouldn't think so," the cop said with a grin.

Derek, meanwhile, had made it past the cop nearest him and out the exit door without attracting any other attention. He grabbed the shoes he'd left in the stairwell and quickly pulled them on. Feeling a bit more confident, he ran down the stairways as quickly as his short legs allowed.

He was just feeling that he was home free, when he turned the corner at the first floor landing and almost literally ran into a plainclothes agent.

"Uh, sorry. Gotta run!" the PI said with barely more than a moment's hesitation. He'd barely taken a step before the agent reached out and grabbed him by the collar.

"Where do you think you're going?" he asked roughly.

"Goddamn it, this is an emergency!" Derek said. "Get someone on your radio and check!"

The agent immediately called Control and got the same response as the LV cop moments earlier.

"You sure?" the PI heard him ask his contact. "Ok, if you say so…" He turned back to Derek. "You're free to go. But take it easy. There are little kids out there."

Who'll be blown to bits if we don't find Marid in the next few minutes! Derek wanted to shout, but he kept quiet and walked away more slowly than he wished.

It was tough sledding moving through the closely packed mass of spectators, but Derek had had plenty of practice moving through crowds. From above it must have looked like a child pushing through a corn field as the crowd parted and then re-formed as he swept past. More than one person called out in alarm as he or she felt something unseen brush against their legs as he went past. Derek didn't even hear them.

When he finally popped out of the crowd he was sweating profusely.

"Derek - over here!" a familiar voice directed from a few yards to his left. He turned to see Brady standing with one of the LV cops who'd been in the chopper that found him.

"Anyone see him yet?" he asked as soon as he was close enough to ask in a normal voice.

"No one. Derek, you remember Officer Ashcroft, don't you?" Brady said, indicating Chester. The cop returned his nod.

"How could I forget? Good to see you again. So, where to?"

"If we're right, the kid's got to get to this area soon, if he's not already here. Probably working his way toward the front. Let's spread out. Keep your phone on!"

Without waiting for a reply, James started for the nearest end of the crowd, while Derek and Chester trotted further down the long line of people pressing against the ropes that separated them from the driveway where the President was supposed to exit.

Brady couldn't help but worry what Marid might do if he realized the President was sitting in his plane out on the tarmac and wouldn't be exiting through the VIP terminal anytime soon. Would he calmly walk away, maybe to put Plan B into effect, or if a security official confronted him would he panic and explode the vest right then and there?

'He's just a kid, and he's never been involved in this kind of thing,' he thought. The conclusion was ominous.

*****

Marid moved slowly through the excited spectators. He was in no rush. He didn't want to draw attention to himself, not now, not so near to his final act of devotion.

Everything was working exactly as al-Zahiri had planned. Perhaps he really did have a vision from Allah that told him how to circumvent the nonbelievers' security. Or perhaps he was just a very smart man. In any case, he had predicted how the Secret Service would react, and up till now he had been right at every turn.

The young man felt almost invisible wearing the Las Vegas Police uniform that al-Zahiri had procured for him. No, better than invisible – powerful! No one gave him a second look as he walked among them, his hair cut short, his beard shaved. Al-Zahiri had said that they would treat the uniform with respect, and they did. He looked no one in the eyes and held himself with a confident, almost arrogant attitude, shoulders back, head held high. Just as he'd been instructed.

It seemed as if he were walking in a dream. The people separated as he approached and came together again as he passed them by. He didn't have to push or demand they move. It was like magic!

This was the kind of power al-Zahiri had been talking about. The kind of power that Muslims never got in the west.

"When was the last time you saw a Muslim cop?" the holy man had asked him. "Or the governor of a state?"

Of course, Marid couldn't name a single one. They were all good Christians, with maybe a Jew or two. He really didn't know. But he was certain that no Muslim would ever be elected until things changed in the U.S.

"We need to stand up for ourselves," al-Zahiri had said. "Until we do, no one else will. And first of all, we must show that the west cannot kill our men, women and children without repercussions. We must show them that an eye for an eye is not just a saying, it is a principle that we live by."

The words echoed in his head as clearly as when his kaaed had first said them to him. "We must show them!"

But the other voice, smaller and not as certain, nagged at him. This voice spoke of the killing of innocents as a crime – worse, a sin. He heard his mother's words and saw her pleading eyes...

Marid shook his head. He was losing his focus. He glanced around and saw a number of police officers and plainclothes security agents combing through the crowd. He would attract attention if he just stood there doing nothing. So he waded into the mass of people and began to walk through them as he saw the others doing.

'Probably looking for me,' he thought.

The irony was not lost on him.

*****

Brady was beginning to think that maybe he'd been wrong, and Derek too. With so many officers scouring the crowd, how could Marid not be found – if he were there?

He caught the PI's eye as he plowed through the spectators just a few yards away. Derek shook his head. Nothing. Brady nodded and went back to the task at hand, but he was losing hope. The faces were beginning to blur. Every other person seemed to be the kid at first glance; none survived a second look.

He was just about to call Steve Lyle and admit that they may have been wrong about Marid coming to the airport, when he saw a young police officer just twenty feet or so to his left moving steadily through the crowd. He was the right height and weight, and although his hair was dark he still looked enough like the kid to catch James' eye. The thing that made him take a second look wasn't his appearance, however. It was his casual, almost nonchalant air as he walked. All the other security people were moving forward with haste, maybe even fear. This young cop looked…well, out of it.

Brady tried to find Derek in the crowd, but the little man was nowhere to be found. He punched the speed-dial on his cell.

"DiLaurain," the PI answered on the first ring.

"Derek," Brady whispered, trying to keep his voice down to avoid panicking the thousands of people all around him. "Take a look at the cop to my left, maybe twenty feet."

He waited. "Could be him," Derek answered. "Can't quite see from this angle."

"Can you get to a position where you can make a positive ID? I'll try from this side."

"I'm on it."

Brady saw his friend change course and push through the packed spectators on an intercept course with the young cop. Brady did the same. He'd only taken a couple of steps, however, when his phone rang.

"It's him!" Derek whispered into the phone. "I've got eyes-on and it's a positive ID!"

"Don't let him see you!" Brady said. "We don't want to provoke a reaction we can't predict. Keep him in sight, but keep your distance."

"Got it."

"I'll call Lyle and see what he suggests."

"I'll be standing by."

Brady turned away from Marid so the kid couldn't accidentally see him, and dialed his cell.

"Lyle, James. We've ID'd Marid. He's here in front of the terminal wearing a Las Vegas police uniform. No beard and he's dyed his hair black. We need to clear some people out of here without making a commotion."

"Brady, don't do anything. Just keep him under observation from a distance. Let me get with my people and see what we can come up with."

"Okay. Let me know."

As he hung up, Brady drifted casually into the shadows at the edge of the terminal, a vantage point from which he could keep an eye on the kid without risking detection. Marid looked composed, if not entirely alert to his surroundings. He moved slowly past person after person, his eyes down as if inspecting their shoes instead of their faces. No sense of urgency. No sense of alarm. He seemed almost drugged to Brady.

'Wonder if that's the result of Alietto's pep talks, or something else?' he thought as he looked around to see if he could find Derek nearby. It took a few seconds to find the PI in the sea of taller bodies, but finally he picked him out standing behind a column maybe twenty-five or thirty feet from Marid. He caught his friend's eye and signaled him to hold pat for a while. Derek nodded his acknowledgement.

As the seconds and minutes dragged by, Brady found his heart racing from anxiety. If anything went wrong… If the kid suddenly saw either of them, or felt their presence… If he just pushed the wrong button or pulled the wrong tab, or whatever he'd do to detonate the vest, then dozens if not hundreds of innocent people would be dead, blown to smithereens. For nothing but the insane machinations of a homegrown terrorist.

Just a couple of minutes later his cell rang.

"Brady, it's me," Lyle said sternly. "We're going to announce that the plane has experienced tire problems and so the President will disembark Air Force One and make his way by vehicle to a different exit from the airport. We'll start loading people on buses to take them there. We've got three full-size buses and a couple of mini-vans all ready to go – borrowed from the press pool and the staffers. I've got my site manager on the way to your location to get with you about handling the crowd. We need to get as many as possible onto the buses without alerting Marid. What do you think?"

"Might work," Brady said. "Will someone pose as the President to leave the plane and make it look real?"

"Good idea. Let me see what we can do. And Brady?"

"Yeh?"

"Thanks. Try to keep you and your little friend safe."

"That will definitely be on my mind."

CHAPTER 26

James watched the crowd impatiently looking for the site agent, all the while keeping one eye on the kid. It was less than five minutes later when a tall, attractive, fit-looking woman in a blue suit sidled up to him. At first he was pleasantly surprised at the attention. Then he saw the earpiece and knew that she was Lyle's manager.

"Mr. James?" she asked.

"I am."

"Rebecca Lester," she said, shaking his hand. He was instantly impressed by her firm handshake and piercing blue eyes. "Can you point out our man?"

Brady waited for Marid's eyes to turn away from the area in which he and the agent stood, and then motioned with his chin.

"That's him. In the police uniform."

"Looks authentic," she said, more to herself than to Brady.

"He sure does. Where do you get a uniform like that?"

"That's what we'll need to find out, once we take him into custody. For now, stay close so we can have someone here he recognizes once we move the people away from the terminal."

Even as she was finishing, a man with a bullhorn was making the announcement a hundred feet or so down the pavement.

"Ladies and Gentlemen, may I have your attention please!" he said. "The President's plane is experiencing some problems with a tire on the landing gear, so it will not be able to taxi up to the VIP terminal as planned. The President will disembark Air Force One and be taken by his armored vehicle through a different exit gate, for security reasons."

A huge groan greeted the announcement.

"But don't worry, you will all still have an opportunity to see the President. We are bringing buses here right now to move you over to the new exit gate, and if you'll just board the buses quickly, without any pushing or shoving, we'll get all of you right over there. Okay?"

The crowd cheered.

"Good. Then please line-up behind the uniformed Las Vegas policemen who are now holding their hands up in the air."

He pointed to a half-dozen LV cops who were standing in front of the crowd, their hands in the air.

Brady glanced over at Marid. He was looking around tentatively, whether it was from confusion or distrust, the reporter couldn't say. What was clear, however, was that he recognized that something important had occurred, something that had changed his plans completely. A thought suddenly struck Brady. He popped open his cellphone.

"Steve, it's Brady. I just had an idea: could you ask one of the uniformed Vegas cops to go over to Marid and tell him to help shepherd the spectators into lines for the bus ride? Act as if he's just another cop. That should distract him for a few minutes. Stop him from changing his plans before we can get these people out of here."

"I don't know, Brady," the Secret Service agent said. "What if he gets a hint that we're playing him? Will he detonate the vest? You know him better than we do – what do you think?"

Brady wished he could reassure the agent, but he could not. "I really don't know, Steve. I don't know the kid well enough to know where his tipping point may be. But if we don't do something, we're just giving him free rein to come up with a new plan. I don't think we want to do that."

"No, no we don't. And we're afraid to take him out, for fear a shot might detonate the vest. Alright – I'll give the order. But watch him closely. Any sign that he thinks something's up, let me know immediately."

"You got it."

As the first of the buses began to roll up to the VIP terminal, Brady saw a uniformed cop come up to Marid and tap him on the shoulder. Maybe it was Brady's nerves, or maybe it was the cop's, but he looked nearly as tense as Marid. The kid jumped as if struck.

The cop smiled as if they'd shared some little private joke, and after his initial flinch Marid responded calmly, nodding his head in agreement. The cop pointed to a nearby staging point, and Marid gave him a thumbs-up. It was only after the cop walked away that Brady saw the kid's face collapse in relief.

'Alietto picked well,' he thought. *'Marid's got guts.'*

The buses came to a stop where long lines of spectators had queued to climb aboard. Everything was going well, and Marid was doing his part to usher the people onboard, when Brady saw movement on the top of the terminal building. At first he couldn't make out what he was seeing. But moments later a black-suited security person, carrying a long, scoped rifle, maneuvered into place overlooking the boarding area.

'*Sniper,*' Brady realized, and his blood turned cold. He shifted his body to see behind him and saw another shooter atop the parking garage, and then another across the way above the administrative buildings. He supposed he couldn't blame Lyle. If everything else failed, a quick end to the situation was the best he could hope for. But not Brady. He'd promised the kid's mother he'd help her son, and he still intended to do exactly that.

The first three buses finished loading and pulled away, with two mini-buses pulling up to take their place. Brady could see Marid much more clearly now, with fewer people standing between the two of them. He was doing his job, helping the last few dozen people get onboard. Across the driveway, Derek lifted his hands as if to ask, 'what now'? Brady had no idea. They'd gotten most of the innocents out of the way, but now they had to get Marid to surrender. That wouldn't be easy.

He was wondering exactly what he could do to persuade the young man, when he noticed Marid's eyes look skyward. From the widened eyes and shocked expression, it was clear that he'd seen the sniper. Would he realize that the marksman was there for him, or just think it was part of the Presidential security plan? The kid scanned the tops of the other buildings, identifying several other snipers as well. He looked confused for just an instant, but as the last person in his line climbed aboard the bus, he turned and followed them.

Brady punched the fast-dial on his cell and Lyle answered in an instant.

"Marid's getting on the mini-bus!" he whispered urgently.

"I know, my men are reporting in real time," the agent answered coolly. "You got any ideas? Otherwise, I think we may need to take him out. He's forcing my hand."

"No!" Brady said, louder than he had intended. "Let me talk to him – please!"

"James, there are two dozen people sitting on that bus. I can't risk their lives."

Brady knew the agent was right. But he still had to try.

"Steve, the kid's been brainwashed. Let me talk to him. I think I can persuade him to surrender."

"And if you're wrong?" Lyle's voice was cutting.

"I'm willing to risk my life that I'm not."

"And the others?" There was a pause. "Hold on. I'm getting a report." Brady waited a few long, tense seconds.

"James?" the agent said, coming back on the phone.

"Yeh?"

"Looks like we'll have to take you up on your offer. The kid's settled down on the bus floor. Apparently waving his service revolver and scaring the crap out of people. Our snipers don't have a clear shot. You're on."

Brady gulped a breath. "Thanks."

"Just stay very calm and try to make a connection with him."

"Will do."

He stepped out from his hiding place and almost immediately his cellphone rang.

"What the hell do you think you're doing!" the PI yelled. "He'll see you!"

"I'm going to talk to him," Brady answered.

"Talk to him! Brady, the kid's a walking bomb! One wrong word and he could blow that bus to kingdom come!"

"Are you *trying* to get me even more nervous than I already am, or are you just the worst coach in history?"

"I may not be John Wooden, but this is nuts!"

"Remember the smack addict I talked down off the bridge in '96?" Brady said calmly.

"Yeh, so?"

"The cops didn't want us to go anywhere near him. Said he'd jump. But he didn't, did he?"

"No. I suppose not."

"This kid's not crazy," Brady said. "I can reach him."

"But…"

"I can reach him." Brady didn't know if he were trying to convince Derek, or himself.

The PI sighed. "All right. I'll be rootin' for you."

"That's better."

A short pause. "Hey Brady, how about if I try to sneak up to the back of the van? If things go badly, I'll try to take him out through the back window."

Brady thought about it. The kid was already sitting down so low in the bus that he couldn't see out of the windows. Why not? Except that it would be putting his friend at ground zero of the blast zone…

"I can't ask you to do that," Brady said, "but if you're game, it does give us one last chance to stop the carnage."

"You think I'm going to let you have all the fun?" the PI said, the tension in his voice belying his cheerfulness.

"Keep your eyes on me," James directed. "If I put my hand to my heart, take him out – head shot." Brady could barely say the words. An image of the kid's mother flashed in his mind.

"I'll be there."

Brady hung up his phone and glanced over to where the PI was hiding. He saw him give a big thumbs-up. He nodded in return.

The police had moved everyone back from the van where Marid was hiding. The scene was surreal: a cordon of police, guns drawn, encircled the van at a distance of fifty feet or more, all of them tucked behind concrete barriers, pillars, or similar. On the rooftops, the three snipers had been joined by a half dozen plainclothes agents.

'Probably communicating directly with Lyle,' Brady thought.

The van was now so close he could see Marid's feet through the entrance door, and could hear his nervous chatter. At first he couldn't make out what he was saying, but as he came within just ten feet it became clear: he was praying.

"Lâ ilâha illâ allâh," the kid kept repeating in a low voice, over and over again. "lâ ilâha illâ allâh."

The prayer contrasted with the moans and sobs he could hear from the others in the van. When he was as near as he dared, he called out.

"Marid! It's me, Brady James – the newspaper guy from DC."

The praying stopped, as did most of the moaning.

"Marid, I just want to talk to you. May I come onboard?"

"Help us!" a woman's voice called out.

"This goddamn guy is nuts!" a young man added.

For a moment, all was quiet.

"Can I come up there, Marid?" Brady pressed. "I'm unarmed."

Brady saw the kid's feet move, and moments later his face came into view as he peered cautiously at the reporter.

"What are you doing here?" the kid asked softly. "Get away!"

"I can't do that, Marid. I promised your mother that I wouldn't let you do this, and I keep my promises."

"Then you'll die with the rest of them." His voice sounded numb, dead to the world.

"Marid, al-Zahiri is a fake. He's not a terrorist. He's not even from the Middle East."

"You're lying!" Marid shouted angrily. "You just want me to surrender!"

"I'm not lying," the reporter insisted. "His real name is Joe Alietto. He's from here, in Las Vegas! He's the leader of a local militia that wants to start a holy war, wants *you* to start a holy war, so they can *kill* Muslims."

"I don't believe you."

Brady closed his eyes to gather his wits. "Marid, can I show you something? I can prove to you al-Zahiri is a phony."

"If this is a trick, you will die with the rest of these people."

"No!" "Stay away from us!" voices called out from the bus.

"It's not a trick," Brady said as calmly as he could. "Please."

The kid was quiet for a long moment. "Come, but keep your hands where I can see them!"

Brady put his hands up and walked slowly toward the van.

"I'm coming now," he said soothingly. "I'm not your enemy."

He saw Marid's eyes following him as he approached. As soon as he stepped up on the van's first step, however, the acquiescence hardened.

"That's close enough!" Marid ordered.

Brady could see fear in the young man's face. But it was nothing compared to the terror he saw in the passengers'.

"All right, all right. I'm stopping here," James said.

For the first time, Brady could see Marid's entire body. He held his right hand inside his partly unbuttoned shirt, Napoleon-like, while aiming the pistol in his left hand directly at James. "What do you want to show me?" he asked suspiciously.

"Can I reach into my pocket to get it?"

"Slowly."

Brady pulled a rumpled piece of paper from his pants pocket.

"Take a look at this, Marid," he said as he unfolded the paper. "It's an arrest photograph of Joe Alietto. You can see it's your man, al-Zahiri." He held out the faxed mugshot that Chester had provided.

"Give it to me," the kid said, reaching out to take the paper.

He snatched the fax from Brady's hands and studied it closely, peering up over the paper from time to time to make sure Brady wasn't up to something.

"It's a fake," Marid said after several seconds. "Al-Zahiri told me you people would try something like this."

"It's *real*, Marid. Al-Zahiri is the fake. He's the imposter. He told you all that crap about jihad and vengeance just to get you to do this. He wants to *destroy* Muslims, not empower them!"

Marid studied the mugshot once again, but for just an instant.

"Why should I trust you? How do I know you're not lying just to get me to abandon my holy mission?" he asked.

Good question. "I guess you'll just have to trust your instincts," Brady said. "Let me ask you – wasn't there ever a time, whether it was when you first met al-Zahiri or later on, when you had a sense that something wasn't right about the guy? That something was…well, phony?"

The look on Marid's face was part consternation, part denial.

"He is a holy man!" he cried out so loudly that a woman sitting near him flinched noticeably.

"He's a con man," Brady responded matter-of-factly. "He's using you, Marid. He doesn't care about you, or Islam, or anything except getting what he wants. You can't help him. He's crazy."

"Crazy?" the kid said softly.

"He's a madman! He'd trying to get you to kill the President so that Americans think that all Muslims are insane terrorists! He wants non-believers to hate Muslims!"

Marid swallowed hard. Brady thought he could make out the slightest glimmer of tears in his eyes. *Just a few more minutes,'* he thought, *'just give me a few more minutes and I'll convince this scared kid that Alietto is the only devil he has to fear.'*

*****

In the security control center, Steve Lyle was watching the whole thing go down via wireless video sent directly from one of his spotters out at the terminal. He saw Brady standing on the steps of the bus, saw the PI creep up to the rear window as the reporter was talking to the kid. All seemed quiet for the moment. That was good.

But he was under tremendous pressure to act. Vegas Police headquarters reported hundreds of phone calls demanding that they do something. He'd even had calls from DC.

Congressmen were asking for explanations. "What are your plans?" "When can we expect a resolution?" "Protect the innocent bus passengers at all costs!"

How the hell could he take action *and* protect the passengers? The second the kid saw anyone approach the bus, he might push the button. *Boom.* It'd be a bloody disaster!

"What should I tell them?" his assistant asked nervously, her hand cupped over the phone mouthpiece.

"Damned if I know," Lyle muttered. But he knew the routine. He had to say something. "Tell them we're moving our people into position. Negotiations are taking place even as we speak. If they fail, then…we'll act."

He winced as he heard her relaying the information over the phone and exhaled deeply.

"Come on, Brady!" he said to the TV screen in front of him. "It's gotta be *now!*"

*****

Derek chanced a peek through the back window of the van. He could see Brady pleading with the kid, even

306   William J. Millman

though he couldn't make out everything he said. From his vantage point it was clear that the kid was fully focused on his friend. Could he sneak in through the back door without alerting Marid, and put him out with a choke hold? He knew it was dangerous. Knew that the kid might push the button. But he'd never seen anyone who was being choked who didn't reach for the arm squeezing the life out of them to try to pull it away. It was an automatic reaction. All he needed was a few seconds…

He wished he could call Brady and get his input. But there was no way. He had to make up his mind and act. And the time was now.

He tapped lightly on the back window. A young black man sitting on the aisle just inches from the window jumped at the sound and turned, eyes wide.

Derek immediately put his index finger to his lips.

Jesus, don't make a goddamn sound!' he thought as he quickly reconsidered whether this was such a good idea after all.

Thankfully, the young guy nodded his understanding. Derek was just about to motion to him to open the back door, when the woman sitting across from him saw his head turn and followed his eyes to Derek.

'Not again!' the PI fretted, but the black kid waved for her to keep quiet.

Derek instinctively ducked down for an instant, then lifted his head very carefully to peek down the aisle of the bus. Marid hadn't noticed a thing.

'Open the door!' he mouthed to the black kid while pantomiming the same.

The kid nodded, and after a quick look at the back of Marid's head to be sure he was still completely engaged with

Brady, he slid out of his seat and carefully lifted the handle that secured the door. Derek's eyes bounced between the kid, the obviously terrified woman sitting across from him, and Marid, now kneeling on the bus floor. With every inch the handle moved, Derek's heart crept closer to his throat. But Marid was completely involved in his discussion with Brady, and he didn't react at all.

'That's it, keep him talking Brady,' he thought. 'Hold his attention.'

As soon as the handle was clear, the PI signaled for the kid to move back into his seat. Derek them reached up to the outside door handle and began to open it as slowly as humanly possible. One squeak, one sound of any kind, and it might be the last they ever heard. The door was moving quite smoothly, without any sound that could spell disaster, when suddenly a red light over the driver's head began to flash and a buzzer sounded.

'Damn it!' the PI fumed as he pushed the door shut, jumped off the bumper and dove under the bus.

He didn't want to die hiding under a passenger van at the Las Vegas Airport! Hell, he didn't want to die at all.

*****

"What is he doing?!!" Lyle yelled at his TV monitor in the control center. "Is he trying to get them all killed!??"

He had watched Derek's attempt to sneak in the rear exit of the bus, and had seen him dive under the vehicle moments later.

"What's going on out there??!" he shouted into a walkie-talkie.

"The midget's hiding under the vehicle and...Hold on – the kid is up and moving toward the rear of the van!" one of Lyle's Agency spotters reported.

"What's he doing?"

"Can't tell. Looks like. Uh oh. He's seen the exit door."

"What do you advise?"

"Can the snipers get a good shot at him?"

"Hang on." Lyle switched channels. "Longshot 1, Longshot 1, this is Merlin. Do you have the suspect in sight?"

"Got 'em Chief. What now?"

"Can you get a clean shot?"

The sniper vacillated. "I, ah, there are at least two civilians between subject and shooter. We might be able to sneak one in there, but it'd be close."

Lye held the walkie-talkie in mid-air as he pondered. "Just keep him under close surveillance for now," he finally said resignedly. "But be ready!"

"Always," the sniper answered.

Lyle changed back to the spotter's channel. "No go on the sniper," he said. "Too much chance of collateral damage."

"Then you'd better hope your journalist buddy is a good talker," the spotter said. "Because it looks from here like the kid is freaking."

Lyle exhaled. Just what they didn't need. A panicked bomber.

'Come on, James!' he thought as he stared at the poorly-lit images on the TV monitor. *'Come on!'*

*****

Brady thought he might be reaching the kid. He seemed to be listening, maybe even coming to believe the truth about Alietto and the whole plot. He was just about to ask Marid if he could take another step up into the bus, when suddenly an alarm started beeping and a red light began to flash over the dashboard!

"What the...??!" he said aloud as he watched Marid jump to his feet and rush toward the back of the bus. People screamed. Cried.

For just an instant, Brady thought it was all over. The end.

But then he realized that the alarm had just sounded because the rear door of the bus had been opened. Derek?

He watched as Marid stormed to the back door and pushed it open violently. He saw him scanning the outside of the bus for any security people that might be hiding there, but he saw no one.

The people sitting on either side of the kid pulled back in horror.

"Did you do this?!" he heard Marid scream at a young black guy seated right next to the door. "Do you *want* to die?!"

The black teen shook his head urgently. "I didn't mean anything!" he yelled.

"Because if you want to die, just tell me! I'm ready to martyr myself!" Marid continued, turning back toward the rest of the bus. "Do all of you want to die?!"

He sounded completely gone. Broken. Brady knew he had to do something fast.

"They don't want to die!" he yelled as he climbed up the second step to face Marid at the opposite end of the van. "None of them want to die! And neither do you."

Suddenly all the screams and tears stopped save for a few whimpers and sniffles. Marid stared at Brady, his face contorted with anger. Brady could see his hands shaking from fifteen feet away.

"Give me one reason why not," the kid said with a shaky voice.

"Because you're not a killer," Brady said softly. "And Islam is not a religion that kills innocents."

"An eye for an eye!" Marid shouted.

"These people have done nothing to you," James continued, sounding more like a plea than a statement of fact. "They are innocent."

"Their President isn't!"

"No perhaps he's not. But their President is not on this bus. You will not go to heaven for killing someone who hasn't wronged you."

"What do you know about Islam?" Marid said, his voice noticeably lower.

"Just what I've read. And what your mother told me about it." Even as he said it, he had an idea. Last gasp Hail Mary? He slipped his cellphone from his pocket.

"Why should I listen to an infidel?!" Marid said, but his anger was half-hearted. When he saw James looking at his cellphone, his tone changed. "What are you doing? Put that down!"

Brady ignored him for the time it took for the phone to ring three times. *Be there!* he implored.

"Hello," a familiar voice answered.

"Nyla, it's Brady James," he said loud enough for her son to hear at the other end of the bus. "I have someone here who wants to talk to you."

"I don't want to talk to anyone!" the kid yelled, but Brady held the phone out to him anyway.

"It's your mother. She wants to talk to you." He moved almost imperceptibly closer to the kid.

"Hang up!"

Instead, Brady punched the speakerphone button. "You're on speakerphone," he announced loudly to Nyla. "Marid's right here in front of me."

"Marid!" the pained cry reverberated throughout the bus. Then she said something quickly in Arabic.

Marid looked as if he'd been slapped. His face fell. "I love you too, Mom," he said softly.

"Do not do this!" Nyla went on. "It is not right. It is not just!"

"They kill Muslims!"

"But we are not *them*! We live by the words of the Holy Koran. We do not kill innocents. You *know* that, Marid. I taught you better!"

Brady could see the kid's mind working. He tried to find the words to contradict her, but he was failing.

Then, Brady saw the rear door open, just a crack. Through the tiny slit of light he saw a familiar face: Derek.

"Please, Marid – Chip, listen to me. I love you. Your friends and family love you. We do not wish you to do this!"

The tears in the kid's eyes were more prominent now.

"Listen to her," Brady urged, his voice louder than necessary to help disguise the opening of the rear exit door.

"You don't want to do this. You have a choice. Make the right choice."

"He's right, Marid!" Nyla continued on the heels of Brady. "You are a good person. You are a good Muslim. You must not do this terrible thing!"

Brady tried to keep his eyes diverted as the PI crept up into the bus and began to crawl toward Marid. It was only six feet or so, but one wrong move…

"You can't correct a wrong by doing another wrong," Brady said. "Especially not to people who had nothing to do with it. Look at these people, Marid. Look at them!"

He waved his hands toward the terrified faces on both side of the aisle. "They are just normal, average people, like you and me. You don't hate them. You don't want to hurt them."

"Marid, PLEEASE!" his mother suddenly cried out on the speakerphone. Marid threw his hands to his ears to block her out.

The moment he did, Derek jumped to his feet and threw himself forward. Grabbing both the kid's arms at the elbows, he pulled them back behind Marid and held on for dear life.

"Brady, a little help here!" the PI yelled as Marid struggled to escape.

James hurried down the aisle, but before he could get to them the young black guy who'd opened the door jumped up and grabbed Marid by the throat with one hand.

"Give it up," he said. "You're not gonna win this one."

Marid squirmed desperately, even as his face turned a deepening shade of purple.

Derek's hands were slipping and the muscles in his arms began to ache; he wasn't certain how much longer he could hold on, when Brady arrived and held his cellphone up to the kid's ear.

"Marid, *please* don't do this," his mother's voice pleaded from the speaker. "For *me*."

The words finally penetrated whatever barriers he had erected around himself. His body went limp and his knees almost buckled. He began to sob, silently.

"Don't worry, Nyla, it'll be okay," Brady said into his phone. "I'll call you back in a short while." He hung up and dialed Lyle.

"The situation is under control," he said. "Get someone in here."

Even before the Secret Service agent responded, uniformed police and plainclothes agents began pouring out from behind every wall and barrier in the area. In seconds, Marid was handcuffed.

"Hey, take it easy on him!" Brady demanded when one of the local cops pushed him roughly to his knees. "He's no threat."

The cop looked up as if he was going to say something, when an agent grabbed him lightly by the elbow.

"Let it go. Let's get him outside where our bomb guy can take that vest apart."

The cop lifted Marid, a bit more gently, to his feet. The tears had stopped but the blank look on his face was painful for Brady.

"Marid, it'll be okay. We'll tell them how Alietto conned you," he said soothingly. He didn't know how much he believed what he was saying himself, but he needed to tell the kid something to get him through the next few hours and days.

He thought he saw a glimmer of understanding in Marid's eyes, and then he was gone, out the rear door to where a heavily padded bomb expert awaited him.

"Jesus, that was too damn close," Derek said from the seat where he'd collapsed when the cops had taken charge.

"You are one bad little dude," the young black guy said, standing a few feet away in seeming awe.

"I'll take that as a compliment," the PI said.

Brady shook his head, trying to decide whether to laugh or explode. "Crazy as all hell," he finally said, "but bad all right. *Very* bad."

"You wouldn't have it any other way," the PI said with a smile.

"Don't tempt me."

"Speaking of which, I could be tempted to accept a cold Bud right about now…"

"You're hopeless," James said, but then relented. He could use one himself. "Give me two minutes while I call his mother."

Derek's smile faded. "Ah, good man. Better you than me."

"For all concerned."

Brady climbed down from the bus slowly, his legs feeling a million years old. The last of the passengers was just being herded to a waiting bus on the opposite side of the terminal. To his right, he could barely make out the top of the bomb expert's head behind a blast barrier as he worked on Marid's vest. Shadows stretched across the buildings and asphalt as the sun dipped toward the mountains in the distance.

He took a deep breath and exhaled. It was good to be alive.

He punched the redial button on his cell and listened to the phone ring. The voice that answered sounded weary.

"Nyla," he began, "your son is going to be okay…"

EPILOGUE

Brady barely heard the incessant ringing and buzzing of the slot machines as he waited for the passengers to disembark the plane. His attention was focused on the gate. Anne hadn't been particularly enthusiastic at first when he'd invited her out to Sin City for a long weekend, but when he explained that he and Derek needed a little 'blow off steam' time, she reconsidered and hopped the next plane west.

Derek had questioned his sanity.

"You're asking her to come out here?!" he'd asked when Brady first suggested the idea. "That's like inviting your mother-in-law to your honeymoon!"

"It's a good thing you like being single," James had answered, "'cause I think you're gonna be that way for a *lonnng* time."

He was smiling to himself as he recalled the conversation, when a familiar face emerged from the jetway.

"Brady!" Anne called out, and a huge smile exploded onto his face. He hurried over to meet her and was rewarded with a heartfelt hug and kiss.

"I missed you!" she said when she caught her breath.

"I know the feeling," James said, and he realized he meant it more than he could say.

"You don't look much the worse for wear," she said, stepping back to appraise him from a distance.

"And you look great!"

Her smile broadened. "So where's Mr. DiLaurain? Couldn't resist the allure of the slot machines?"

"Derek had to park the car. We were running a little late."

"Still tying up loose ends?"

"Actually," Brady began, but just then he saw Anne's eyes widen and her eyebrows shoot upward. He followed her gaze.

Across the terminal, emerging from a crowd of passengers who stepped back as though allowing a dignitary to pass, strode Derek, hand-in-hand with an absolutely gorgeous showgirl type who must have stood six foot two. Derek barely came up to her navel.

"My god," Anne said involuntarily.

"Don't let him hear you say that," Brady replied. "He'll take you seriously and ask for regular prayer services."

Before Anne could marshal another thought, Derek called out to them.

"There are the two lovebirds! Welcome to Las Vegas!"

Brady could see a blush come to Anne's face, but she hid her discomfort easily.

"Derek! You look like this place suits you," she said. The tiny PI came up to her and took her hand, kissing it with gusto.

"I'm a Vegas kind of guy," he agreed, and then turning to his escort said, "Anne, this is Jennifer. Jen, Anne."

The tall, leggy blonde batted her fan-like eyelashes as she took Anne's hand. "Derek has told me so much about you two!"

Brady cringed. "Some of it may even be true," he said.

"Always the joker!" the PI said much too loudly. "Do you have luggage?"

If there was anyone within 50 feet of the four of them who wasn't staring openly at the spectacle, Brady couldn't see them.

"Just one bag," Anne mumbled.

"Then let's go get it! We've got shows to see, banks to bust!" Derek said as he took Jennifer's hand.

"Only one bag?" the showgirl said as they began walking through the terminal. "I can never seem to travel with less than three!"

Brady glanced over at Anne out of the corner of his eye. It must have made quite the picture, the four of them traipsing through the slot machines.

'Follow the Yellow Brick Road,' he thought, and before he knew it, he was humming.

www.ingramcontent.com/pod-product-compliance
Lightning Source LLC
Chambersburg PA
CBHW021457240626
47154CB00002B/408